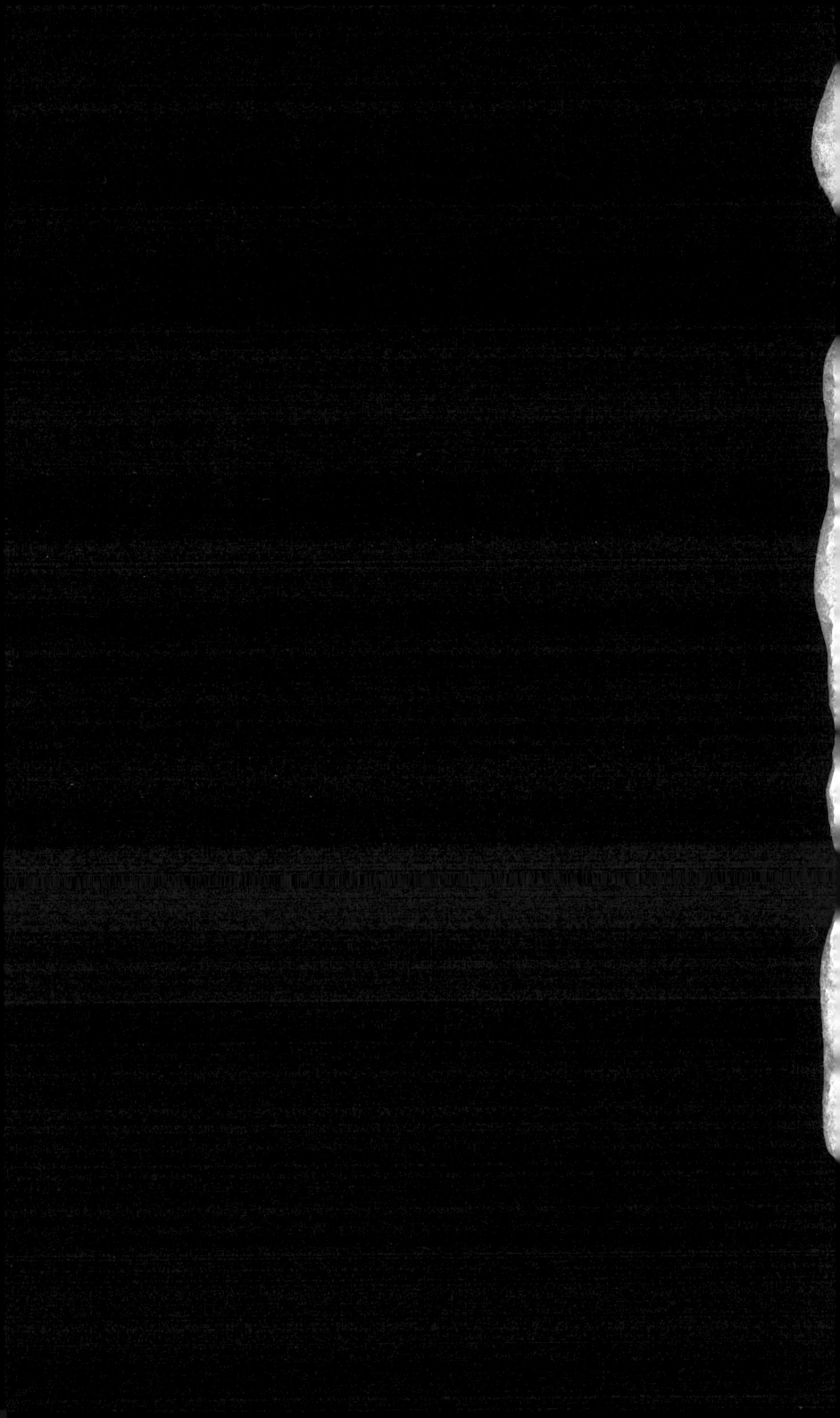

I enjoyed this romantic musicological novel. As someone who has made editions of Monteverdi's Orfeo and been deeply involved in three different productions of the opera, I was naturally intrigued by the story, and particularly the imaginative recreation of musical Mantua, Pisa, and Florence in the early 1600s. In Part Two ... a strange paradox develops between historically informed performance and appalling forgeries of text ... a well-researched and entertaining read.

– Sir Roger Norrington

BY THE SAME AUTHOR

Drama/Theatre Studies
Carry On, Understudies (theatre)
Five Plays (drama)
Post-war British Drama: Looking Back in Gender
Wandor: Plays and Dramatisations. Digital Archive

Poetry
Gardens of Eden Revisited
Musica Transalpina
The Music of the Prophets
Natural Chemistry
Travellers

Short Stories
Guests in the Body
False Relations
Four Times EightyOne

Creative Writing
The Author is Not Dead, Merely Somewhere Else:
Creative Writing Reconceived
Critical-Creative Writing: Two Sides of the Same Coin – A Reader
The Art of Writing Drama

As editor
Plays by Women (4 Vols)
On Gender and Writing
The Body Politic
Once a Feminist

CD
CD: Salamone Rossi Hebreo Mantovano

ORFEO'S LAST ACT

ORFEO'S LAST ACT

MICHELENE WANDOR

GREENWICH EXCHANGE
LONDON

Greenwich Exchange, London

First published in Great Britain in 2023
All rights reserved

Orfeo's Last Act: A Novel in Two Parts
Michelene Wandor © 2023

This book is sold subject to the conditions that it shall not, by way of trade or
otherwise, be lent, resold, hired out or otherwise circulated without the
publisher's prior consent in any form of binding
or cover other than that in which it is published and without
a similar condition including this condition being imposed
on the subsequent purchaser.

Printed and bound by imprintdigital.com
Cover design: December Publications
Tel: 07951511275

Greenwich Exchange Website: www.greenex.co.uk

Cataloguing in Publication Data
is available from the British Library

ISBN: 978-1-910996-68-3

For Adam, with thanks; and for Thomas,
Ivan, Sophie, Lila and Oliver

PROLOGUE

Mantova, Italy: early 1700s

Walking and walking, across the stone causeway, mists to the right and left, towards the Castello di San Giorgio, mists rising from the ground as the rain plummets down, splashing up a dark, fetid dampness from the receiving ground.

My right foot catches the hard edge of the causeway, slipping, doubling, over the edge. I flounder up to my knees in mud, clutch at the grass clumps on the side, and clamber out again. I see the dim outline of the Castello ahead of me.

PROLOGUE

East Anglia, the United Kingdom: early 2000s
Low clouds release dashes of sleet and rain beneath a grey East Anglian sky. I turn left at the Madingley signpost, along a winding lane, past a cluster of half-a-dozen small cottages and a dilapidated barn. Then, right at The Coach and Horses pub, second left, signposted Catchpole Manor. Right, into the drive, lined with clumps of daffodils. My car wheels crunch on the gravel.

Prima Parte

ONE

THE MIST MIXES WITH spatters of mud, the stench of shit and sweat, wet and warm, mud drops on my arms, my face and round my eyes, till I blink and breathe water, human and animal detritus, the fertile muck of the fields. It reminds me of the rains of 1599. *Mutazione di secolo.* The end of the century, or the end of the world.

I climb up the bank from the lake, skirt the Castello di San Giorgio, and walk round the Cattedrale di San Pietro. I stand for a moment: across the Piazza di San Pietro, I see the Palazzo Ducale.

I walk along the side of the piazza, thinking I must be careful not to tread on any of the cracks in the cobbles. If I do, the ground will heave and throb under the sucking impact of my soft, silent shoes, and I will be sucked down into the marshes until there is nothing left of me but my voice.

Seconda Parte

ONE

LOW CLOUDS RELEASE DASHES of sleet and rain beneath a grey East Anglian sky. I turn left at the Madingley signpost, along a winding lane, past a cluster of half-a-dozen small cottages and a dilapidated barn. Then, right at The Coach and Horses pub, second left, signposted Catchpole Manor. Right, into the drive, lined with clumps of daffodils. My car wheels crunch on the gravel.

I get out of the car and stretch, and, as if on cue, music bursts into the air. Above the open front door, behind a low stone balustrade, stands a group of people playing what look like trombones and short, slightly curved black instruments. Some high notes crack, lower notes stumble out of tune, but it's all enthusiasm.

As the piece ends, a battered red estate car slithers to a halt beside me. An elderly man climbs out. He wears

PRIMA PARTE

I know this is ridiculous. First of all, the cobbles are so small, that I can't help treading on the joins between them, and nothing happens when I do. Anyway, it is a long time since the marshes threatened anyone at this end of the island, this fiercely covered and protected end. The marshes have long been drained, filled in, built upon.

There are still canals, remnants of the many rivers and waterways which criss-crossed the island. And yet, I am safer here than in Venice, where canals haunt at every turn, where it is easy to disappear in the middle of the black night. I am safer here than on the hills of Florence, where any passing mercenary could kill me for my empty purse. I am safe, above all, because no-one knows I am here.

I pass the Castiglione palace, and reach the Basilica di San Andrea. I slip in through one of the church doors. The air is chill, damp, with that acrid marsh smell which is stronger at dusk. A handful of candles flicker in the altar gloom.

I stop at the chapel to the right of the front door. Mantegna's tomb. If I were a Catholic, I would cross myself with respect. Footsteps shuffle towards me. The caretaker, carrying a dim lamp. The service is over, he shouts at me, in a mountain dialect I haven't heard for years. He must go home. His wife and dinner are waiting. Out. Get out. Go home.

I hurry out of the church. You should cross yourself, he shouts after me. I never cross myself, I shout back, without turning my head. He swears and bangs the door closed behind me.

Out in the piazza, candles in the houses begin to streak against the blue grey of the evening. The ground floor window in the merchant's house opposite is open, and through the gauze

baggy brown trousers, and a fairisle cardigan, in faded tones of blue, green and red. From the passenger side an equally elderly woman emerges. Her grey hair is tied back in a fifties-style pony-tail. She's wearing a grey tracksuit and white plimsolls. We exchange smiles.

The front door is propped open by a small, weighty brass dog. I wheel my case into the house. It is dim after the bright sun. Inside, oak panels shine from soft wall lights. A wide staircase with a red stair-runner carpet is in the background. A scrubbed pine kitchen table stands between the staircase and the front door.

Behind the table is a dumpy, middle-aged woman in a floral blouse. 'Edinburgh Woollen Mill and jumble sale fairy cakes,' I think uncharitably. She smiles at me. 'Hello,' she says. 'Welcome to Catchpole Manor. What's your name?'

'Emilia Constantine,' I say.

She looks along the rows of badges on the table in alphabetical order, each backed by a safety-pin. 'Here we are,' she says, handing me a badge with my name on it. She puts a tick against a column in a black plastic A4 folder. To the right of the folder are bunches of keys, each with a numbered tag.

Mrs Dean (her name is on a badge, just above ample breast-level) hands me a bunch of keys. 'The small key is for your room, and the other two are for the front door. We close up at eleven pm.' She gives me a sheet of paper with a map of the house. 'We are here.' She puts a cross by the front door in blue biro, and deftly draws a series of arrows, up the stairs, left along a winding corridor, ending with a cross on a building at the back. 'Room 27 is in the new annexe.'

curtain, I can see a maid putting plates on a table. I wonder if Daniele Norsa is still alive.

I need somewhere to eat my bread, drink my wine, and sleep. I retrace my steps, across a corner of the Piazza di San Pietro, then skirt round the streets behind the Palazzo Ducale. By a small doorway lurk three small boys, tiny Magi, with nowhere to go, giggling with some sort of nameless intent. One of them looks like Giacomo, son of Massarano, the dancing teacher. His head is bare. I think, I should warn him, the night air is cold here, he must protect his voice. And then I think, it can't possibly be Giacomo. Even if he were still alive, he must be at least my age.

The boys run off. I realise I have made my way, as if by instinct, to the door to which Giovanni once gave me the key. The wind has dropped and the moon is pale and waxy, hazed round the edge, two-thirds full. A dog whimpers. In the right angle between two walls, behind some bushes, there is a bare patch of earth. The bricks cradle my back. I lean against my bag and wrap my woollen cloak round me. In the distance, I can see the dim crenellations of the tower of San Giorgio. I am safe here from the chill of the water. I will be sheltered from the early morning dew.

I eat my bread, drink my wine, relieve myself against a tree, and sleep.

❖ SECUNDA PARTE ❖

I pick up the keys and map. 'There's tea and a biscuit in the Great Hall, just behind me, at four o'clock. You can have more than one biscuit, of course. I never understand why it's tea and *a* biscuit. The other meals are in the dining hall, in the annexe. Just below your room, in fact.'

'Barbara!'

The elderly couple, carrying battered canvas holdalls, have followed me in.

'Gabriel. Netta.'

Mrs Dean comes out from behind the table, to touch right and left cheeks with the woman. 'How was the drive?'

'A nightmare,' says Netta. 'We're exhausted.'

'Nonsense, my dear one. We're fit as the proverbial. Same old Catchpole, I see,' beams Gabriel. He has a slight West country burr.

'Even better,' says Mrs Dean. 'The annexe is finished, and there are new carpets in the bedrooms.'

'Wonderful,' says Netta. 'Gabriel will be pleased.'

'It's not I *will* be pleased, my love. It's that I *am* pleased.'

'Pedant!' says Netta. 'The boxes of music are in the boot.'

'I'll get the girls to put them in the hall,' says Mrs Dean.

'Thank you,' says Netta. 'Gabriel is a little tired.'

'Nonsense,' says Gabriel. 'I'm as fit as the proverbial.'

I carry my case upstairs and along a corridor with double-glazed windows and a slight smell of new paint. The passage twists to the left and then to the right, and finally through a fire door into a small square vestibule, carpeted in cool grey. On a pale butterscotch pine door is my room – number 27.

◈ PRIMA PARTE ◈

TWO

NEXT MORNING I WAKE to a heavy dawn mist. Through it glows a pale promise of sunshine. I am stiff. Too old to sleep out. A woman comes towards me, carrying a basket. I brace myself to receive insults suitable for a beggar. She is holding an orange. When she sees me, she stretches out her hand. I take the orange, and, without waiting for thanks, she walks on. I peel the orange, savouring the oily zest on my fingers.

I go through the open double doors into the courtyard behind the Palatine Church of Santa Barbara. One door hangs precariously from its heavy iron hinges. I could have sheltered more securely within the palace walls. But then, I would have missed the orange.

I look up at the church. Bird droppings everywhere. Branches blown by the wind litter the clearing by the main door. A broken carriage on its side, with just one wheel. A sad place; memories calling to me, without knowing the right words. I turn away, walking quickly across the space towards the door which leads down, deep down, below the Castello di San Giorgio, facing the Lago Inferiore.

I dip my head to avoid the low lintel. The rooms are cold, damp and empty. No sign of the rich stores of hams, vegetables, the paraphernalia of a busy palace kitchen. I come into the vast dining hall, once full of linens, the smell of hot stones, the pleasures of food. Now messy. Littered.

On greying wooden tables lie the rancid remains of food –

❖ SECUNDA PARTE ❖

The door weighs shut. A narrow, single bed, a small bedside table with a lamp on it. A folding door in the corner leads into a tiny *en suite*, with toilet, shower and sink. A slightly larger table also has a lamp on it, together with a red plastic folder: safety instructions, a map with fire exits, and a brochure listing courses for the whole year. An up-to-date student bedroom, nothing like the drab accommodation when I was an undergraduate. However, for a moment I feel as lost and scared as I did on my first day at (admittedly, a prestigious) university.

I'm used to academic conferences, being admired by snappy young PhD students, flattered and feted for my paper or keynote speech. This is different. From what little I have already seen, I am due to spend the next few days surrounded by old-age pensioners enjoying retirement activities. Oh, well. It's research, and I will just have to be an anthropologist, studying the weird ways of amateur musicians in the wild.

I look out of the window. The annexe forms an L-shape at the back of the house, and I can just see the loop of the gravel drive leading to the front door. As I watch, a taxi drives up and stops, half out of view. A tall figure emerges. Long black hair, a black leather jacket; he (it must be a he) takes out a rucksack and a large instrument case, pays the driver, slings the instrument over one shoulder by a strap and disappears.

In the distance, a clock strikes four. It is tea-time. I am about to go and find a welcome cuppa, when I hear a rough backfiring. I go to the window again. A motorcycle idles, spewing out dark grey exhaust fumes. The passenger, wearing a long multi-coloured dress, with an instrument case strapped on her back, dismounts. The

some sort of meat, a grey, congealed coating, hunks of stale, mouldy bread, shrivelled, rotting mushrooms. The army must have rampaged through here, taking everything they could.

Faded grey and yellow drawings on the walls look down on the detritus. These are Pisanello's ladies, still watching a tournament, their necks elegantly inclined, like the swans who accompanied them. A deep, deep dark blue, almost black, holds soldiers, horses, armour, ladies, lances, dogs, trees in the distance. I pluck at my memory. 'This,' Giovanni once told me, 'is a story, a legend, which comes from across the sea, from far away. From England. From hundreds of years ago. From King Arthur.'

A figure lies alone, his legs relaxed and open, his armour for all the world like a soft, comfortable sleeping suit. I touch the chill, cold plaster. My hand feels a vibration, a long, slow, deep sound. I take my hand away from the wall and the note stops. I put my hand back on the wall, and it is there again. I sing the note. It echoes round the stone walls.

High above, I can see the Tudor rose. A frieze at the top of the wall with intertwined collars, Lancastrian collars, the Tudor rose and marigolds, one of the emblems of the Gonzaga family.

I clamber back up into the courtyard. There is a pile of planks of wood, fresh and fragrant. I pick up two of the smaller planks, and make my way along the cloisters, to the broad tower on the opposite side; paved with tiny red bricks, wide, shallow steps lead upwards, shallow enough for the ceremonial horses to climb.

If anyone sees me, I think, I will pretend to be a workman, going about my business of repairing the Palazzo. I climb higher, the silence enveloping me. I walk through rooms grubby with

❖ SECUNDA PARTE ❖

driver unfastens one of the panniers. The figure removes the helmet, shaking long blonde hair free, and picks up the pannier. It's Xan.

The motorbike revs up, slews round on the gravel and roars away down the hill.

TWO

I RETRACE MY STEPS to the front of the house. A slow straggle mills round Mrs Dean's table. As I thought, a preponderance of grey heads, mostly women. I follow a trail into the Great Hall. It bustles with the chink of crockery, chatter, groups of people standing or sitting on black plastic chairs.

Even to my architecturally untutored eye, the Hall is impressive. Dark wooden panels warm a space which soars upwards to exposed roof beams. Above a massive fireplace hangs a portrait of an Elizabethan family. At the far end, Gabriel and Netta are arranging piles of folders on trestle tables.

Two young women stand in front of a large open serving hatch, pouring tea from large brown teapots. On a nearby table are milk, sugar and biscuits. Two grey-haired, dumpy ladies are ahead of me in the queue. They wear identical cardigans, one pale blue, the other pale green. When it's my turn, I get my tea and go towards the milk, almost bumping into the man from the taxi.

the victory of strangers, aiming for a small, familiar, domestic door, at the end of a narrow hall.

I take out the key I have kept for so long; the door is ajar, as if someone has just opened it for me. Inside, I put the planks on the floor. The red velvet curtains over the window are ragged. I draw one back carefully. All round the walls; men and women and children; servants, animals, horses and dogs, wooden, immobile. Above me, the familiar blue oculus. Too many memories. Too much past.

For a moment, I think I am mad to imagine I could come back and find anything the same. But yes, there it is. Tucked into the fireplace, a chest, the top elaborately carved with dolphins, sea creatures; Neptune's sceptre on the lid. Carefully, I lift the lid. Scraps of paper. Mouse droppings. Feathers from some large bird. Fragments of plaster from walls or ceiling. Small jagged pieces of metal. Torn pieces of fabric; impossible to tell what they were: silk, cotton, velvet, linen. Emptied of everything, just as the rest of the palace has been emptied of everything.

A rush of disappointment dizzies me. Steadying myself, I almost fall into the chest. One hand hits the bottom, and makes contact with something more solid than the other ragged fragments. I feel round the shape, and lift a package: the blush of the green velvet surface has faded unevenly, worn down to the underlying weave. Somehow, miraculously or simply through carelessness, it has stayed here, where I left it. Relieved that no-one has cared enough to take it, I tuck it into my belt, under my blanket.

No-one stops me as I make my way back out of the palazzo. I walk back across the Piazza di San Pietro, the Piazza Erbe,

❖ SECUNDA PARTE ❖

His hair is tied back, and he's wearing a cream sweater, jeans and trainers. He picks up a plate with biscuits and offers it to me. 'Thank you,' I say. 'Prego,' he says, a perfect Italian rolled 'r'. His profile is neat, sharp. He wears rimless glasses. Apart from myself and the tea-pourers, he's the youngest person I've seen so far.

'I saw you arrive,' I say. 'You came in a taxi.'

'I did,' he says.

'Are you Italian?'

'How did you guess? I should have said "you are welcome" instead of "prego". And you?'

'From London,' I say.

'Are you a singer?'

I shake my head. 'Have you been here before?'

'No. You?'

'It's my first time too,' I say. I put my cup down and look at my watch. 'I must finish unpacking. Excuse me.'

THREE

THE DINING HALL, DOWN two flights of stairs from my room, is modern, high and vaulted, with beige beams, white walls, and a tiled floor. Tables are crowded, with the odd empty chair tipped forward; places saved for friends. I am about to sit with a group of complete strangers, when a warm arm snakes round my waist.

'Emmy. I knew you'd be here before me!'

past the Rotonda and the Palazzo Ragione. Thunder follows me. A procession of horses races past me on the cobbles. Saddleless mountain riders. Sauntering calmly in their wake, comes a donkey. On its back, the woman from this morning. Leather panniers on either side, vegetables spilling out over the tops. Leeks. Cabbages. Fluffy parsley and onions. She plays on a pipe as the donkey sashays. A pretty tune, wandering and wavering, in a flexible rhythm.

I recognise the melody. It was played by the blind *flauto* player, Jacob van Eyck, a young Dutch musician who visited Mantova when we worked on *Orfeo*. Every day at noon, he stood on the steps of the Church of San Andrea. When the bells died away, he began playing, first in imitation of the bells, then improvising, until his notes raced faster and faster. The woman is playing *Lachrimae*, sad, slow, poignant. Tears. A long note, then a tumbling minor third to the next long note.

I can still feel van Eyck's golden O of sound. Articulated with fingers, breath and tongue, gliding from note to note. A steady, liquid stream of breath, round and full, came from deep in his body. The golden O, held in the ear's air. The instrument poised on his lips, loosely clasped round the mouthpiece, no precious air seeping out from the edges, tongue flicking invisibly backwards and forwards against the tip and edge of the fipple, cheeks loose, fingers moving like a salamander, up and down in a blur.

I have been trying to find the golden O of sound throughout my life. Sometimes it has shone through the haze of the world. For a brief moment I hear it again as I tread across the familiar cobbles. Then the woman waves to me, and she is gone.

I walk quickly round the edge of the Castello di San Giorgio

Xan leads me to the table where Gabriel and Netta are sitting. On the way, Xan whispers: 'By the way, everyone here calls me Anna. Is that ok?' I am puzzled, but I nod.

We sit, to a chorus of hellos to Xan.

'This is Emilia, everyone. My cousin. She's a singer.'

I smile. I am neither her cousin, nor a singer. One of the men opposite me has grey hair and a neat, pointed beard. He stands up, says 'Edison', and shakes my hand. 'This is Nora-Jane, my wife', indicating a woman, with short, dyed gold-blonde hair curling about her ears. She says: 'Do sit down, dear.' Next to her is a burly man, wearing red and blue plaid shorts, with the waistband belted below his paunch, sandals and bright green socks. 'This is Luther,' says Xan. 'He makes viols.' Finally a small, slight woman who looks terrified. 'I'm Ellen,' she says, without looking up.

I sit next to Gabriel. 'We arrived together,' I say.

'Yes, of course. Anna tells me you are a producer for Radio 3. That must be fun.' I am not Xan's cousin, or a singer, or a producer for Radio 3. Luckily, I needn't reply, because the soup arrives. It is followed by roast beef on large serving dishes, placed in the middle of each table. It's a good icebreaker, as we pass the food round. Slices of meat, small Yorkshire puddings, roast potatoes, pale cauliflower florets and sliced carrots. Dessert is fairy cakes with the tops sliced off and replaced as butterfly wings, resting on dabs of butter cream, topped with glacé cherries. This is wonderfully familiar British food. I suppress the desire for an avocado.

In the middle of dessert, bursts of familiar sounds come from both ends of the hall. Instruments alternate and then finally surround us. There are cracked notes, broken

and down to the shingle shore. The bank is firm, the marshes at bay. There, ahead of me, is the boat, bobbing at the edge of the Mincio.

Franco helps me in. I am shivering. As he rows in rhythmic silence, I remember his father. A strong fisherman, he risked his life, helping Jews escape when the Emperor invaded. I remember an Englishman called Thomas Coryate, who came to Mantova many years before that. We met briefly, but he caught a shivery cold, and left without seeing any of the paintings or sculptures. Now there are no paintings or sculptures to look at. Just walls and ceilings, each with its own silent story.

Coryate did find time to walk round the streets, sit in one of the gardens and write: 'This is the citie which of all other places in the world I would wish to make my habitation ... ' He sent me a copy of his book, when he got home, to England. I still have it, in my room in Venice.

The boat bumps onto the bank. I hug Franco, and he reaches into his pocket and takes out a small linen bag. '*Mandorle*,' he says. 'It's got a bit wet, I'm afraid. But still. *Mandorle*.' I hug him again. For the last time, I have left the city which was my habitation, and return to Venice which has become my habitation.

❖ SECUNDA PARTE ❖

phrases, and the applause is explosive. It is the group I heard on my arrival. The players wave at everyone, and go back to their table.

Gabriel stands up. The applause dies away. 'A most appropriate beginning. Gabrieli's *Canzon primi toni*. Thank you, gentlemen. And lady. You can always rely on the Midland Eight.' There are cheers and table-thumps from the players.

Gabriel continues: 'Friends. Welcome to Catchpole Manor for our twentieth anniversary.' Cheers and whistles. 'I am, as you know, a man of few words.' Laughter. 'My better half is the one who does the talking.' More laughter. Xan whispers under the laughter: 'Gabriel makes all the decisions, and Netta does all the work.'

'As you also know, I owe everything to Arnold Dolmetsch, with his pioneering work on early music. Without his passion, devoted acolytes and brilliance, I would not be here, and you would not be here.'

There is gentle applause. 'I have a few announcements,' continues Gabriel, 'and then I'll hand over to my better half. We are delighted to have the annexe this year – the old stables – converted into rather neat bedrooms, with what I am reliably told are called *en suite* facilities. I am sure you will agree that this dining room is a splendid advance on our previous cramped quarters.'

There is a commotion at the door. A couple, wearing walking clothes – heavy boots, waterproof jackets, and rucksacks – come in. Everyone cheers and applauds. Gabriel beckons with both hands. The pair clump across the hall towards our table. 'Welcome also to Catherine and Barton. Better late than never.'

As the new arrivals sit down, Netta stands up and

PRIMA PARTE

THREE

I'VE BEEN BACK FOR a day, and no matter how many blankets I snuggle into, I still can't stop shivering. From my window, I watch two monks hurry across the Piazza di San Marco, their hoods shielding them from the wet.

Last night I dreamed of Daniele Norsa's synagogue. Painted birds flew down from the walls, each with a flower in its beak. They sat on my arms and shoulders, round my feet on the floor, and sang to me. I knew I had written the music, but did not recognise it. Then, with a great flapping of their wings, the birds flew out of enormous holes gouged in the walls, and I woke up. At first I thought I was back in the Scuola Grande in Mantova, the Grand Synagogue. Then I remembered. I am safe, here in the Canonica, where Christ and the Virgin Mary (in both of whom I do not believe) watch over me. But this is where I now live. This is where I have lived for over ten years, behind San Marco.

The door opens. Emilia comes in. She puts a tray down on the table. 'It's hot,' she says. 'Eat. No point you getting ill as well.'

'How is Claudio?' I ask.

'Sleeping.' She gestures towards the ragged green package on the table. 'Have you opened it?'

'Not yet. I'll open it with Claudio.' I indicate the craggy *mandorle*, half unwrapped, half eaten. 'Have some. It got wet. It's a bit salty.'

speaks with quiet authority: 'By tomorrow morning, there will be a list of groups on the noticeboard in the hall. Tonight's choir with Barton will meet at eight sharp, in the Great Hall. Mrs Dean, the warden, has asked me to remind you about some of the usual housekeeping arrangements. Please don't practise before seven in the morning, or after ten-thirty at night.'

The kitchen door swings open and the young women from tea-time emerge, carrying trays with tiny posies made up of two daffodils, stalks cut short, each tied with a bright red ribbon. 'Oh,' says Netta. 'Today is Mothering Sunday. Mrs Dean has kindly made nosegays for all the ladies.'

Gabriel gets to his feet again.

'We are specially honoured this year with a new tutor. Roberto Castelli. All the way from America and Venice.' He indicates another table, and my tea-time companion stands up. 'Robert – you don't mind if I call you Robert, do you?' Roberto makes a bow of acceptance. 'Robert has a Fellowship at London University this year, to prepare a new edition of Monteverdi's *Orfeo*. Some of you may well find yourselves called on to be guineapigs.'

Barton and Catherine look up sharply. 'Do have a wonderful time this week,' says Gabriel. 'Music does more than merely soothe the savage breast. Music is a civilising influence. Making music is the most harmonious thing we can all do. If all the nations in the world made music instead of war, the world would be a better place.'

He sits, as the hall fills with murmurs. Netta puts her hand firmly on Gabriel's arm. 'Gabriel dear, you must take your pills.'

She breaks a piece off and puts it in her mouth. 'It's good. The salt goes well with the almonds.'

I hug her and the tears come. 'Silly,' she says. 'Eat. The mushrooms are fresh. Don't stay up too late.' She closes the door softly.

I devour the polenta, with its coating of grated cheese, and creamy, fragrant mushrooms. The tempting smells mix with the musty, salty odours of the package. The aroma of sea salt reminds me of the moment I first saw Venice rising from the sea.

The boat then was packed with frightened, hungry people, desperate children. In 1630, after centuries of grandeur and peace, the story of Mantova, we believed, was now over for us. The French and the Spanish had fought over the city, and now the Austrian army was finishing the job. The Jews had helped to build the fortifications on the edge of the city, and paid for the privilege. The soldiers brought the plague, but the Jews were blamed for it. The invading army took everything they could from the palace and looted the ghetto. We had a choice. Stay and be killed, run away and risk being killed. If we wanted to leave, we could take three ducats each, and nothing else.

I arrived, shivering, in Venice. The plague had arrived before us. I knew only three people: Claudio, Leone da Modena and Sara Coppio. At first I stayed with Leone in the ghetto, but love him as I did, his house was too noisy, resounding with the sound of his angry, passionate voice, and I could not work. I could have stayed with Sara, but her house was the opposite. Too quiet, stuffed with precious objects, invaded once a week by her intellectual, literary salon. Among them I felt like a small, provincial composer.

❖ SECUNDA PARTE ❖

'Don't fuss, Netta,' says Gabriel. 'Come on, dear,' says Netta, getting up. The hall begins to empty, and our table follows suit, until Xan and I are the only ones left sitting.

'What's going on, Xan? Your cousin? A singer? A Radio 3 producer?'

'Em, it's fine. I just tweaked things a bit, to make sure Gabriel would give you a place. The course is always oversubscribed. You can sing, can't you?'

'I have no idea!'

'Oh, I'm sure you can. You're a clever clogs. I couldn't tell them you are – what is it? – '

'Researching amateur music-making in the UK. Don't pretend you've forgotten.'

Xan squeezes my hand. 'I don't want my friends to feel they're being watched. You'll get to know people. Some of them are a bit weird, but they're all very friendly. Remember, you're my first cousin on my mother's side, and you're preparing a programme about early music for Radio 3. I must go. See you at eight in the Hall. Don't be late. Barton always starts on time.'

FOUR

AT A QUARTER TO eight, I go into the Great Hall. Floral curtains are drawn across the huge bay window. A gigantic chandelier in the middle of the hall glitters with candle-shaped electric light bulbs.

PRIMA PARTE

For weeks I could hardly speak. And yet, as is the way, time passed and music came to be my consolation again. Claudio was my saviour. He let me sit in his room during the day, silent, sometimes weeping. The quiet of the cloisters, the church, Claudio's room, did their job. One afternoon, I fell asleep, and no-one woke me till the following morning. I stayed there the next night and the next, and within a few days a room was cleared for me, and Claudio brought me back to music.

As Claudio's copyist, his *scrittore*, I am accorded some – limited – privileges. I am freer than I would be in the ghetto, but life in the ghetto is not as rigid as foreigners think. Our young men go to study at Padua university, living and working alongside their Catholic comrades. They behave like any other young Italians. They swagger, moving with a grace which comes from living freely in the city. The guards at the ghetto gates are supposed to be gentiles, but it is not a popular or well-paid job, and so some are Jewish. There is a thriving illegal market in keys to the ghetto gates. Young men enjoy parties, and Christian women enjoy young Jewish men. Circumcision is a curio. A notch on the bedpost.

Warmed by Emilia's food, I brush dried salt from my blanket. I have work to do. I have the end of a madrigal to finish. Claudio has never been good at endings. As usual, he is leaving the final moments to me. *Zefiro Torna*. Like so many composers, I have already set this to music, and now I must finish Claudio's version. Two high voices over a bass line. Something new in the land. Something to soar into the future.

I sharpen my quill. I mix the ink. Even though my room is untidy – littered with clothes, discarded pieces of paper – my

❖ SECUNDA PARTE ❖

Netta and Gabriel are arranging plastic chairs in large semi-circles, facing the fireplace. The two pastel-cardiganed ladies (I'm sure they would rather be called 'ladies' than 'women') are already sitting in the front row. Other people put down bags and start unpacking instrument cases. I take refuge on one side of the bay window.

In front of the fireplace is an oblong wooden box, with one side propped open with a stick. I can see a keyboard. Barton and Catherine enter; he carries an elaborately carved music stand, and she has an armful of music, which she puts down on one of the chairs at the front.

She sits at the keyboard and produces a flurry of notes. Then she plays just one note, followed by another. They jangle; she leans forward, holding an object which looks like a small corkscrew, and does something inside the box of the instrument, until the two notes merge into one. I realise she is tuning the instrument. I don't know how she can hear over all the noise in the hall.

Roberto comes in, carrying his instrument case, followed by Xan, who goes over to talk to Barton. Together they divide a large pile of paper into smaller groups. Roberto comes over to me.

'I knew you were a singer,' he says.

'Not really,' I say. 'You didn't tell me you were a visiting celebrity.'

'You didn't ask,' he replies. 'Touché,' I say. 'Sorry. That's French. I don't know the word in Italian.'

'I'm going to play up my Italian accent,' he says. 'The old ladies will love it.'

Catherine has finished tuning. Barton stands in front of the harpsichord and claps his hands loudly. The desk is an oasis of order. One small pile of paper waits, ready drawn with staves. I write a note. It dazzles and dances. It does not want to be still. My hand shakes. I can't tell whether I am shivering with cold, exhaustion, or excitement. I want to be held by the unwritten music, the security of notes lasting for a reliable time-span, at a reliable pitch, something new, never written before. The notes dance. The devil is in the detail.

I lift a pile of paper from the floor, onto my desk. The pages are covered with scrawly, spidery handwriting – a rushed Hebrew, as if Leone da Modena hadn't had enough time to write everything down. Every page has scribbled notes in the margins. Leone entrusted the manuscript to me last year. He asked me to translate it into Italian, so that his children – and the Italian, Christian world – can read it.

I began with great eagerness, and have translated about half of it. I have not been able to finish it. I am not sure why. Perhaps because it is about a real life, with real feelings and passions, terrible sorrows and great hopes. Music has none of that. Just the purity of its sound on paper. And yet. *Hayei Yehuda*, the life of Judah. 'These are the stories of Judah Aryeh ... ' Judah, Aryeh, the lion, Leone in Italian and Latin. My roaring lion friend, Leone da Modena. He reminds me of another Leone, Zio Leone di Sommi, my family's muse and guide, long, long gone. Both lions by name, lions by nature.

I fix my eyes on a place in the wall, where the plaster is dark with damp. Light and shadow pass across the wall; there are darker patches, lines and dots, swirling and moving, taking shape and then losing their shape again.

I open my eyes. I must have fallen asleep in my chair. Outside, I hear the Nona sounding midday from the San Marco

hubbub dies down. 'Choir in the middle, please. Sopranos in front. Agnes. Sheila. Please take up your descants and walk. To the right. Unless you want to sing solos?' The pastel ladies twitter with pleasure at the attention. They pick up their bags and instruments. 'Recorders, please form up behind Agnes and Sheila. Viols, on the left. Cornetts, sackbuts and the kitchen sink, at the back, behind the choir.'

Roberto takes out a large string instrument from its case, and then he sits on a chair near Catherine.

Amid the now purposeful bustle, Xan comes to lead me to the third row of the singers. Netta is distributing sheets of music to voices and instruments.

'Would you like to tune, Bob?' says Barton.

'Certo,' says Roberto, sonorously.

Catherine sounds a single note on the harpsichord. Roberto bows a string. The sounds jangle. Catherine continues sounding the same note, while Roberto bows with one hand, turning a peg with the other, the instrument held firmly between his calves. The two sounds merge into one. My stomach jumps with pleasure. Catherine plays a higher note, and the process is repeated until each string has been tuned – there are seven strings. I am mesmerised by the bow's movement, smooth and rhythmic, backwards and forwards.

Singers round me shuffle their music impatiently. One soprano in particular, in front of us, can't stand still. She has red streaks in her blonde hair, and dark red, almost black, fingernails.

'Thank you, Bob,' says Barton. He raises his baton. 'Choir,' he says. 'Your notes.' Catherine plays a series of

campanile. That's what has woken me up. I have slept for nearly twelve hours.

A hand is on my shoulder. It is Emilia. I smell camomile tea. A bowl sits on the table in front of me. Emilia smooths my hair, cups my cheeks in her hands and kisses me softly on the lips. Then she leaves, as quietly as she arrived. I sip the tea and remember my own story.

FOUR

MY MOTHER SOAKS STALE bread in milk, and when it is soft, we throw it to the chickens. We keep eggs for ourselves, and we sell eggs to our neighbours. Sometimes I carry some in a basket lined with straw to one of the small doors at the back of the Palazzo Ducale. The servants give me money, pieces of stale cake, or tiny, pink, green and yellow iced sweets. If you dip the stale cake in hot milk, it is delicious, almond and buttery. I don't give cake to the chickens.

Chickens cluck when you give them food; they cluster round your feet, clucking even more. I cluck with the chickens. I make tunes out of the sounds. There are squawks and the chickens flap away from me. One flutters over the low fence, and into the road. I run after, clucking to make it stop. It flaps its wings and runs even faster. My mother will be angry if I lose one of the chickens.

notes, and Barton sings three rising notes. 'Your first hymn sheet. *Vieni Imeneo.*'

Beside me, Xan's voice is pure and ringing and true. I can't follow the written music, so I mouth the words, just as I used to do at school assembly all those years ago. Initially, I was excused, along with the two Muslim girls, a Quaker boy and another Jewish girl. Being excused and being excluded were the same thing, and I wanted to belong. So I joined assembly. I loved the hymn tunes, but could not bring myself to utter out loud the words 'God' and 'Christ' and 'Our Lord'. So, I suppose, yes, I can sing after a fashion.

Here the words are in Italian and there are no divinities invoked. We sing it all through once – well, they sing it through once. At the end, Barton applauds very slowly and says 'Congratulations, choir. An exemplary noise. It gives me a lot to work with. Let me tell you who you are and what you have just about been singing. Nymphs and shepherds to a man.' Everyone laughs, Streaky louder than anyone else.

'This is a hymn to Hymen, the god of marriage. Let your passionate rays rival the rising sun which brings happiness to these lovers. Banish horrors and doubts, torments and grief. *Vieni Imeneo*, from Monteverdi's *Orfeo.*'

Barton nurtures now one part, now another. He hears everything. When one voice falters, he sings their missing notes, so that they can find their place again. He directs us on musical and verbal stresses, phrasing, volume. The atmosphere is intense, professional. As we repeat sections, I begin to remember the notes. With Xan beside me, I tune my voice to hers, and disappear into her sound. I

I decide to sing instead. *Yitgadal ve yitkadash.* Ahead of me the chicken stops. A man has blocked its way and grabbed it by one wing. Deftly, he grasps the chicken's legs and turns it upside down.

'Thank you,' I say.

'You're welcome, Salamone.'

'How do you know my name?'

'I have seen you with your Zio Leone. Come. I will walk home with you.'

'Thank you.' As we walk, he asks me: 'What were you singing?'

'The beginning of a Jewish blessing,' I say.

'What tune were you singing for the blessing?'

'Oh, I just made it up.'

By this time we are back home. The escaped chicken joins its friends, with lots of squawking.

I rush straight in through the front door. Loud voices fall silent. My father and Zio Leone sit at the table; my brother and sister are playing quietly in the corner, and my mother sits by the window, sewing some red material.

'I see you have met Signor Gastoldi, Salamone,' says Zio Leone. He puts his arm around me. The atmosphere softens. My mother smooths her skirt and puts on her welcome smile. My father is looking puzzled.

'Azariah, this is Signor Giovanni Gastoldi. He conducts the choir of Santa Barbara,' continues Zio Leone.

My father holds out his hand. 'Please. Signor. I hope my son has done nothing wrong?'

'The opposite,' says Signor Gastoldi. 'I heard him singing.' My mother bustles, bringing wine and glasses and a plate of

❖ SECUNDA PARTE ❖

have never experienced anything like it; totally absorbing, Barton our guru and guide.

'Well done, choir.' He turns to the instruments. 'I am sure you have been taking careful note of all my instructions.' An amused, slightly embarrassed sound ripples across the instruments. He raises his arms, baton poised. 'All together. Choir and instruments.'

The sound is oddly magnificent, even with wrong notes. Loud and confident, we celebrate the hymn to marriage. Agnes's wobbly recorder finishes a bar after everyone else. We all laugh, and Barton applauds.

'That was so good,' says Barton. 'We'll do it all over again tomorrow evening.'

There is a soft, relaxed buzz as everyone packs up and leaves the Great Hall. I'm in a daze.

'I knew you'd be fine. Did you enjoy it?' asks Xan.

I nod. 'Barton is amazing, isn't he?' I have become pure sound. I can listen. I can follow. I can sing. It is somehow both strange and comfortable.

We go into the dining hall. Huge plates with chunks of buttered fruit cake are on the tables. Hot, strong tea in large teapots, one on each table. I eat and drink. Musical phrases, bass rhythms enclose me. Xan is surrounded by people. She turns to me.

'Are you tired?' I shake my head.

'Come and listen to us,' she says. 'We're playing Dowland in Roberto's room.'

I force words out: 'Where is Roberto's room?' I wonder whether Dowland is some kind of board game.

'The Red Room. Top of the main stairs.'

We stop briefly to greet Gabriel and Netta. He looks pale. Netta takes a phial of pills from her pocket, and

cakes. 'Help yourself to *bozzolani*.' The men sit down, and I stand by my father's chair. My mother goes back to her sewing, and there is silence again, apart from the sounds of my brother and sister in the corner.

Signor Gastoldi lifts his glass and drinks. Then: 'Forgive me. If I am interrupting something, I can come back another time.'

'We were discussing business problems,' says my father.

'You may be able to help, Signor Gastoldi,' says Zio Leone.

My father takes over: '*Strazzaria*. We used to make woollen cloth. Now we are forced to trade in used clothes. Patching, mending.' He indicates my mother, bent over her sewing. 'We are s*trazzaroli*. Second-hand Jewish cloth merchants. I am sure this is not news to you, Signor Gastoldi.'

'It isn't really as bad as that.' My mother looks up. 'There is still plenty of work.'

'It is as bad as that, even if there is plenty of work. It is worse than that.'

My mother puts her sewing down. 'My loom, Signor Gastoldi, is gathering dust. In the past two years, we have found it harder and harder to sell the cloth we make.'

'More and more woollen cloth is being imported from France and England,' says my father. 'First, they restrict our production of silk, now the wool. Italian wool is the best in the world. Italian workmen are the most skilled. So other countries tempt our men to set up factories with them.'

'Feel, Signor Gastoldi,' says my mother, taking a red woollen shirt to him. 'When I have finished mending this, you will not be able to tell the difference between it and a shirt made of new wool.' Gastoldi passes the cloth between his fingers.

'Wonderfully smooth, Signora.'

gives some to Gabriel. He swallows them with a swig of tea.

'How's it going, Emily?' he asks.

'It's Emilia,' I say gently. 'It's wonderful. Thank you for letting me come.'

Xan and I go up the stairs, and through a half-open door. On chairs arranged in a circle are three of the people who were at our table at dinner. Edison and Nora-Jane and the man with the paunch. Xan takes a small viol from a case in the corner of the room. The rest are already seated, holding their instruments, music stands in front of them. So Dowland is not a board game!

'Do you want to follow the score? We're playing from a modern edition, but there's a spare facsimile.' Roberto indicates two large books on the bed.

'I'll just listen.' Xan smiles at me encouragingly. I open the modern edition to the first page. John Dowland. Ah. A composer. I sit on the bed as they all tune. Roberto's bass is rich and full, Xan's sweet and full. There is something tender about the way everyone supports and contains their instrument between their knees, legs and/or calves. At close quarters, I can see the delicate sweep of each bow, backwards and forwards. There is something vulnerable in each upturned palm, fingers and thumb delicately curled round the wood and hair of the bow, belying the subtlety, power and control of each bowing movement.

They finish tuning, smile at each other and play. The sound is like nothing I have ever heard. It's pure, not like violins and cellos, though I couldn't define the difference. The first part of the – what is it, the tune? – ends with a long note. Just before it, there's a wrong note; they repeat

'I told you, Azariah,' says my mother, going back to her chair. 'There is still enough work.'

'The Duke is the worst offender,' says my father sharply. 'He wants to be on good terms with England and France. He has led the move to import foreign cloth. It's purely political. We can only sell our cloth to poorer people, and they can't afford the finer stuff.'

'That's exactly why I prefer to mend the good wool,' says my mother.

'We have gone from being dignified cloth weavers: *lanaioli*, to being scavengers. *Strazzaroli*.'

My mother looks up. 'Azariah, that's enough. Excuse us, Signor Gastoldi. We should not be washing our dirty wool in public. In a manner of speaking.'

Zio Leone laughs at the joke. His laugh turns into a cough. 'What about the guilds?' asks Signor Gastoldi.

'With all due respect, Signor Gastoldi,' says my father. 'They are Christian guilds.'

'I have been trying to persuade Azariah to join the Christian guild,' says Zio Leone. 'They would find trade easier.'

'Rubbish.' My father is emphatic. 'They may say they want us to join. It's a ruse to restrict us from trading in wool and silk, because they'll have more control over us. Plus they have meetings on Shabbat, to make sure we can't be there.'

'If we join the guild, you can argue with them from the inside,' says my mother.

'We have our own guild,' says my father, banging the table. 'The Jewish community. The *universita*. We got round their attempt to restrict our trade in silk, and we can do the same again.'

the music and the wrong note sounds again. I quiver, but no-one seems to mind. I don't know why it seems like a wrong note. Maybe it isn't wrong. Xan and Roberto exchange looks. I can't tell if it is one of understanding, embarrassment or collusion at someone else's mistake.

At the end of the first piece, they retune in silence. I look more closely at one of the books. It has a heavy cream paper cover, with a pastiche Elizabethan picture on it. The other book is larger, with a heavy, royal blue frontispiece, like an elaborate tomb carving, set on a linen-look paper cover. Inside, the pages have lines and squiggles and symbols. On the title page it says: *Lachrimae, or Seaven Teares Figured in Seaven Passionate* ... my eye skips to *By Iohn Dowland, Bacheler of Musicke*. I flip through the pages. Blocks of music face different ways on the page, so that I have to turn the book round to see each chunk the right way up.

I don't know how long they have been playing; the chimes of the clock tower sound eleven o'clock. Roberto interrupts the music: 'Oh, my God. I must be going to a tutors' meeting. Please stay. There is four-part music to play.' He loosens the bow hair and puts it, with his viol, in the crushed yellow velvet lining of the instrument's case.

The others are already looking at some other music. I follow Roberto out. He hurries lightly down the stairs. I make my way back to my room.

My mother sighs. 'Azariah, please think. In the end, they can punish us in any way they want. We heard rumours this week that they may stop us from selling cakes to Christians. You had better finish yours, Signor Gastoldi, before someone sees you eating a Jewish cake.'

'Rebecca, please.' My father is nervous.

'Signor Gastoldi understands. I can tell a good man by the way he holds his shoulders. You won't say anything about this, will you?'

'Of course not,' says Signor Gastoldi.

'Good. Now finish your cake. Otherwise the chickens will get too fat.'

'Actually, that's where I met Salamone,' says Signor Gastoldi. 'Feeding your chickens.' I am grateful for the lie. 'He was singing – he has a real talent. I would very much like to take him into Santa Barbara, to see how his voice sounds there. May I have your permission?'

My mother and father exchange looks. Zio Leone says: 'I am sure they don't mind. I've been in Santa Barbara many times.'

'Is it true,' my mother asks, 'that there is a drop of the blood of Jesus Christ in Santa Barbara?'

Signor Gastoldi smiles. 'Well, they claim there is a sacred relic – a drop of the most Precious Blood.' He finishes his wine. 'I don't know if it is true. The cake is delicious, Signora,' he says. 'And please, Signor, I understand the difficulties of your *università*. May I teach your son music?'

I look at my father, then at my mother. My brother and sister have fallen silent in the corner.

'The choir in Santa Barbara is – a little ragged. It's not their

❖ SECUNDA PARTE ❖

FIVE

❖

I FIRST MET XAN in a café on Marylebone High Street during the early 1990s. The 1980s recession was, appropriately, receding. New shops open, and café culture moves in.

I spend a lot of time in cafés now. Reading, sometimes writing, but mainly just looking and thinking. It may sound odd from an academic, but I am fed up with libraries. Don't listen to what people say about academia. Long holidays, seeking out dusty old manuscripts, making new discoveries, giving the world new knowledges. I love the teaching, the contact with students, but I hate the bureaucratic systems, universities behaving as if they are businesses, taking money from students and not always giving them what they need.

At first, I loved working in the spanking new British Library on the Euston Road: the soaring foyer, hushed reading rooms, a private light for each reader, comfortable blue leather easy chairs, power points for laptops. I bought a heavy, expensive metal lock for my computer. The ritual of plugging in, winding the wire from the lock round the table leg and then securing it into the computer, was a comforting preparation for peaceful labour. Looking up, I see a landscape of moving heads, punctuated by bell-like signals as other members of the congregation turn their machines on and off – random calls to secular, intellectual prayer.

Uncertainty sets in when my father meets me for

fault. It's a good choir. But Giaches de Wert has had malaria again, so at the moment, I am in charge of the *cappella*. I want to strengthen the choir. I think Salamone would fit in very well.'

'Will he have to sing in Latin?' asks my mother.

'Yes,' says Signor Gastoldi. He is clear and firm and gentle, all at the same time.

'I can learn Latin,' I say eagerly.

'What do you think, Leone?' asks my father. 'Will we get into trouble?'

'The Lord would like to hear his voice,' says Signor Gastoldi.

'Whose Lord are we talking about?' I ask. I really do want to know, but for some reason everyone finds it funny.

'Well,' says my mother, 'I think it is an excellent idea. Salamone will get the best possible musical education with Signor Gastoldi.'

'And what happens when de Wert comes back?' asks my father, 'and finds a Jewish boy in his choir?'

'I am sure de Wert will not make a fuss. All he cares about is having a good choir.'

'And,' added Leone, 'remember that the *universita* is due to present our Purim play to the Duke. Salamone can teach the other children in the troupe.'

'I can play my violin quite well already,' says Menahem from the corner. 'And I know how to sing,' adds Esther. Everyone laughs.

Signor Gastoldi stands up. 'I promise I will look after Salamone. I will bring him home after rehearsals. And you are right. Duke Vincenzo has no hostility towards the *universita*.'

❖ SECUNDA PARTE ❖

coffee. He hates the building. The outside reminds him of a smart concentration camp, he says. I tell him the library is a miracle of twenty-first century architecture, cheek by jowl with the newly refurbished gothic vampire Frankenstein redbrick, Cadbury's flake chocolate towers of St Pancras Station. The perfect place for journeys of the mind, I say. So what, he hates the building.

Gradually, my concentration drifts. I order books and turn pages without following the words. Am I overworked? My teaching load is relatively light. It is a tough call to admit that my academic life is no longer enough. I have a first-class degree in English Literature, finished my PhD in the required three years, on the stories and novellas of Henry James. It is snapped up by a respectable American East Coast academic press, and is on Eng Lit reading lists world-wide. I am serious, and popular, in demand at conferences as a James expert.

My first job is at one of the more prestigious new universities of the 1960s, the University of Lavenham, in East Anglia. Like all universities, the government gives them money for research – as long as their academics keep up their publication record. Heads of department transfer the pressure onto their teaching staff.

In the London Library I find the manuscript of an unknown short story by Henry James. Little more than four hand-written pages, it is tucked in one of the many volumes of *The Golden Bowl* on the crowded shelves. The book hasn't been borrowed for decades, so it is not surprising that the treasure has lain undiscovered. It is one of James's Italian stories – a postscript, a codicil, even, to *The Aspern Papers*.

The story is on frontispiece pages from various books

'Until some bastard whips up another riot.' My father is still doubtful, but he is outnumbered.

My mother comes over and puts the red woollen shirt round Signor Gastoldi's shoulders. 'Please, Signor. Accept this as a present from us.'

'Thank you, Signora. You are very kind. I will try and have a word with the Duchess about the woollen cloth,' says Signor Gastoldi. 'She is easier to approach than the Duke.'

My father is disarmed. 'Signor, you are kindness itself. You will always be welcome in my house.'

FIVE

NEXT MORNING SIGNOR GASTOLDI takes me round the high walls of the Palazzo Ducale, through a low door and into a courtyard. Across it, and a little to the right, are the large, imposing doors of a church.

Inside, it is cool, peaceful. 'Sing your blessing, Salamone.'

'I don't think I should sing in Hebrew in a church.'

'The Lord won't mind. Anyway, I won't tell him.'

I am not sure whether he is joking, but I sing *Yitgadal ve yitkadash*.

'What tune is that?' he asks.

'My tune,' I say. 'I made it up.'

I sing again. He joins in, singing low notes, below my sound.

published in the 1880s. James must have grabbed for the nearest blank sheets of paper. Here and there the handwriting is a little shaky. One page has his signature – and this clinches the discovery, after it is officially authenticated, along with the ink, paper and the writing implement he'd used.

A major British academic press publishes a special, leather-bound edition. This includes my detailed linguistic analysis of the correspondences between this and James's other Italian stories, and an imaginative reconstruction (by me, with footnote references to other manuscripts) of three other possible draft versions of the story. Essays in *The New York Review of Books* and the *London Review of Books* vie with each other for the length and extent of their praise, and the *New Yorker* offers me an entire issue in which to tell my personal story about my quest for the authentic voice of the Italian Henry James.

I am head-hunted by a number of universities, and Lavenham, to keep me, offers a Professorship. I move up to a lofty office, on the seventh floor of a smart new glass and concrete building overlooking the river Orwell. I buy a *pied-à-terre* in leafy Hampstead, with a view across London, and spend my time reading Joanna Trollope, Maeve Binchy, Agatha Christie, C.J. Sansom, Catherine Cookson.

Then Frank, my Head of Department, invites me for an end of year drink. Over the second glass of cheap chilled white wine, he asks how my research is going.

'Oh, fine,' I say.

'Your publication record over the past three years is the lowest in the department, Emilia. The Vice-Chancellor

'How did you know what I was singing?'

'I didn't,' he says. 'I made mine up too.'

He sings a short, wordless melody. I copy him. He sings the next phrase, and again, I copy. Then we sing together, his voice deeper than mine, singing the same notes. There is a wide corridor between both voices, but both are facing in the same direction.

We repeat, and now he punctuates my tune with long, slow, rolling notes. At the end, the sound swirls round the space so fast that my eyes and ears can't follow it. It is the most beautiful sound I have ever heard. It is like an echo, but it is not an echo. It is still our voices. As the sound dies away, I hear our breathing, mine higher and quicker than his.

'Can you read music?' he asks.

I shake my head.

He leads me towards the altar. It is a tall, flat table, not like our *bima*, which is like a little stage, with steps for the rabbi to go up and stand behind. To one side of the altar is a higher table. On it is a large book, open, with lines and shapes and words on it.

'The words are Latin,' he says. He sings, pointing to each blob or shape as he changes the note. We repeat, together.

'That's very good,' he says. 'Read the words, as if they are in Italian.'

We sing again. After the first few notes, he stops pointing, and I try and follow what is written, moving up or down – with his voice still low and slow beneath mine. I trip and fumble now and again, but because I am listening to him, I find my way back to the right place. Once he joins in with me to put me back on track, then goes back to his own sound.

is on all our backs. Remind me what exactly you are working on at the moment?'

I wait.

'The university is under pressure to become a teaching, rather than a research, institution. I don't want that to happen.'

'You can't fire me just because I haven't published anything recently.'

'I can't fire you anyway. I don't want to fire you. I don't want to lose you.' He pauses. 'I've been given an ultimatum by Human bloody Resources.'

Frank has been a good friend over the years.

'Are they threatening you?'

'I know there are times when the research just doesn't flow. But – '

He doesn't need to finish the sentence. Panic makes my imagination take flight. 'Actually, Frank, I have been doing some work on the Jacobean masque, and on the compositional relationship between words and music.'

'Terrific,' says Frank. 'That's all I need to know. How soon can you publish?'

I laugh. 'It's early days.'

'You're due for a sabbatical. If you want a year, I'll support you. I might be able to swing full salary.'

My heart leaps at the idea of a year away. 'That would be great,' I say, and then, with the prospect of freedom, my imagination goes to town: 'I'm thinking of something with a performance element – authentic reconstructions of a couple of the masques? Some cross-disciplinary work, between departments?' It was beginning to sound plausible, even to me.

'Now,' he says, 'I'll sing your tune, but lower than your voice, and you make something up that fits. No words.'

He sings, and I leap from his notes to mine, up and around and away and then back to him again; for a little while I sing the same as him, my voice merging with his, then I soar away again, and finally, we end together.

'*Supra librum*,' he says. 'Extemporisation, improvisation against a line of plainsong. The English call it *faburdon*, the French call it *faux-bourdon*. The chickens have taught you well.'

'No-one taught me.'

He laughs. 'Your voice is special,' he says. 'Would you like to sing here, in Santa Barbara, with the choir?'

My heart jumps. 'Oh, yes.'

We walk towards the door. I have to run a little to keep up. 'Your church is like our synagogue. Your rabbi faces the people, just like ours.'

'We don't call him a rabbi. He's a priest.'

'Of course,' I say, as if I knew all the time.

SIX

FROM THEN ON, EVERY day I stand round the huge choir book with the other boys. I learn the round, empty shapes, the diamonds and the squares, some joined with lines, some

'Excellent. We might be able to apply for further research money to cover that. Another drink, Emilia?'

SIX

❖

MY PARENTS ARE PUZZLED. A whole year off work? They don't understand academia, though they are proud of my successes. They display my degree ceremony photographs (BA, PhD) with gowns and mortar boards. They have all my books on their shelves; they don't read them, and wouldn't understand them anyway.

My father's pride reached its zenith on their twenty-fifth wedding anniversary. As we posed for family photographs in the garden, he whispered: 'I'm proud of you, Emilia. You beat them at their own game.'

'Who's them?'

'The *goyim*. You beat the *goyim* at their own game.'

'I don't think of it that way.'

'Well, you should,' he insists. 'One day they will turn on you for being cleverer than they are. That's why you must show them first that you are cleverer than they are, then they won't be able to turn on you.'

'That doesn't make sense. If I'm cleverer than they are, they'll turn on me even more, so why should I try to be cleverer than they are? You think they'll turn on me anyway, don't you?'

separate, our voices easing between the lines and round the spaces, always in relation to each other. I learn fast. I sing in Latin: to the Virgin Mary, to the Father and the Son and to the Spirito Sancto, whoever they may be.

Some of the older boys play instruments. I have seen viols before. Some of our *universita* play them, but I have never been so close. The sound shimmers in the church, coming to meet us as we sing, blending with our voices as if the instruments had eyes to see and ears to hear.

During a rehearsal break, I pick up one of the small viols and hold it under my chin, as if it is a violin. It is too fat. I rest the instrument on my knees. It feels snug, comfortable, natural. From then on, after the singing, Signor Gastoldi teaches me to play the viola da gamba. It is so comfortable that I think I was born with a treble viol resting between my knees, the scroll nestling close to my chest.

At first, I use my fingers to pluck the strings, to find out where each note is, then I bow and sing. I can play what I hear and hear what I play. The frets welcome me, and my fingers and voice move together. When the one falters, the other guides it to the right note. I take the instrument home, wrapping it in wool and canvas, and in the evening I play and sing with my brother and sister, while my mother sews and my father reads by candlelight. My mother makes a strong linen covering for the viol, lined with remnants of softer material: wool and silk. Sometimes Signor Gastoldi comes to eat with us and hears us sing and play. I take the instrument to bed, and place it carefully on the floor, between my bed and the wall, resting my hand on it when I close my eyes. That way I can hear music in my sleep.

'Who knows. Just remember your Jewish values. Whatever happens, you beat them at their own game.'

I am about to head into an argument about 'Jewish values', then think better of it. My parents fast on Yom Kippur, have a Seder at Pesach, and light candles at Chanuka. They don't keep kosher, and aren't averse to bacon or prawns. In restaurants, of course. Not at home.

They are just 'Jewish' with unthinking pride. In my first year at university, my father asks me whether I have met any nice Jewish boys. A man who would look after me.

I come close once. Larry was giving a psychoanalytic paper on omissions and lacunae in nineteenth-century novels by women writers at a conference in Chicago. He concludes that these 'gaps' are related to sexual repression – what cannot be expressed directly. Australian charm and shoulder-length blonde hair. Over coffee, I go up to him: 'When you mentioned "omissions", I honestly thought you had said "emissions".' He stares at me with his bright blue eyes and says: 'Are you trying to pick me up?'

'Of course.'

It didn't need any more. Affairs at conferences are common; sizzling with intellectual competition and being away from home and everyday life. We meet once or twice a year for a couple of years, and then excitedly plan a weekend in Paris. Disaster. Out of the intellectual limelight he is a pernickety fusspot – complaining about the food, the wine, the crowds in the Louvre. The sex is still fantastic, but I'm not stupid enough to think a lasting

At home I sing Hebrew words to the music I have learned. Hebrew works as well as Latin, although sometimes the stresses are in different places. I teach my brother and sister the Latin words. My mother and father approve. If we want to be scholars, they say, we should learn Latin, just as real Italian scholars learn Hebrew. Zio Leone di Sommi writes in Hebrew, Italian and Latin. He has written a book about plays and stages and performance, and he jokes that one day I can translate that from Hebrew to Latin, and then to Italian. I say, 'Yes, yes, I will do that for you, Zio Leone.' My father ruffles my head and says I am an 'accommodating boy'. My father is a stern man in the community, but he can be a gentle man at home.

One day, after rehearsal, Signor Gastoldi takes me into the palace kitchen. We walk through a large hall, full of hurrying, shouting people. The walls are covered with painted figures. That night, I dream of the hall, partly below ground, flakes of *stucco* straining away from the walls. A deep, deep dark blue, an almost black distance holds soldiers, horses, armour, ladies, lances, dogs, trees. Gastoldi walks beside me. This is a legend, he says, from across the sea, from England, hundreds of years ago.

A figure lies alone, his legs relaxed and open, his armour keeping him warm. This is the English King Arthur, says Gastoldi. I put my hand on the wall. The plaster is chill. I feel a vibration, a long, slow, deep sound.

At the top of the wall is a frieze, with intertwined collars, Lancastrian collars, the Tudor rose and marigolds. These are English, says Signor Gastoldi, though the marigold is also an emblem of the Gonzaga family. I do not know where England

relationship can just depend on sex. I heave a sigh of relief when we say goodbye, with a quick peck on the cheek. No more conferences for me.

SEVEN

❖

WITH MY SABBATICAL COMES café culture. One morning, at my usual faux-French wicker table in Marylebone High Street, a young woman breezes in, carrying a multi-coloured striped shoulder bag. She drops a leaflet on each table. A pageant for Henry the Eighth, it promises, down at Hampton Court. The information nudges my academic guilt. Too early for my Jacobean masques (about which, by the way, I know nothing), but perhaps this will get some curiosity going.

Hampton Court on an August Sunday afternoon is crammed with tourists: Americans and Japanese, festooned with cameras. I wander round the garden. I hear piping music: a trio of costumed musicians play under a tree. A tall thin man with a floppy maroon velvet hat, and two women in long yellow and red velvet dresses. It sounds like the signature tune of 'Blackadder' and is perfectly pleasant. I listen for a while, and then go to find the café.

I've just about finished my coffee and banana cake, when: 'May I?' I nod assent. A young woman with a pony tail sits down with a mug of strong-smelling peppermint

is, but it sounds like a place I would like to visit. As I begin to wake, the roses and marigolds drift down to the ground. I take my shoes off and walk on the warm, soft petals.

SEVEN

I GO DOWNSTAIRS TO see Claudio. At first I think he is sleeping, and I sit quietly beside his bed, while Emilia tends the fire. His breathing is deep, a little raspy, regular and rhythmic. Not too frightening. Just an old man recovering from a bad cold.

I shift in my chair. At the creak, he opens his eyes. 'Well? Have you got it?'

'Of course,' I say, holding up the faded green velvet package, which has been resting on my knees. Claudio struggles to sit up. 'Well?'

'I haven't opened it yet. I wanted us to do it together.'

'So get on with it.' He gestures impatiently at me, and has a bout of coughing. Emilia brings some water for him to sip, then moves his pillows to support him better.

'Well?' he says again, impatiently.

I take the package to a small table near the fire and begin to unwrap the cloth, carefully, worried that it will disintegrate. The basic weave is strong, and it holds. The papers are tied with a black ribbon. I untie the bow, and pick up the first page.

tea. She puts her bag on the floor. I recognise the bag and smile. She smiles back. A man comes towards the table.

'Sorry, Terry,' she says. 'I'm meeting someone for tea. Do you mind?'

'You didn't tell me.'

'I forgot.' As he walks away she says softly: 'Do you mind talking to me for a few minutes?'

'Not at all. What about?'

'Oh, anything. Do you like my hair?'

'Yes, I do. Brilliant pony tail.'

'More,' she orders, stirring her tea.

'Nice T-shirt. Bit short, though.'

She looks down at her midriff. 'Oh, God, is it?'

'Not really,' I say. 'By the way, I couldn't find the pageant. Did I miss it?'

'There's no pageant. That's the name of our group. The Tudor Pageant. I told Terry it was a crap name,' she says. 'Tacky costumes and a crap name.'

'Was that you playing in the garden?' I ask.

'God, yes. Terrible, wasn't it?'

'I don't know. If you hate the name and you hate the costumes, and the music was terrible, why do you do it?'

'Because Terry asked me. I haven't got any work lined up.'

'Are you a musician?'

'Officially. I'm not going to do this any more, though. It's too amateur.'

She laughs. A wide laugh, a wide mouth, the whole of her face crinkled and lit up; a lock of hair falls from the single clip holding it at the back of her head. She opens the clip, and the rest of her hair tumbles down.

'No, no,' says Claudio. 'I'm not interested in the beginning. Go to Act Five.'

I look carefully for Act Five. 'It's here,' I say.

'Good,' says Claudio, sinking back onto his pillows, his eyes closing.

'Do you want to look at it?'

'No, no. As long as it's there. You look after it.' I replace the pages and wrap the cloth round them. Claudio is imperative.

'You've got more important things to do than sit here staring at me. Get on with my music.'

'You're an irritable old bastard. You don't deserve me.'

'Of course I don't deserve you. When did I ever get what I deserve? Don't answer that. I want the opera finished.'

'What opera? This is news to me.'

'It's news to me as well. It came to me this morning. *L'incoronazione di Poppea*.' He opens his eyes. They are shining. 'Get going.' He points to a sheet of paper on his bed. 'Take that. Some words for you.'

'Where shall I start?' I can't tell if he is actually serious.

'At the end, of course. Always start at the end.'

'What happens at the end?'

'They live happily ever after. You should know that by now. Now get out. I'm tired.' He coughs.

I pick up the package, and turn round when I get to the door: 'What instruments does my lord desire?'

Claudio laughs and waves me away, as if to say: 'Who cares?'

'You could always leave it unfinished,' I tease.

'It will be unfinished, unless you write it,' he retorts.

'Claudio,' I say, 'I think you may be Jewish.'

'That's better,' she says. 'Look, would you like to hear some proper early music?'

'Early – '

She doesn't wait for me to finish my sentence. 'What you've just heard. Only better. What are you doing next Thursday?'

'Going to hear music with you.'

'The Wigmore Hall. Give me your phone number. I'll ring you this evening. Is that ok?'

I write my phone number on my serviette.

'Thanks.' She takes the serviette and puts it in her bag. 'Terry is fretting. I'd better go and make peace. My name is Xan, by the way.'

'Emilia,' I say.

She picks up her bag and hurries away, pinning her hair up as she goes. The back of her neck is smooth and sleek, like a swan gliding, wings outstretched.

EIGHT

I'M NOT A CONCERT-GOER. I don't do live performance. I prefer books. My mother played the cello, and she tried to teach me; I learned to read music a bit, but neither of us were really interested.

The Wigmore Hall is a cosy space, compact, almost like a school hall, with a vaulted ceiling over the stage, and two doors at the corners. At the back of the stage

'Oh, yes,' he replies sarcastically, 'how do you make that out?'

'Because,' I say, 'you are in mourning for the destruction of the Second Temple of the Jews by the Romans. Wise men have ruled that whatever you do, you should leave a little bit unfinished, in memory of the destruction of –'

He finishes my sentence for me: ' – the destruction of the Second Temple of the Jews by the Romans. The Greeks also say that every house should have a corner which is unfinished. Does that make me a Greek?'

'It certainly doesn't make you a Roman.'

'End of catechism,' says Claudio.

'So now you are making me into a Catholic?' I say.

Claudio says: 'Next year in Jerusalem', and I answer: 'Next year, who knows?'

EIGHT

BACK IN MY ROOM, I look at the words:

Pur ti miro
Pur di godo
Pur t'annodo
Pur ti stringo
Pur t'annodo, piu' non peno, piu' non moro, non moro, o

❖ SECUNDA PARTE ❖

wavy, pre-Raphaelite figures stream upwards in modest eroticism. The audience is mostly grey-haired elderly, with a scattering of younger people, possibly students. Xan and I sit near the front.

The lights dim and five musicians file onstage, bow to the audience and sit in a semi-circle. Two women with neat, short haircuts, three men with long hair, two with beards. They wear smocks in variations of green, over black trousers. Two small string instruments, like violins, are balanced on two of the players' knees. One slightly larger instrument is supported between another player's knees, and the two largest instruments, supported low down between the calves, look like cellos, but have no spikes.

I can't say I enjoy the first half very much. The sound is – thin, I suppose is the best word. After the first two pieces, the musicians stand and bow. We clap. They leave the stage. The audience rustles into chatter. An usherette in black comes and moves the stands around. She brings another stand and positions it at the apex of the semi-circle of chairs. The musicians file back on and bow. We clap. I'm getting bored.

The right-hand door at the back opens and a young man, with spiky blonde hair, comes on. He is wearing a dinner jacket and black bow tie. He bows, and we applaud again. He stands behind the new music stand, and sings in a high, falsetto voice, accompanied by the instruments. The audience loves it. Xan leans forwards, her face in her hands. At the end of the song, she claps enthusiastically. I don't know what to make of it.

In the interval, we go downstairs to the bar. I look at Xan's programme. The singer, it says is one of the world's

mia vita
O mio tesoro

I see myself in your eyes. We are entwined. I shall not be in pain, nor shall I die. Oh, my life, oh, my treasure.

I say the words out loud: in Italian, in Hebrew. Short, rhythmic phrases. A psalm of love. Nero and Poppea combine in a stately rhythmic dance, their cloaks and robes creating breezes around my head. I shiver. There is nothing fanciful here. Emilia has left the window open to air the room. The night dew is chill and damp. I close the window.

My hand is bold and clear, with fat, schoolboy letters. They serve well for clear musical notes, which must obey the discipline of line and space and note value. My handwriting is much clearer than Claudio's, perhaps because Hebrew lettering is not joined up in the same way as Italian or Latin. Each letter of the Hebrew alphabet is distinct. Claudio's hand rushes on – looping above, looping below, slanting to the right, rush, rush rushing, as if he is trying to get as many notes as possible onto the page as quickly as possible. He has not slowed up with age, and I am one of the few people who can read his handwriting clearly.

Pur ti miro. Two voices, poignant, lilting, and loving, will duck and weave; their notes will harmonise, clash and soar in discords which are sweet to the ear, because they are aiming for harmony. I can hear it in my mind, and all that remains is the slow and painful labour of writing it out.

The bells sound midnight. The moon glimmers faintly on the canal. The smoke from a thousand fires swirls light and grey in the dark, shades and shapes of shifting figures. I am

leading counter-tenors. He is singing as a guest with the group, who are from one of the American universities which specialises in 'early music'.

Perhaps it is chocolate chip ice cream, the warmth of the hall, or Xan, listening raptly beside me, but the second half is much better. I'm no longer taken by surprise by the sounds, of either instruments or voice, and, indeed, I begin to detect subtleties of tone and volume, and variety. At the end, even I clap with some appreciation. Xan says: 'I'd take you backstage, but Terry will be there. He knows the group.'

As we hurry out of the hall, I ask: 'What's your relationship with Terry?'

'Oh, we're on and off,' she says carelessly. 'He doesn't *talk*. You know? Sometimes it's very peaceful. But mostly, it's boring.'

I nod. 'I understand. Everyone I know talks a lot.'

'He loves the music, and he's ambitious. He just doesn't talk. Are you hungry?'

'Er, yes. Yes, I am.'

We have an Indian takeaway and a bottle of white wine in her flat, in one of the mansion blocks along Wimpole Street. The curries are gentle, and we eat them with thick, chunky, fragrant mango chutney, which Xan has made herself.

'Is Xan short for Susan?'

'Good God, no. It's short for Xantippe.'

'Xantippe? That's Socrates' wife.'

'Really? Who's she?'

'Xantippe was a spirited woman. Some say she was bad-tempered, argumentative, jealous of other women. Some people called her a nagging shrew.'

surrounded by the dying. They reach out their arms towards me. At first, I shrink back, my shoulders contracting. Then I see they are smiling. I stretch out my arms towards them and open my hands. As I do so, I hear the sound of an instrument. I can hear the pitch in my head, but I hear no articulation at the beginning of the note, so I can't tell if it is wind or string, viol or recorder. I decide it is King David's lyre. The dead hear it and they are calmed, turn away from me and go. I shiver and close the window.

NINE

ONE DAY, WALKING HOME from rehearsal in Santa Barbara, I feel a thump in the middle of my back. I turn round, and something hits me on the arm. I stumble. Two boys from the choir are chasing me. I run as fast as I can. I hear them shouting: Jew, Jew-boy, Christ-killer, plague-bringer. I reach home just as my father comes out to see what the noise is. He shouts at the boys and they turn and run. My head is bleeding.

I lie in bed for two days, shivering, though I have no fever. Signor Gastoldi comes to see me, and I can hear him talking to my mother and father. He promises that the boys concerned will leave the choir. That makes me feel better. Zio Leone comes and puts his hand on my forehead and sings to me. It is Friday night, and I am well enough to go to synagogue, the

'Well, I'm not like that. How do you know all this?' She leans back in the chair, her legs slightly apart, her long skirt draped modestly between them.

'I read it somewhere. Does anyone call you Xantippe?'

'No. When I went to school, no-one could pronounce it, so everyone called me Anna. Then, at college, I played the Telemann trio sonata. You know it?'

I shook my head. 'I'm a musical philistine.'

'Would you like to hear some really good music?'

She puts on a CD. It's a solo recorder, she says. Not Telemann. At the end: 'What do you think?'

'I don't know,' I say.

'It's Van Eyck.'

'Van Eyck, the painter?'

'I don't know whether he was a painter as well.'

'Maybe there was more than one Van Eyck. Who's playing on the CD?' Xan hands me the sleeve. Her picture is on the back.

'It's not a very good photo,' she says.

'You're amazing. Have you recorded anything else?' She shakes her head. 'What do you like about the recorder?'

'I love it because it's got perspective. It goes deep, deep, into the distance, into the hollow space behind all sound. It keeps time, and it shows you the way out of time. Through the hollow, you can see into the past, into other countries and other times and deep into the bellies of all those you love, have loved and will love. When you play, you breathe into the soul of you. It's the golden O.'

'That's poetry,' I say gently.

'I don't know anything about poetry,' she says. 'It's just fact.'

room at the top of Daniele Norsa's house. My father invites Gastoldi to come too. I don't need to listen to the prayers; the painted birds and flowers on the walls calm me.

Afterwards, Signor Gastoldi comes home to eat with us. Menahem kicks me under the table. Everyone is looking at me. I haven't been listening.

'The wedding, Salamone.' My mother's voice is gentle. 'Signor Gastoldi would like you to play some music at the wedding.'

'I would like you to compose and play music. Together with Emanuele and Esther,' says Signor Gastoldi.

'What wedding? Are you getting married?' I ask him. Everyone laughs.

'Duke Gugliemo's son, Vincenzo, is getting married,' says Signor Gastoldi.

'But he is already married. Is he going to have two wives? Isn't that greedy?'

My father explains: 'His wife has decided to go into a convent, so he must find another wife.'

My mother mutters: 'Sent to a convent, more like. No children. That's the problem.'

'The official wedding has already taken place, in Florence,' explains Signor Gastoldi. 'But there will be celebrations in Mantova.'

'More taxes,' says my brother, showing off that he understands the ways of the grownups.

'Will you compose something?' asks Signor Gastoldi. 'One of your *canzonette*. Perhaps even more than one.'

'What are their names?' I ask.

'Vincenzo Gonzaga, and Eleonora de' Medici.'

I want to know more about her. 'How long have you been living here?'

'It's not mine, if that's what you mean. It's my grandmother's. She died last year. Her grand domestic pile is falling to bits. Probate is taking ages. My grandfather is in an old-age home. He doesn't know what time of day it is.'

I yawn. I'm quite drunk. 'I should go,' I say, not moving.

'You can stay here. You can have my bed.'

Xan leans forward and stands up. Her breasts stretch taut from her body, rounded, her collar bone elegant, creamy marble. She takes my hand. My eyes stroke down her body, down one slim buttock and thigh, to the smooth, lithe calf above her bare foot. Her skin is an even colour, not pale or freckled, but the kind of skin which tans evenly, and which looks wan and sallow-yellow if she is ill. I imagine myself tending to her in bed, when she has a fever, bringing her tea with lemon and honey.

In the bedroom, a red paisley bedspread hangs at the window. Xan turns down the green quilt on the bed. A flutter of breath at my cheek, a hand on the inside of my upper right arm, fingers stroking my arm, a soft kiss on my cheek. 'Sleep well,' she says. 'I'll leave a towel and toothbrush for you in the bathroom.' I lie down on the bed, fully dressed, warm. Above me, on the ceiling, a round, multi-coloured glass lampshade glows. My eyes close.

I wake next morning with Xan curled round me. She kisses me on the cheek and says: 'Go back to sleep.' When I get up, she has gone. There is a note on the kitchen table with a telephone number:

'Phone me. Xan.'

TEN

SIGNOR GASTOLDI LEADS US through room after room. Bright with candles, colours, perfumes. I recognise jasmine and lavender, and then everything merges into clouds of light and haze and smells. We wait in a small chamber. A servant brings us some cool, red drink, in long glasses. It tastes like summer and strawberries.

We tune our viols, and mouth our way silently through the words. My brother and sister are always confident when they sing, but for some reason, this evening I am afraid I may forget my words. Then the door opens and we are beckoned in.

Vincenzo and Eleonora sit on raised chairs in the middle of the room, on a red carpet covered with rose petals. More people sit round the sides of the room. We bow. We sit and tune and sing.

Voi due terrestri numi
V'ergete a vol sopra i celesti lumi
Vincenzo e Leonora
Si che la terra e'l ciel chino v'adora

You are our Gods on earth
Vincenzo and Leonora
The heavens sing in harmony
May Vincenzo and Leonora live together in happiness.

❖ SECUNDA PARTE ❖

NINE

❖

OVER THE NEXT FEW months, Xan takes me to hear music by Byrd, Gibbons, Jenkins, Lawes. The last one sounds very modern, and I don't like it very much. We hear Handel oratorios on the South Bank, Bach cello sonatas in London churches. Xan explains that these were at the outer edge of her musical taste, which really ends at around 1700, with Corelli's Opus V sonatas for violin. We hear these played by a young Polish violinist, giving his final recital at the Royal Academy of Music. His bow soars and flutters, strokes and fizzes. Xan knows everyone. 'The trouble with early music in this country,' she says, 'is that you could cram us all into one telephone box.'

We hear a flamboyant Spanish recorder player, who wears bullfighter shoes, to compensate for his lack of height, clicks his heels in mock toreador style before he begins playing, and then mesmerises us with his dexterity and soaring sound. He plays modern pieces, written specially for the instrument, making strange, unmusical sounds, singing and playing simultaneously.

The Spanish musician was her recorder teacher, in Basel. 'He's the sexiest player in the world. It doesn't mean anything when I say he is sexy, Everyone falls in love with their music teacher. That's because music is sexy, and when you get near someone who is making it, you find them sexy.'

I imagine my fingers stroking her collarbone, tracing their way up and under her left ear, and down the side of

We sing it twice; the second time Esther decorates and soars over the top line. I have forgotten that we have an audience and am startled when I hear the applause. We stand, and Signor Gastoldi leads us in a bow.

They insist on hearing the music again. This time my voice misses one or two notes, and I wonder if I am getting a cold. At the end, they clap and laugh, and Eleonora beckons us to her. She kisses me on the cheek, while Vincenzo talks to my brother and sister. Servants carry plates of food, and trays of glasses, filled with different coloured liquids. Sweat trickles down my face. Eleonora keeps tight hold of my right hand. She has rings on all her fingers, and we are so close that I see the thick powder on her cheeks and smell her perfume.

A servant brings a plate of small cakes for us to take home. Polenta and almonds and sugar. My mother eats one. 'Hmm,' she says. 'Mine are better.'

My voice misses notes more frequently after that, and soon it is no longer pure, like a boy's or even a girl's. At first, I am deeply upset. I strain, trying to reach the high notes I love. Signor Gastoldi moves me to a lower voice in the choir. It takes me a while to adjust to singing inside the texture, instead of soaring over the top. I exchange my beloved treble viol for a bass viol. The strings are lower in pitch, and soon we are comfortable with each other.

Now my voice is low, like his, Signor Gastoldi says I may call him Giovanni. He encourages me to compose, till I have a collection of three-part *canzonette*. We are in great demand, for Jewish wedding parties and other community celebrations, and for the great houses in the *città*. We call ourselves the *concerto dei giovani*.

❖ SECUNDA PARTE ❖

her neck. Xan's intense concentration at concerts makes it easy to listen. Once Terry comes with us, sitting silently next to Xan. I try to make conversation in the interval, but he is monosyllabic to a fault, and I give up.

One day, Xan gives me a leaflet about an early music course. She is going. Why don't I come? I thank her, and say it isn't really my thing.

That evening, Frank phones me. How is my research going?

'Very excited about your Jacobean masque project,' he says. 'There is some funding in the Music Department. We might be able to do an interdepartmental deal. What do you think?'

'I'm still at an early stage.'

'Well, we don't want to lose the money. Can you give me a paragraph?'

'Oh, no problem. I should have something by next term.'

I drink innumerable cups of strong coffee, while I roam round the internet. Nothing piques my interest. I get up for more coffee and knock over a pile of concert programmes. As I gather them up, I realise that I have found new, wordless pleasures in music. I think about life when I return to teaching, and the prospect seems bleak. I phone Xan, and ask her if she thinks there will still be places on the early music course. Can I just come and listen? She says she knows the organisers, and she will see what she can do.

I phone Frank. I have a meeting with a musicologist – an expert in the Jacobean masque. Frank is delighted that I am on the case.

I feel a little uncomfortable at lying, delaying the

Then Duke Gugliemo dies and Vincenzo becomes Duke. We watch from the top of our house as the royal party parades through the streets, beneath a canopy of silver cloth, just the edge of a white satin robe fluttering in the breeze. The cheers are deafening. The new Duke has abolished half the tax on wine. They say that his treasurers throw gold and silver to the people.

The celebrations continue for weeks. Zio Leone brings a request for the Jewish troupes to provide dancing and music, with a special request for the *concerto dei giovani*. We must wear new, rich costumes, suitable for such a celebration. My mother and all the women in our street spend days sewing velvet and silk, turning old clothes inside out, covering fraying seams with new lengths of brightly coloured cloth.

Giovanni leads us through the Palazzo. New rooms. New corridors. We arrive in one of the wide halls, lined with busts of Greek and Roman emperors, and he holds up a hand for us to stop. 'Salamone,' he says, 'they would like to hear you play first. Alone.'

I follow him to another room. He closes the door. 'This is the Camera dei Cani, the Room of the Dogs. Wait here.'

I look round. Deep blue paint swirls across the walls and the ceiling. I swim in the depths of a deep blue sky. Six sharp, shining white lines radiate outwards from Diana, driving her chariot, drawn by dogs. They ride on a cloud resting on a floating female figure, its hand outstretched. On Diana's forehead is a crescent moon. Stars twinkle. Vincenzo is born from Duke Gugliemo, and Eleonora surveys the scene. The stars are disposed in a favourable astrological formation for the rule of Mantova. It should be called the Room of the Zodiac.

moment when I will either have to come up with a real project, or admit that it has fallen through. Lies upon lies. I don't feel guilty. My mind drifts back to the time when I discovered the James story. I didn't feel guilty then. When the news broke, the London Library were delighted. Their membership increased – more academics, rifling in the stacks for undiscovered documents to boost their careers, no doubt.

American universities made a strong pitch for the manuscript. Frank and I felt it should stay in this country. I photographed the pages. The plan was to have a formal handover, with dignitaries from the London Library and the Mayor of Ipswich present.

The week before the ceremony, I visit my parents in London. It's only after I get to Liverpool Street station that I realise I haven't got my briefcase. I must have been so absorbed in the newest Joanna Trollope that I forgot to pick it up when I got off the train. Was there anything valuable in it? Well, yes. There was a valuable manuscript. In the honourable tradition of Thomas Carlyle and T.E. Lawrence, I join those who have left precious manuscripts on a train. Newspapers and TV stations report the loss, but there is no trace of the briefcase or its contents.

Luckily, I have photographs. The University has no choice. The photographs, or nothing. The James Estate are justifiably annoyed that I have not handed the manuscript over to them, but they too have no choice. The photographs *in lieu* are displayed in the library at the University of Lavenham.

I am not ashamed of what I did. I always had a good eye, and a facility for copying. At school I forged notes from parents, to help friends get out of games or school

PRIMA PARTE

I am sucked into the sky and whirled past a centaur. He thrusts his spear towards a bear, whose half-open mouth reveals a flickering red tongue. I fly round a crab, over which a foreshortened lion hovers. Naked twin cherubs clutch each other, stroking my cheeks as I pass.

Giovanni returns and conducts me into another room. In the centre, just as they sat at their wedding, are the Duke and the Duchess. Vincenzo and Eleonora. A semi-circle of courtiers stands behind them.

Giovanni sits at a small, plain wooden harpsichord. I tune my strings. He plays a series of chords: *La Spagna*. I play the chords alone, and then improvise as he repeats the sequence. I dance up and down the instrument, reaching to the lowest bass string, stretching to the highest point way above the frets, tightly to the top of the fingerboard. The rhythms beat with the blood of my heartbeat. I am flying with Diana through the deep blue sky. My heart and soul are inside the belly of the instrument, flying and flaunting with the sound buzzing through my body and the instrument. We are one, and we are at one. I rest on the final chord.

We bow and return to Diana's room. My brother and sister run to perform with the dancing troupe. Giovanni follows them. The door closes behind him, and I hear the sound of rustling silk. I turn. The Duchess is there, her Moorish maid by her side.

Voi due terrestri numi
V'ergete a vol sopra i celesti lumi
Vincenzo e Leonora
Si che la terra e 'l ciel chino v'adora

'You see,' says the Duchess. 'I remember your song.' I bow,

trips. I copied signatures faithfully, and no-one ever suspected anything. The idea of imitating James' handwriting started as a lazy experiment, light relief from serious study. I spend so much time with manuscripts and old books, that I wondered whether recreating authentic handwriting, with authentic implements on authentic paper might enable me to inhabit – imaginatively, at any rate – the mind of Henry James. I suppose it is a bit like people who visit Charles Dickens's house, and by touching his desk, feel they are in touch with his imagination.

I felt a pang of guilt for plundering rare books for their blank pages, but others have vandalised libraries in far worse ways. I wanted to see how far I could go in fooling people. I meant to own up, and use the experience to encourage discussions about how close we could ever get to the imaginations of geniuses. But I was far too clever. My success ran away with me. My discovery was taken so seriously that I realised that if I told the truth, I would never work again in academia.

I have one regret. I wanted to confess to my parents, if only for them to absolve me: 'Never mind, you're our daughter, and you beat the *goyim* at their own game,' but they might have shopped me – to the library, to the university, to the police. Blood might not have been thicker than morality. My need to confess was suppressed, and then, as time flew by, forgotten.

my eyes fixed on the maid. She is dark, her skin almost black, her eyes challenging. Out of the corner of my eye I see a ship at the edge of the ceiling. I want to jump into it and sail away. Twin cherubs jostle me back down into the room with their soft naked bodies.

'And you write beautiful music,' she adds.

'Thank you,' I say. And then: 'I am preparing a collection of *canzonette* – may I dedicate it to you?'

'I would be honoured,' she says. There is a small silence. 'Do you know the palazzo well?'

I shake my head. 'Just Santa Barbara, really.'

'Come, then.' There is an imperious tone to her voice. She is like a breeze which blows gently, and then gusts cold. I do not know what to say. I am still holding my viol.

'You can leave the instrument here with Emilia. It will be quite safe.'

I wrap the viol and secure it in its canvas covering. Emilia's hands briefly touch mine as she takes the instrument from me. I follow the Duchess, watching her green and gold silk cloak billow and puff smoothly over the marble floors. We walk along a long, wide gallery, lofty and airy. 'This is the *Corridorio dei Mori*.' Plaster and wood splinters lie in small piles in the marble corners.

'The Duke is designing this as his new *Logion Serato*. He plans to have music played in here. What do you think?'

I sing a line of melody and listen to the way the walls receive it. 'It is pleasing,' I say. She is amused at my formality. 'I want mirrors along one side. On the ceiling, I want a painted horse which changes direction as you look at it. The Duke loves riding.'

❖ SECUNDA PARTE ❖

TEN

❖

THE MORNING AFTER MY arrival at Catchpole, I wake before my alarm goes off. I draw back the curtain. Two figures jog past the back of the house. Barton and Catherine wear matching grey tracksuit bottoms and red and orange fleecy tops.

Breakfast is help-yourself. Cereals. scrambled egg, bacon and sausage, tea, coffee and a huge revolving toaster for sliced white and brown bread. Everyone wears their name badge. I've forgotten mine. I collect cornflakes and a cup of tea.

I join Gabriel and Netta at their table. 'Emilia.' Gabriel indicates the chair next to him. 'Could you pass the sugar, Netta dear?'

'Nice try,' she says. 'You know you mustn't.' She takes some sweeteners out of her pocket and gives them to Gabriel. He turns to me. 'Do tell us more about your project, my dear.' Roberto and Xan arrive and join us.

It's a bit early in the day to have to invent a new life, but I give it my best shot. 'It's a series of three programmes. About amateur music-making in the UK. We're doing one on choirs, another on orchestral music, and one on early music.'

'Fascinating,' says Gabriel. 'I shall look forward to them. I only listen to the Third Programme anyway.'

'It's called Radio 3 now, dear,' says Netta.

'Can't see why,' says Gabriel. He turns to Roberto. 'Well, Robert. Have you decided?'

PRIMA PARTE

We walk out into the Piazza di Santa Barbara, like two friends out for an evening stroll. The evening mist surrounds the oil lamps on the walls with steamy haloes. She leads me to one of the towers in the Castello di San Giorgio. A wide spiral staircase leads up to a corridor with Greek and Roman heads and torsos tucked into niches. At the end is a small door. She takes a key out of her pocket and opens the door. I follow her in and she closes and locks the door. Colours glow dimly from the walls. The only sound is the crack of the flickering blaze in the fireplace.

She opens one of the windows. Frogs have begun their hymn to the night. Far below, the rain rustles wetly on the lake. A hazy moon shines. She takes a taper and lights a series of candles round the room. A bed, canopied in white silk, almost fills the room. By the window is a large wooden chest.

Soft hands cup my cheeks. A light kiss on the lips, too swift for me to even think of responding or withdrawing. She takes my hands and leads me to the bed. The candles warm the pinks and browns and the flesh of figures peopleing the walls. The candles warm her face. Her cheek is against mine.

'*La Camera degli Sposi,*' she whispers. 'Mantegna's *Camera Dipinta.*' She draws back the cover. 'Neapolitan silk. Not Mantovan. This is the most beautiful material your body will ever feel.'

She takes my hand and guides it under her dress. The skin is soft, delicate. She urges me gently onto the bed, under the white canopy, then under covers of yellow and red silk. She wears nothing under her dress. My fingers play with this new softness, slightly damp, and then I feel her hand against me. A stiffness, felt not for the first time, but felt for the first time

'Decided what?' Xan chips in.

'Gabriel thinks Roberto might give a talk about his research.' Netta says 'Roberto', as against Gabriel's anglicised 'Robert'.

'I don't know,' says Roberto.

'Explain how someone puts together an edition of a piece of early music,' urges Netta. She turns to me. 'Roberto is working on a new edition of *Orfeo*.'

'I don't want to upset anyone,' says Roberto.

'He means Barton.' Netta has lowered her voice.

Roberto nods. 'Yes.'

'Do him good,' says Netta. 'He thinks he owns Monteverdi.'

'That's a little harsh, my dear,' says Gabriel gently. 'By that token, he would own Schutz and Gabrieli and Tallis – and even Bach – every composer before Mozart.'

'Well,' says Roberto, 'I could talk about the history – the context of early opera, that sort of thing.'

'I'm sure Barton won't mind. After all, his edition is at least ten years old.' Gabriel gets slowly to his feet. His face is shiny with perspiration. 'We'll call it: Monteverdi and the Golden Age.' He and Netta walk down the hall, stopping here and there to chat to people.

Xan butters a piece of toast. 'What are you doing this morning, Emmy?'

'I might go for a walk,' I say.

'Roberto – give Emilia a viol lesson. She'll love it.'

'A what?' I say.

'Are you free this afternoon?' asks Roberto.

'Well – '

Xan puts her hand over Roberto's. 'Emilia can borrow my viol,' she says.

with purpose. I hesitate. 'You need not worry,' she whispers, against my neck. 'I am pregnant. Remember, that is my job.'

We are friends, two lovers like any other couple. My hands run over the faintly rounded stomach, smooth and full of promise. There are no words for what follows. Just a sequence of rapidly climbing notes, a phrase, a fanfare.

We lie together quietly. I laugh. She strokes my face. 'What is funny?'

'You are a very good guide,' I say.

The sky has come into the room, through a round eye in the ceiling. Clouds look down. Over the rim of the circle, a Moor in a striped, headdress exchanges a smile of approval with me. A servant looks severe, disapproving. A handful of gleeful cherubs peer down. One holds an apple in his hand, another pokes his bottom out over the edge in impertinent display.

'The *putti* will keep our secret,' she says, kissing my ear and cheek and face. She springs out of bed, her dress covering her. I wonder who else she has brought here. As if she can hear my thoughts, she says: 'Vincenzo has gone to his mistress tonight. You should keep an eye on your sister. She is very pretty. You are a wonderful musician, and you are one of the most beautiful men I have seen since I left Florence. Normally, I don't like Jews.'

This was too close to an insult. 'We are not all the same. We're just like everyone else, I mean. Different, and not all the same.'

'That was tactless of me. I am sorry.'

A lovers' tiff. An apology. She paces, a nervous energy filling the room. 'I hate this room. It is full of old, dead Gonzagas. Marriages arranged, more children, more misery. It took nearly

'Don't you need it?' I ask. She shakes her head. 'I'm rehearsing La Musica with Barton.' I have no idea what she's talking about. 'See you later.' She's up and away before I can say anything. I'm embarrassed.

'You don't need to take any notice of her.'

'No, no,' says Roberto. 'It will be a nice idea.'

Catherine comes towards us. 'Rob, can you tune the harpsichord for my continuo class after coffee?'

'Of course.' He is all smiles, but as Catherine moves away, he says: 'I don't think she likes me. And Barton is moody. Don't you think so?'

'I don't really know them.'

'Well. I must do the teaching now.' He stands, with the hint of a bow towards me. I watch him walk away. A tight, rhythmic sway of the hips. I wonder if he is gay. I wonder how well Xan knows him.

ELEVEN

❖

I WANDER BACK PAST my room to the fire escape door at the end of the corridor. Down a small flight of iron steps. It's breezy, with a warming sun. At the back of the house is a walled kitchen garden. Runner beans slant lazily in the air, and there are untidy groups of herbs; overgrown sage and rosemary bushes, parsley in a couple of chipped pots, rangy chives, with purple flowers sprouting.

ten years to paint. Time goes slowly for the Gonzagas.'

'Aren't you happy? You must have everything you could want.'

She sits on the bed, and strokes my head, as if I am a child with a fever. She kisses my forehead, and moves down to my mouth. A long, gentle touch of her lips on mine. Now sad friends, sad lovers.

A candle flickers and flares, the wall behind it glowing and flickering with gold flashes of paint. She snuffs out the candle with her fingers.

I am dressed. I stand awkwardly. 'Why did you bring me here?'

'Important visitors are sometimes received in this room. You are my visitor. You are like me. You do not belong here.'

'I was born in Mantova,' I said. 'You were not. I belong here.'

'You could be my clown. My court Jew, who knows nothing and must be told everything.'

Not just a lovers' tiff now, but a full-scale rift. 'If that's how you think of me, you should not have used me.'

'I'm sorry. The Duchess begs your pardon.'

'I don't want to talk to the Duchess. I want to talk to you.' I am a boy, a sulky man, a disappointed suitor who can see his princess receding into the distance.

There is a tiny pause. 'You may not believe me, but you are the only person I have ever brought here.'

I put my arms around her. Lovers again, gentle, loving. 'You may not believe me,' I say, 'but you are the first Duchess with whom I have shared a bed.' I kiss her cheek, confident, assured, dignified again.

❖ SECUNDA PARTE ❖

Open windows release competing sounds, instruments and chatter. I sit on a bench against the wall. Inside, recorders play. The music stops and starts. Sometimes it is horribly discordant, then it settles into a neat, warm sound, then back into discord and laughter. A door opens and the playing stops.

After welcoming voices, a single, more authoritative voice. It's Catherine. 'What have you been playing?' There is an answer, then she says: 'Play it through for me.' At the end, she says 'Well done. Shall we tune the final chord?'

The tuning starts with a low note from one of the recorders, followed by another and another, with Catherine directing 'up' or 'down'. Finally, they all play together. It is strong, rather beautiful, even. I didn't know recorders could sound like this.

Catherine repeats the process with other chords, and each time my shoulders tingle as the sound comes good. I don't understand how tuning a single chord can make a difference to the rest of the playing, but somehow it does. Catherine homes in on shorter sections, just as Barton did last night. Sometimes she asks someone to play on their own, sometimes two or three instruments play together. These fragments sound lovely. Perhaps, I think, the more you play the better it sounds. Perhaps it is just a matter of familiarity.

After the piece is played all the way through, Catherine says, 'Very well done. You could play that in the concert.' I hear the door close and someone says: 'Isn't she marvellous?' Someone else says: 'That's a lovely piece.' A third voice: 'We don't really want to play it in the concert, do we?' There's a chorus of replies, the upshot of which

I pull the covers back over the bed, neatening the wayward heavy silk cover, which slips and slides with a will of its own. She watches me, amused.

'You are the first man I have ever seen who makes his own bed.' She opens the chest under the window and takes out a key on a length of yellow silk. She holds it out to me.

'You remind me of the real world. Jews must wear pieces of yellow fabric to identify us,' I say.

'But you don't wear the badge in the palazzo.'

'No. Jewish musicians have dispensation from your Duke to come and go without the yellow badge.'

We leave the room in silence. Outside, she locks the door, then wraps the key in the yellow silk square and gives it to me. We hold hands until we reach the first staircase, and then she precedes me. Noble lovers parting.

We cross the Piazza di Santa Barbara, now dark and silent, torches on the turrets smoking into the night sky. We reach the side door. I open it. We stand for a moment. She kisses me on the cheek.

'Keep the key safe,' she says.

The night dew is heavy. I walk round the Piazza di San Pietro, and then round to San Andrea. I go in. Two old women are sweeping away the damp and soiled rushes, and putting new straw down. It smells sweet, like the fields with the sun upon them.

The clock strikes, startling me. A man stands up from one of the pews near the front.

'Where have you been?' It is Giovanni. He puts his hands together in a gesture of prayer. 'If you are not careful, everyone else will know.'

is 'no', and then the third voice says: 'Shall we play something else?'

The tower clock strikes eleven and I walk to the front of the house. Animated groups stand around, balancing coffee cups. Sheila and Agnes, now in matching yellow cardigans, with embroidered yellow and red daisies on their fronts. are talking to Streaky. I collect coffee, milk, sugar and a ginger biscuit and wander back out. Rapid footsteps follow me.

'Emilia.' It's Roberto, two biscuits sitting in his saucer, while he eats a third. He says my name with a lilt on the second syllable. 'How is your morning?'

Before I can answer, Streaky joins us. Today she has bright blue false eyelashes. She stands sideways on to me, so she can face Roberto as if they are just on their own. I don't like the look of her. She's too trendy for this provincial, dowdy crowd.

'Signor Castelli,' says Streaky, in a broad Manchester accent. 'Barton said you would be taking the sopranos and contraltos this afternoon.'

'Did he?'

'In the library. After tea. We need to learn the notes to *Fortunato Giorno.*'

I cringe at her anglicised accent. She makes no attempt to sound Italian.

'Really?' says Roberto.

'Thank you, Maestro,' she flutters. 'See you later.' She trips away on ridiculously high-heeled red shoes. Her tight black leggings finish just above fine white ankles. I have a sudden vision of the shoes flying into the air, the eyelashes flapping right off her face and flying free, into the spring sky, to join the fluffy white clouds.

'Leonora won't let anyone harm me.'

'Leonora?'

'Yes. She is lonely. She is bored. And she is pregnant.'

'Do you know what you have done?'

'Yes. And I'll get better at it.' Giovanni almost smiles. My defiance goes. 'What shall I do now?'

'Forget it ever happened. You're not the first man to be favoured in this way.'

'Do you think it was wrong of me?'

'I'm a good Catholic, but I don't believe in original sin. Unlike the Pope, I am celibate. I don't know whether it is right or wrong. But I told your parents I would look after you, and I feel responsible. Tell them we rehearsed late, and that you stayed the night with me. That will be at least partly true.'

'Thank you.'

We pick our way over the slippery cobbles. 'Do you know the story of Santa Barbara?' I shake my head.

'Barbara was very beautiful. Her father was afraid that she would be carried away by an unsuitable suitor, so he imprisoned her at the top of a tall tower. He went away to fight, and Barbara was converted to Christianity. She had three windows built in the tower: one for the Father, one for the Son and one for the Holy Ghost. When her father returned, he was appalled, and he tried to kill her. Miraculously, she was carried to the top of a mountain. But her father followed her and did kill her. Since then, Barbara has been the patron saint of war. She is also the patron saint of prisoners, stonemasons, and a protection against thunderstorms.'

'And of Jewish musicians.'

'So now I'm just a *repetiteur*,' mutters Roberto.

'A what?'

'Keyboard dogsbody,' he says. 'Bloody Barton treats me like a musical slave. I thought Gabriel was in charge. Look. I can give you a viol lesson at two. It will be nice. After lunch. I meet you by Reception.'

There is something imperious about him, but also – let's say masterful, in the old-fashioned use of the term. Anyway, I have no plans for this afternoon.

I take my cup back into the house. Mrs Dean is in a floral apron, carrying a bucket of cleaning things, a bright yellow duster peeping out of the top. 'Were you off for a stroll?' I nod.

She looks at her watch: 'Would you like to see some of the house?'

'I don't want to take up your time,' I say, meaning exactly the opposite.

'Not at all. You look a bit lost.' She puts the cleaning things down and takes me across the hall and through an arch at the end. To the right, stairs lead down to toilets. A rope blocks off a spiral stairway on the left, with a sign: 'Private'. Mrs Dean lifts the rope, and we climb a broad, shallow spiral staircase. On a narrow triangular landing, there is a low door on the right.

Mrs Dean unlocks the door. 'Mind your head.' We duck into a small room, with dark wooden panels, books piled higgledy-piggledy on an old bookcase, and a formica-topped kitchen table, with some paint-spattered chairs round it. 'I suppose the table and chairs are original?' I say. Mrs Dean smiles. 'Oh, yes,' she says. 'We're going to donate them to the V&A. We have Catchpole Board Meetings in this room. It used to be servants'

'I doubt whether she can protect you if you draw the Duke's fire.'

'I shall charm him with music, Giovanni.'

'You can charm the angels, but the Duke is not an angel.'

I sing a phrase. 'Four voices. Psalm 137. *By the rivers of Babylon.* Do you want to hear more? I will teach you the Hebrew.'

ELEVEN

I SLEEP IN GIOVANNI'S room for the few hours left of the night. I dream of the painted room. One of the putti drops an apple on my head, and laughs. I jump up and throw the fruit back. It is caught by the peacock, which throws it to the black Moor servant, who throws it to the white woman servant, whose face is Leonora's. She flies down to lie on the pillow next to me, her strong, straight nose in profile, her dark eyes looking at me. I put out my hand to stroke her cheek, and she turns into the scowling face of Vincenzo. Above us the putti shriek and giggle. I wake to hear the clatter of horses' hooves on the cobbles outside. I am sweating.

I hurry to the window. Far below, wild horses from the mountains near Lake Garda gallop at great speed along the street, bareback riders whipping and whooping. Behind them they leave steaming brown piles, already being shovelled into

❖ SECUNDA PARTE ❖

quarters, we think. The original house was built in the 1540s. The south-east tower – where we are now – dates from then. I'll show you the real treasure.' We back out and she locks the door.

'Is it safe?' I ask, indicating upwards.

'Oh, yes. We just don't want people wandering around during the restoration.'

The wide spiral stairs have gaps between the triangular treads. The wood is greyish, flecks of peeling white paint scratching the wooden surface. I hold on to the newel post. 'This comes from a single tree,' says Mrs Dean. 'Probably brought over from Norway. It goes all the way to the top of the tower.'

On the next landing is a doorless opening to the left. We bow our heads and turn into an uneven space, with a low window on the left. Through leaded panes, I can see fields stretching away, Cambridge in the dim distance. On the floor are neat piles of plaster. The walls are a muddy grey, a mixture of white and discoloured brick. Opposite the door, where the ceiling comes down to about shoulder height, is a tapestry, hammered into the wall with heavy nails. It is riddled with holes, and the bottom edge is frayed. It is dirty, vaguely greeny-yellowy-brown, and it's difficult to see the picture.

'We've taken down one tapestry,' says Mrs Dean. 'The rats have been at that one.'

I look up. The timbers are massive. Mrs Dean touches a roughly chiselled beam, and points out some markings carved into the wood. 'We think this means the roof timbers probably came from another building in the area. Catchpole Abbey, perhaps. Henry the Eighth took that

carts and wheelbarrows by women and children, who wheel them away to gardens and farmlands

Weeks later, Giovanni and I rehearse alone in the church. We sing, in Hebrew.

> *By the rivers of Babylon, there we sat down, yea, we wept, when we remembered Zion.*
> *We hanged our harps upon the willows in the midst thereof*
> *For there they that carried us away captive required of us mirth, saying, Sing us one of the songs of Zion.*
> *How shall we sing the Lord's song in a strange land?*
> *If I forget thee, O Jerusalem, let my right hand forget her cunning.*
> *If I do not remember thee, let my tongue cleave to the roof of my mouth; if I prefer not Jerusalem above my chief joy.*

Our voices soar up into the church tower. We laugh and clap. There is applause above us. I look up, and there, in the gallery, where a corridor leads into the palazzo, stand the Duke and Duchess. The Duke says, loud enough for us to hear: 'I see the little Jew has forgotten his Latin.' Giovanni bows to the Duke, who turns on his heel, and leaves. The Duchess follows him, not looking back or down.

As her time approaches, the Duchess retreats to her own rooms. She does not join Vincenzo and the court at the musical entertainments. She does not come to see the play the Jewish troupe puts on during carnival (at our own expense, of course). We do not play at the baby's christening in Santa Barbara.

I keep the key warm, wrapped in its fragment of yellow silk. It is in my pocket, nestling against my thigh. As she did, just once.

to pieces. They may even have been ship's timbers originally.'

'Do the rafters go all the way across the house?' I ask.

'Well, certainly over the Great Hall. Here – '

She raps her knuckles against a hollow-sounding wall – 'it was probably open, and possibly a minstrels' gallery, overlooking one end of the Hall. The building itself originally extended over two floors. A new ceiling was put in during the eighteenth century, so the Great Hall – where everyone plays – is now just one storey high. The house was in a terrible state until the 1920s. If it hadn't been for these roof timbers, the whole lot would probably have collapsed.'

'How much restoration is there to do?'

'Just this tower. It should be finished by next summer. We hope.'

The silvery tones of the clock interrupt us. Mrs Dean looks at her watch, and turns to go. I follow. As I pass the tapestry, I can't resist stretching out my hand to touch it. A cloud of grey dust fluffs out. I move my hand quickly, and one of my nails catches the edge of the fabric. 'Oh, shit.'

Mrs Dean turns. I'm expecting tight-lipped disapproval, but she laughs, and treads carefully over to the wall. Gently, she lifts the corner of the frayed tapestry. A rounded, reddish-brown shape. She lifts it a little further; it looks like the rear end of an animal. 'Good heavens. There must be a wall painting under there. How exciting.' She bends down to look, moving the tapestry carefully. 'A spear – a hunting scene, perhaps. Oh, this is exciting.' She looks at her watch again. 'Excuse me. I must go and keep an eye on lunch.'

TWELVE

ZIO LEONE HAS MOVED in with us. He began coughing last winter, continued through the spring, and the heat and humidity of summer. My mother fills the room with the scent of lemon, ginger and honey. It is my favourite hot drink, and Zio Leone and I cup our hands round bowls of steaming liquid. When Giovanni comes to our house, my mother brings him a bowl too.

Giovanni compliments my mother, clears his throat, then announces in a portentous voice: 'A marriage has been arranged. The Grand Duke, Ferdinando de' Medici and Christine de Lorraine.'

'A political alliance, you mean,' corrects my mother. 'We know all about it. Another marriage of convenience, binding the Florentines to the French.'

Giovanni turns to me: 'How would you like to go to Florence, Salamone?'

'Just a minute.' My mother joins us at the table. 'What for, and for how long?'

'For the wedding celebrations. The Duke of Florence would like us to send some of our Jewish musicians.'

Zio Leone laughs and that sets his cough going. When he has recovered, he says: 'Typical Medici behaviour. They boast that their actors and singers and musicians are the best, and then, in a crisis, they have to admit they need the Jews. Who else is going?'

At the bottom of the staircase, I call my thanks to Mrs Dean. My hands are still covered with dust. In the downstairs Ladies, I wipe my hands with a tissue before washing them thoroughly.

TWELVE

❖

LUNCH IS ALSO SELF-SERVICE. Large dishes of salad, sliced ham, scotch eggs, shallow bowls of sardines, chunks of cheddar cheese, and potato and cauliflower salad, probably left over from last night. Hunks of French bread and butter, and various mustards, ketchups, brown sauce and chutneys bunch at one end of the table.

Xan is sitting with the raucous Midland group. I go to an empty table, where I'm joined by Roberto, followed closely by Streaky. She tumbles question after question at him. He responds with courtesy and careful attention. Where were you born, Maestro? Where do you live in Italy? Where did you get that wonderful accent? Her voice is really annoying, but I glean information about Roberto. He studied music in Bologna, then in Basel, then in America, where he has been teaching and playing for the past ten years. There are academic mafiosi in America and Italy, he confides. He is hoping that this year's Fellowship, and his research, will help him get tenure in the US.

Streaky giggles at each reply. Her perfume is very

Giovanni senses interest. 'I understand there will be contributions from Rome, Siena – the *Accademia degli Intronati*, I believe. And the *Compagnia dei Gelosi* –'

Zio Leone interrupts. '*Commedia.* Fairground entertainers.'

Giovanni inclines his head. 'Well – something for everyone. I would like Salamone to come with us.'

'We shall have to ask Azariah.' My mother says 'we'. That means she thinks it's a good idea. I hug and kiss her. She smiles and says: 'Just you, Salamone. Menahem and Esther are too young. When is this?'

'The wedding is taking place by proxy. Christine will arrive in Florence around the end of April. Will you let me know what Signor Rossi says?'

'Of course,' says my mother.

I walk out with Giovanni. 'I have finished my collection,' I say. 'As many pieces as I have years.'

'Nineteen is a good number,' says Giovanni. 'Congratulations.'

'I would like to dedicate it to the Duchess,' I say.

Giovanni stops. 'No,' he says.

'But why not?' It is hard to believe that nearly two years have passed since that afternoon. I might have imagined it, except that the key, securely wrapped in yellow silk, comes with me everywhere, sewn into a small bag I keep on a twisted velvet cord round my neck.

Giovanni puts an arm round my shoulders. 'Dedicate the book to the Duke. It is both politic and safe.'

'*Alla Serenissima Signora, et patronna mia.*'

'*Al Serenissimo Signor, et patron mio.* You haven't done anything else stupid, have you?'

❖ SECUNDA PARTE ❖

strong. I sneeze, take a tissue from my pocket, and as I wipe my nose, I feel something grainy. The tissue has grey dust on it. I probably didn't wash my hands properly.

I get to Reception just before two o'clock. Mrs Dean is busy on her computer. Roberto arrives, his viol over his shoulder, a smaller case in one hand, and a music stand under his other arm.

'Where shall we go?'

'You can go up to the old Servants' Room, if you like,' says Mrs Dean. She unhooks a key hanging on a nail and hands it to me. 'You know where it is. Bring the key back when you've finished.'

In the room, Roberto puts the instruments down. 'Look,' I say. 'I'm probably wasting your time. I can just about read music, but I have never had a music lesson in my life. I was pretending to sing last night.'

'I think you can sing, because I heard you in the choir.'

'You couldn't have heard me.'

'I have a good hear,' he says sharply, as if I have insulted him. He pronounces 'ear' with an extra 'h' at the beginning, as many Italians do. It is wrong, but rather charming.

Roberto sets up the music stand, opens the large viol case and takes out the instrument, laying it gently on its side on the worn brown carpet. Then he opens the smaller case. Inside, a silk lilac and red paisley-patterned scarf covers a smaller viol. He picks it up by the neck. It looks tiny in his large, slender hands. He gestures to me to sit down.

He sits opposite and tunes the treble, easily, quickly. The strings sound sweet and light. His fingers look

◈ PRIMA PARTE ◈

THIRTEEN

◈

THE SMELL OF WOODSMOKE is everywhere. Farmers squat in the alleys and narrow streets around the campanile, their meagre produce spread out on the cobbles. Watermelons, courgettes, cabbages. Tired green leaves, as creased as their growers' faces. A couple of ragged chickens croak feebly in wicker cages. An old woman sits by the side of the road, a length of red woollen cloth in one hand. Her companion's black shawl, wrapped close about her hunched head, flaps in the bitter evening wind. Pisa doesn't feel very welcoming.

I have been ill ever since we left Mantova. Giovanni is by my side, an arm ready when I falter. We walk into the Cattedrale di Pisa, out of the wind. The smell of woodsmoke gives way to heavy candle perfume. My eyes adjust to the gloom. We are dwarfed by the soaring canopy. I hold onto the wooden panels for security. My finger touches something jagged. The *intarsia* panelling; patterned lines of purfling round the edges of the panels. I remember the softened outline of my viol, wrapped in its canvas cloth, its purfling held safe from the threats of wind and weather. This thin strip of wood inlaid to decorate and strengthen the instrument has wound itself round the edges of my body, carrying me here safely.

As well as my viol and a change of clothes, I have brought my first book of music, wrapped in my best red woollen shirt. It will be published in a few months in Venice, thanks to Giovanni's help. He took the manuscript to Venice, to

enormous on the tiny fretboard. I wonder how he knows what the notes should be.

He gets up and stands behind me. Warmth, and the aroma of camomile and lily of the valley. His right arm comes round my right shoulder, and he places the instrument on my knees. Instinctively, I open them slightly, so that the round base of the instrument rests between them.

'Hold onto it,' he says.

I put out my right hand. 'No. The left hand. Here. Just under the scroll. Where my hand is.'

My left hand goes out to meet his right hand. Our fingers touch. He clasps my fingers firmly round the neck of the viol, and goes to his viol case. I can still feel his fingers over mine. My hand relaxes, and my fingers enclose the slim neck. It feels grateful. I hold the smooth wood and lift the instrument. Suddenly it feels large and awkward. It begins to slip from my hand, and I get it back on my knees in time.

Roberto unclips a bow from his viol case, tightens the hair by turning the round knob on the top, at the widest part of the bow, picks up his viol, parts his legs, supporting the viol on his calves, holds the bow in his right hand and rests it low down on the strings. It is the same hold I have seen in so many concerts, but always from a distance. He and the instrument look complete. They belong to each other. Neither can function without the other.

His hand is palm upwards, holding the stick as if it is a gigantic pencil, with the thumb and first finger holding the wood, and the taut horse-hair held between the middle and ring finger. It looks easy and natural.

Ricciardo Amadino, the publishers. I wrote out another copy, in my best handwriting. I am very proud of this little collection of three-part pieces. They are for voices to sing, or instruments to play, and I have been experimenting with a combination of sound which particularly interests me: two high voices, and a more measured bass line. The day before we were due to leave, I was hoping to perform some of them to the family and some invited neighbours. But I caught cold, began coughing and lost my voice.

I insisted on travelling, and on the journey, the bumps and sweats mingled with a headache, dizziness, and a delirium which kept me from confessing to Giovanni that I had, indeed, done something stupid.

A week earlier, after Vespers in Santa Barbara, someone takes my arm at the church door. It is Emilia, the Duchess's Moorish maidservant. She draws me into the shadows. She speaks rapidly: 'Have you got the key the Duchess gave you?' My heart is beating fast. She wants to see me again. 'Yes,' I whisper. 'She would like you to return it,' she says. 'Come to the side door this evening. When it's dark.'

That evening my mother tries to stop me going out. 'The cold night air. You must protect your throat.' I promise to take an extra cloak and tuck the small key, still in its yellow silk, into my sleeve.

I stamp my feet at the low, barred door. The evening mist is chill, wetly searing the edges of my cloak, and sitting on the surface of the wool like droplets of dew. I am beginning to wonder if the whole thing is some stupid hoax. The rusty, protesting screech of the grille interrupts my thoughts.

Emilia pushes the door open and holds out her hand. I have

❖ SECUNDA PARTE ❖

'Remember that the weight of the bow is what keeps it on the strings, not the weight of your arm. The bow must rest just above the bridge.'

He puts his instrument down and takes the treble bow out of its case. It is fine, delicate. He tightens the hair and again comes to stand behind me. He takes my right hand and folds it round the bow, guiding my fingers gently into the right position. His hand is strong and warm. The bow, for all its delicacy, feels heavy. Roberto guides my right hand to balance the bow on the strings, just above the bridge. It slides off. He catches it.

'Hold the bow lightly. If you are tense, the bow will not stay on the strings. Breathe.' After what seems like an age, the bow, slanting upwards, but firm, stays on the string. My right arm is heavy. 'Allow your elbow to come out slightly from your body. Don't lean forward. Feel the connection between your shoulder and the strings.'

He moves away, and the bow falls. I replace it on the strings. Roberto nods. 'That's better.' He sits, picks up his viol, and bows a flurry of notes. My back tingles. 'Steady the viol with your left hand. Move the bow over an open string. Any open string.'

The bow creaks and squeaks, and I giggle with embarrassment. 'How does it feel?'

'I don't know.'

'Imagine that the strings are moving the bow up to your shoulder, round your back, and back down your left arm to the fretboard. It must feel so circular that you do not know where you begin and where the instrument ends.'

He speaks, gently, rhythmically: 'Forward. Good. Back. Flex your wrist back, to change the direction of the bow.

the key ready. She takes my hand, with the key still in it, draws me in, closes and locks the door. She speeds ahead, through door after door, and then along a winding corridor. Now and again servants pass us, hurrying, carrying linen, jugs, bowls, chairs, nodding deferentially to my companion, and ignoring me.

'Where are we going?'

'Just follow me.'

I overtake her and bar her way. 'Tell me where we are going.'

'Or what? You will call for help? A Jewish musician, wandering round the palazzo alone, accosting an innocent maidservant?'

Her pace slows. We are in a quiet corridor. Through the windows, I can see a peaceful courtyard with a fountain in the middle, neatly tended flower beds and small fruit trees round an oasis of green. Torches at each corner.

'This is the Corta Vecchia. The Duchess's secret apartments. The *grotto*, the *studiolo* and a garden.'

Of course. Leonora must meet me in her secret, private apartments.

Through a low arch, a milky marble doorway, noble and squared, with sculpted heads and shapes I have no time to register, into a narrow room. A single thick, church candle burns gently. The ceiling glitters, drawing me up into its blue and gold barrel. A glowing geometry. I want to stay here forever.

Emilia takes a taper and lights a series of candles round the walls. 'Riddle: how do you move a room from one place to another? Answer: you change your name to Gonzaga.'

She takes my hand.

'This *studiolo* was on the second floor in the Castello, the

❖ SECUNDA PARTE ❖

Good. Forward. Back. Keep moving. Forward. Good. Back. Good.'

I float on his voice, moving from word to word. As the bow moves faster, the sound is clearer. His words speed up and my bow responds. He controls my movement, my sound, my rhythm. I change to another string. There is a scrunch of sound, and then it is smoother and more rhythmic.

'Good,' says Roberto. 'Very good. Your sense of rhythm is good. Keep going.'

He bows his viol, playing notes which fit with my long, regular bows. I hear singing. I stop bowing. It is the clock chiming. Three o'clock. We have been here for an hour.

Roberto is all efficiency. He replaces both viols and bows in their cases. He folds the music stand. 'Same time tomorrow?'

He doesn't wait for my reply. I sit alone for a few moments, not moving. My legs are empty. My hands are warm with the memory of his fingers. I hear my breathing, and there is birdsong outside. Finally, I stand up, stiff and tired, as if I have been walking for hours. I lock the door and take the key downstairs. There is no-one in the Reception cubicle, so I hang the key back up on its hook.

piano nobile. After Duke Francesco's death, in 1519, Isabella d'Este Gonzaga moved the *studiolo* and the *grotto* here. The story goes that she had put on a lot of weight, and her legs were not as agile as they once were. The ground floor was more congenial. Her son moved her down here.'

'Did he force her to move?'

'Perhaps. Preparations for the move began before Francesco died, so we can't blame Federico for banishing her. A son does not do that to his mother.'

'I would certainly not do that to mine.'

'Of course not. But you are a little Jewish boy.'

'Not so little, Madam.'

'Please call me Emilia. When the Duchess scolds me, she calls me Isabella. She hates the way Isabella's presence is everywhere. Even her perfume lingers in this room, she says.'

Emilia begins singing. The French words are tinged with an Italian accent, delicate, tender:

Prenez sur moy vostre exemple amoureux
commencement d'amours est savoureux.
E le moyen plein de peine et tristesse,
Et la fin est d'avoir plaisant maitresse.
Mis au saillir sont les pas dangereux.

As she sings, she leads me to one of the wooden panels on the wall. *Intarsiatura*, the exquisitely carved and inlaid wooden marquetry, makes a living picture. A series of buildings and towers hovers, one behind the other, along the edge of the water, boats and fishermen in the distance. Emilia points to the bottom of the panel – and there it is. The music, inlaid,

❖ SECUNDA PARTE ❖

THIRTEEN

❖

THERE'S NO SIGN OF Xan at tea-time. I take my tea and a couple of biscuits round to the sheltered kitchen garden. I sit on a bench bordering the herb beds. Bees flit across the chive flowers. I hear a hiccupping sound, then Catherine's voice: 'He hasn't done it on purpose, Barton.' A man speaks: 'He has. He has.' It's a sob. Barton is crying. They are somewhere on the other side of the wall.

'Gabriel invited him because he thought he would be an interesting addition to the course.'

'He didn't tell us about that man's new edition of *Orfeo*,' says Barton, his voice firm and angry. 'Gabriel knows that mine is the definitive edition. Every professional baroque opera production of *Orfeo* uses my edition.'

'Gabriel doesn't understand the professional music world. You know that.' Catherine is soothing.

'Stop pretending it isn't a disaster. Bloody Italians.'

'Monteverdi was Italian, Barton.'

'This is no time for stupid jokes.'

There is silence. They move away. The sun is still warm, but the world has become hard and angular. I close my eyes.

Light, rapid footsteps stop beside me. It's Xan. 'Ah,' she says. 'Great minds. What a lovely day.' She sits beside me.

'What? Heavens. I must have fallen asleep. What time is it?'

laid into the wood, waiting to be revived. Okeghem. A canon. Words. She sings the first line again.

Prenez sur moy vostre exemple amoureux

'Take your understanding of love from me, for the beginning of love is delicious. The middle of love is full of pain and sadness, and the end of love is no more than the memory of a pleasing mistress. When you leave, you begin a dangerous journey.'

I join in, my voice an octave below hers, following and chasing. We arrive at the end together, our hands joined, our eyes meeting, our bodies touching.

She opens one of the panel doors and takes out a bottle and two thick, green glasses. I follow her to a low couch, covered with blue and gold velvet cushions. She pours the wine in the flickering candlelight.

We drink and hum our tongues into a kiss. The cushions receive us. There is no floor, no walls, just a blue and gold sky, and her warm breath on my neck. Her breath is sweet, cloves and musk.

'Imagine, Salamone,' she whispers, 'imagine I am the Duchess of Mantova.'

'Emilia. You are my Duchess.'

'A black Duchess, and a Jewish Duke.'

'Where do you really come from?'

'My father was white. Coloured by the summer sun, but never as dark as I am, and never as dark as my mother.'

I have forgotten Leonora. There never was a Leonora. Just this smooth woman, whose eyes and skin flash and move below and above me, with velvet legs and a vaulted mouth and blue

❖ SECUNDA PARTE ❖

'Nearly dinner time. I'm starving.'
'What have you been doing?'
'La Musica, with Barton, till tea-time.'
'What's La Musica?'
'I forgot. You're my ignorant friend. It's the prologue to *Orfeo*.'
'*Orfeo*, by Monteverdi?'
Xan laughs. 'Not so ignorant after all. Barton is the main authority in this country. He's a brilliant musician.'
We walk back to the house. 'Tell me about the woman with red streaks in her hair?'
'Tanya. She was one of Barton's students. She follows him round the country.'
'Where does he teach?'
'At the National Academy of Music.'
'And Agnes and Sheila?'
'Well. They live in a cottage in the Chilterns, and they are sisters or cousins. No-one knows for sure. They've been coming on Gabriel's courses forever. They wear each others' clothes and argue all the time, and everyone hates playing with them. Gabriel thinks it teaches people tolerance to be put in a group with them.'
'How old are they?'
'Ancient. They used to play with the Dolmetsches. When they started coming on Gabriel's courses, the Dolmetsches shunned them.'
I am about to ask her who the Dolmetsches are and how she knows Roberto, but we have reached the dining hall. We join the table with the viol players from last night. I learn more about them. Edison works in a bank; Nora-Jane, his wife, is a French teacher. Luther is Canadian, makes viols and has a silver stud in his right ear.

and gold moments. Above us, the ceiling watches and protects our modesty. We lie companionably.

'Imagine,' she says, 'taking this ceiling apart and bringing it here, piece by beautiful piece. I suppose Isabella wanted everything to stay as it had always been.'

I read the device on the ceiling: '*Nec spe nec metu*. Neither hope nor fear. *Venti-sette*. XXVII. What does it mean?'

'Twenty-seven. *Vinte le sette*. You will be conquered. If only that were true. If only we were not prisoners.'

'I don't understand.'

'I brought you here so that you could forget her.'

'Did Leonora tell you to do this?'

'No. Leonora was drawn to you because you were young, fresh. I am drawn to you because you are like me. You don't belong here, but, like me, you could not live anywhere else.'

Emilia stands, takes the bottle and glasses back to the cupboard, her feet soft and silent on the stone tiles. 'Come and look round our heaven. Floor tiles with the *imprese* of the Gonzaga family.'

She leads me round the small chamber. On the ceiling: a musical stave, a clef, time signatures of three and four, a perfect circle cut in half, a bisected C, and rests, shaped like towers and turrets.

We sing in canon, facing each other:

Prenez sur moy vostre exemple amoureux
commencement d'amours est savoureux.
E le moyen plein de peine et tristesse,
Et la fin est d'avoir plaisant maitresse.
Mis au saillir sont les pas dangereux.

Everyone is eager to hear about Luther's new bass viol, which he has just finished and is playing here for the first time. Terms fly round the table: curved fronts, soundposts, purfling, authenticity. I am happy to let it all wash over my head. I eavesdrop on a conversation at the next table.

'I loved what you did with *Vieni Imeneo* last night, Barton.' It's Roberto.

'Thank you,' says Barton, his mouth full of chicken. Roberto continues: 'I have been very impressed with your edition of *Orfeo*.'

'But you still think a new edition is necessary?' says Barton.

'Well, it is a matter of new research.'

'What new research?'

'I don't want to talk about it before it is published.'

'No point talking about it at all, then, is there?' Barton stands up. 'Excuse me.'

I go to the Great Hall for choir. It is full of people putting up music stands, taking instruments out of cases. At the front, a boy plays a tiny instrument, like a shepherd's pipe, loud and shrill, trilling up and down like a dextrous, hysterical bird. At the back of the hall are three extraordinary objects: strange, tree-like oblong structures, made from what looks like plywood, each with a curved metal crook coming out half way down. Their players sit on stacks of piled-up chairs, and the instruments emit low sounds which are like a cross between a trumpeting elephant and a mooing cow. I think I have blundered into the bit of Wonderland Alice didn't dare venture into.

I go back to check the noticeboard: 'Recorder

We sing, near doors of mellow, warm and glowing wood. Different grains and veneer make pictures and perspectives, reaching into the distance. Now you see it, now you don't. Now flat, now reaching away to remote fields, rivers, mountains and castles. Some of the wood is almost black, scorched by being passed through trays of hot silver sand.

A half-open lattice door, a door within a door. Behind, in the inlaid cupboard, a bouquet of musical instruments. A fretted guitar, with a flat, even body, its head nestling against a two-string instrument, with pegs at the neck. Between these, two recorders, one smaller than the other, pointing downwards onto the *trompe l'oeil* shelf, the windways like the eyes of an animal. Resting on one shoulder of the guitar, the lower end of a shawm stretches up out of sight into the top, left-hand corner of the frame.

Next comes the upturned base of a spinet. Above it, diagonally poised, a three-and-a-half octave keyboard. On the upper left-hand side, the top of a small harp, and on the right, facing the keyboard in two-thirds profile, a lute, the top of the neck bent back at right angles in parallel with the frame.

'It is time to go,' Emilia says softly.

'You are beautiful,' I say. '*Pulchra es.*'

'*Nigra sum,*' she answers. 'I am black.'

I kiss her.

Orchestra, conductor: Catherine Noble.' I am in the wrong place. Another notice announces the choir, in the dining hall. Half an hour's grace while the tables are cleared.

In the dining hall, Barton hands out music quickly and efficiently. With no harpsichord there, I wonder how we will know how to start. Barton takes a medium-sized recorder from a plastic case and stuns us into complete silence with a short series of virtuosic passages. We applaud, he makes a mock bow, and says: 'Choir: your notes.' He plays three notes in rapid succession, then raises his arms to start. I see that we have five and a half bars rest. It gives me a chance to glance at the translation. *O fortunato giorno* ... oh, fortunate day, when heaven and earth sing together.

Four small groups of singers alternate, and then we do, indeed, all sing together. Barton conducts us with huge sweeps of his arms into a united group. It is an extraordinary piece. Sometimes the groups are smaller groups within the large choir.

I pick up a few words here and there – earth, sky, and Ferdinando seem to figure, and there is a lot of joy. I still rely on Xan's voice beside me, but I am learning fast, because my attention is less and less on her, and more on the written music and Barton's urgent intensity, his clear arm and hand signals, his complete familiarity with the music. The hour and a half pass quickly.

Afterwards, I go to the bar and buy a pineapple juice. Streaky Tanya has joined Barton and Catherine. Roberto and Xan are sitting at a small table in one of the alcoves. I finish my drink and go to bed, the music still in my head.

FOURTEEN

WHEN WE LEAVE THE cathedral in Pisa, it is almost dark, and the farmers and beggars have melted into the shadows. We pass the stables where the rest of the travelling troup is spending the night. Giovanni has persuaded the *maestro di capella* to let us stay in his house. We eat a thick vegetable soup, hot bread and drink deep red Tuscan wine. I can hardly keep my eyes open, and am asleep as soon as I lie down on the straw mattress by Giovanni's bed.

My fever must have returned, because I remember little about the following days. Men shouting, animals and objects clanking on cobbles, the creak and sway of the boat on the final stretch of our journey down the Arno to Florence. Without Giovanni I would not have eaten and drunk, and would doubtless have festered in my own filth.

Our cluster of five Jewish musicians is met in Florence by a small delegation from the Jewish community. Reuben da Pisa and his cousins embrace us. Giovanni takes my viol and goes with the rest of the contingent in one direction, while Reuben takes me to his home.

We walk past the magnificent Cattedrale and its separate *battisteria* and *campanile*, through a bustling market-place, as big as all of our three market squares put together, down narrow streets, through an arch, between two heavy iron gates, into an alley. A thin strip of sky, far above us, gives a little light. To right and left are covered shops, a bakery, a butcher, a shop

❖ SECUNDA PARTE ❖

FOURTEEN

❖

NEXT MORNING, I WALK down to the village. A cluster of houses and a tiny village shop/post office. I wander round, looking for a café. Nothing. I hurry back, but I am too late for coffee. The entrance hall is empty and peaceful, with Mrs Dean dusting the banisters. 'Missed coffee?' I nod, and she beckons me through the swing door behind the main staircase, into the kitchen.

At one end, the young women are putting food out on trays for lunch. Mrs Dean takes me to the other end, and brings out a cafetière from a cupboard. She switches on a kettle, and measures out some coffee. 'That smells wonderful,' I say. 'Well,' Mrs Dean smiles, 'it's only for special people.'

'I don't think I'm special,' I say. 'Well, only to myself.'

'Gabriel asked me to keep an eye on you. Because you came with Xan. With Anna.'

'Is Anna special?'

Mrs Dean pours boiling water into the cafetière. 'Hasn't she told you?' I shake my head. She gets out cups, milk from a small fridge by the sink, spoons and sugar, stirs the coffee, plunges and pours, as she continues talking. 'It's no secret. Gabriel and Netta more or less brought Xan up. After Catchpole was sold.'

'I don't understand. Are you saying Xan is from here, from Catchpole?'

Mrs Dean nods. 'Not exactly from.' There is a crash from the other end of the kitchen. Mrs Dean winces and

with ragged clothes hanging outside it. My mother would take this in hand. I miss her.

Inside Reuben's house, it is quieter, but also more airless. We climb up endless stairs. Reuben's wife, Hannah, feeds us with a fragrant stew, rice and vegetables, and a light, dry wine. Reuben tells me proudly that it comes from his family farm, and adds: 'This is the last bottle. When we were forced to move into the ghetto, we had to leave our farm.'

In Mantova we are not closed in by walls, gates and guards. We are free to come and go, and rarely challenged if we aren't wearing our square of yellow or orange cloth. As we eat, Reuben tells me they came here nearly twenty years ago, a few months after he and Hannah married. Families flooded in from the Tuscan countryside, and tensions flared between people used to open fields, small villages and the smells of animals and crops. Over the years, in these two small squares, bordered by the market square, the buildings grew higher. There is one well for the whole community, in the Piazza della Fonte.

'We have no ghetto in Mantova,' I explain.

Reuben nods gently. 'It is only a matter of time, I'm afraid. Come. You will be comfortable in the children's room. They will sleep with us.'

There is little rest for me that night. When the household sounds have finally died down, I fall asleep, to be woken suddenly by shouts, raucous singing, the clatter of objects breaking in the courtyard below. The sound is magnified as it echoes upwards. People open windows and shout; the noise ebbs and flows until light begins to show through the ragged canvas flap covering my window.

calls out, without looking round: 'Never mind, Deirdre. Just sweep it up carefully.'

'Xan's grandparents were the last Catchpoles here. After the war, the house was falling to bits, and they persuaded the National Trust to buy it. They went on living here, in a flat at the top of the house. After the war, the Trust sold the house to the University of Woodbridge, and set up adult education courses here. When Xan's parents died in a car crash, the grandparents brought her here, to live with them. I was at university with Gabriel and Netta. He ran a course here, in the early 1950s. They were looking for a resident caretaker. I needed a job.'

'How did Gabriel and Netta get to know Xan?'

'Well, when her grandmother died, she was sent to a foster family. She kept running away and coming back to Catchpole. She hid in the stables. On one of Gabriel's courses, she slipped into the hall and joined in the singing. We thought she belonged to someone on the course, and then I noticed she wore the same dress every day – well, anyway. It's a long story, but eventually Gabriel and Netta adopted her.'

'How amazing,' I say. 'That makes her – how old?'

Mrs Dean shrugged. 'I'm not sure. Late twenties? A bit older?'

'Good heavens. She doesn't look it.'

Deirdre is hovering. 'Shall we put out the ham or the corned beef, Mrs Dean?'

I get up to leave. 'Thanks for the coffee, Mrs Dean.'

'You're welcome, dear. I'll come and show you, Deirdre.'

PRIMA PARTE

Hannah bakes fresh bread for breakfast, with creamy butter and a strongly flavoured cream cheese. I can't stay here. It is too claustrophobic, too full of threat, although my hosts are the kindest possible, putting every comfort at my disposal, at the expense of theirs. I leave with thanks and offers of hospitality in return, if they ever come to Mantova, and then I say that I don't know when I will be back, because my *maestro di cappella* needs my services.

Carts and children and people rattle across the courtyard in the busy noise of early morning. I slip through the ghetto gate. Once through the arch, there is more sky. People walk freely, their arms swinging. I look back at the arch. Above it is a coat of arms. I read the inscription below.

Cosimo dei Medici, Grand Duke of Tuscany, and his Son, the Most Serene Prince Francesco, moved by great mercy for all, wanted the Jews enclosed in this place, separate from the Christians but not expelled, so that they could, through the example of good men, subject their stiff necks to the light yoke of Christ. Year 1571.

A wave of rage heats me. I want to run as far away from here as possible, to go home. I walk rapidly, until I come into the Piazza del Duomo. The vast open doors draw me into the soaring height of the church. It is peaceful. Footsteps echo gently. My heart slows. I fancy I can hear my mother's chickens clucking. Tears come to my eyes. Then I laugh. The sound is real. A woman chases a bright brown chicken across the skidding marble floor, while people watch, amused.

I join the chase, and collide with a man who is also pursuing

❖ SECUNDA PARTE ❖

FIFTEEN

❖

I AM PUNCTUAL FOR my two o'clock lesson. This time I take the viol out of its case myself, tighten the bow and tune to Roberto's strings. This is hard. I can't tell when my sound disappears into his. I rely on his nod to tell me when it is in tune. 'Don't worry,' he says. 'It will come.'

I bow the open strings, and he tells me the pitch name of each string. From the top down: D, A, E, C, G and D again. As I move from one string to the next, I say the name of the new one. I continue this for the whole hour, skipping a string, and finally going from the top string to the bottom string. It feels like a massive arc.

The clock interrupts us. 'How much practice have you done?' he asks.

'I haven't done any practice. I haven't got a viol.'

'Keep Xan's viol,' he says. 'She won't need it. She's too busy singing with Barton.'

'What do you mean by "practice"?'

'Repeat what we've been doing. Get better at it. That's practice.'

Now I have something to do. After tea, I go back to the Servants' Room. I get bored with the open strings, and put one finger on a fret. The sound is different, dull. It isn't the same without Roberto there.

the chicken. It is Giovanni. Between us we corner the fowl. I pick it up deftly by the legs, and return it to the grateful woman, who crosses herself, before hurrying out, the chicken squawking rebelliously under her arm.

'Wherever there are chickens,' I say, 'there is Signor Giovanni Gastoldi.'

'Who is taking my friend's name in vain?' A slim Pierrot dances up to us, putting an arm around Giovanni. 'And who is this beautiful boy? Young sir. Jacopo Peri at your service.'

The Pierrot sweeps a large bow, his head almost touching the ground. He is like an overgrown toy acrobat. He stands upright, and swiftly undoes all the fastening down the front of his costume. He opens the costume with an extravagant theatrical gesture. For a moment I think he is going to be naked, but underneath he is wearing ordinary clothes. He takes off his cap, and his hair falls down in a haze of red-gold ringlets. 'Jacopo Peri, *Il Zazzerino*. Please, Giovanni, dear, introduce me to your little provincial friend.'

'Salamone Rossi,' I say. 'At your service, Signor Peri.'

'Polite,' says Jacopo approvingly. 'Any relation to Bastiano de Rossi? No, of course not. Bastiano is far too puffed up to have provincial relatives.'

He folds up the costume and tucks it under one arm. He puts his other arm round my waist, and we walk towards the door and the sunlight, like two old friends taking a stroll. Giovanni walks with us, smiling with pleasure.

'You must be a musician, young sir.' He dashes a glance at Giovanni, who nods. 'I thought so. I feel it in the rhythm of your step.'

'How is Reuben?' asks Giovanni.

❖ SECUNDA PARTE ❖

SIXTEEN

❖

FOR ROBERTO'S TALK THIS evening, Netta has made an impressive hand-drawn poster, with the title 'Monteverdi and the Golden Age of Music', full of flourishes. The talk is in the library, a neat room, behind the Reception cubicle. A dozen or so chairs, five or six people already there. We're competing with Barton and the choir, and Catherine and the Recorder Orchestra. A shock of streaked red hair attests to Tanya, sitting in the first row. No Xan. Our audience numbers swell to ten.

Roberto says he was hoping to show some slides of Monteverdi's birthplace of Cremona, and of Mantua and Venice, the two cities in which he did his most important work, plus the church, where he is buried. Unfortunately, the slide machine is broken.

He talks about the beauty that is the Italian Renaissance. About the Medici in Florence, the Este family in Ferrara, the Gonzaga in Mantua. This, he says, was the Golden Age of courtly beauty, elegance, richness, culture and patronage. Painters, sculptors, musicians and architects. Celebrations, weddings and festivals which lasted for weeks. Lavish cloth of gold and precious stones. A Golden Age. This was Monteverdi's world. He invented opera, and he transformed music from its medieval hangovers to the aural world of today. Monteverdi, the pioneer, was eternal and universal. *Orfeo* was the first opera – as we know the term – and marked the beginning of the present day. We owe everything to Monteverdi.

PRIMA PARTE

I stop walking. 'I'm sorry, Giovanni, I can't stay in the ghetto.'

'Oh, my God,' says Jacopo. 'You won't get any peace in the ghetto. You can stay with us. There are Jews who live near the Pitti, and anyway, it is chaos, my dear, utter chaos everywhere. No-one will notice. No-one will mind.'

'Are you sure? Will I meet my non-relative? This Bastiano?'

'Ah. He is magic. Now you see him, now you don't. He is nowhere and everywhere. He makes notes, he draws, he keeps detailed records, so that everyone will know about our magnificent celebrations. In short, he's a creep. He was there at the beginning, and he will be there at the end. He is Bardi's friend, and he sucks up to Cavalieri. Bardi and Cavalieri can't stand each other. Duke Ferdinando loves him. Bastiano, that is.'

I am completely confused. Luckily we have walked into the middle of a whirl of buzzing, babbling, distracting activity.

'This, my friend, is the Palazzo Vecchio.'

Jacopo takes his arm out of mine. The inside of my elbow is warm and moist, where our sweat has mingled. He leads us along the shady side of a building into an open space littered with wood, furniture, groups of men sawing and hammering and banging. We dodge past horses and goats, tied behind small carts, waywardly trying to wander off. The sounds follow us up a broad staircase and through a half-built arch into a space which soars upwards for two high storeys. Jacopo twirls round with a grand gesture.

'My friends. *La gran sala sopra gli edifizi de' magistrati.* Once merely administrative offices, now our proud, magnificent

❖ SECUNDA PARTE ❖

I remember what I know about the sixteenth and seventeenth centuries: dirt, disease, wars, high mortality – and then I stop myself. I am not here to find academic fault. Everyone here is absorbed. Why shouldn't they have their Golden Age?

Finally, Roberto tells us about his research. He has discovered a completely unknown manuscript of the original music of *Orfeo*. This will revolutionise Monteverdi scholarship. He can't say any more at the moment, we understand. He hopes we will all come to the performance of his new discovery. Any questions?

Tanya dives in. 'Maestro, I hope you don't mind my asking, but are you sure that *Orfeo* is the first opera? In my studies, I have read about Peri's *La Dafne*, in 1597 – '

Roberto interrupts her: 'None of the music by Peri survives.'

Tanya won't give up: 'But Jacopo Peri's *Euridice* of 1600 is before 1607.' Roberto is fast, sharp: 'Peri didn't write all the music for that opera.' Tanya is about to pursue it, when Roberto holds up his hand: 'I don't think we should bore people with academic details – '

Tanya changes tack: 'Maestro, did everyone in those olden days know they were part of a Golden Age?'

'Oh, yes,' says Roberto, now on comfortable ground. 'Each city state competed with the next city state to show how cultured and full of humanist beauty they were.'

'Where will the revolutionary performance of your new edition be?'

'I hope it will be in this country. You have the best musicians and the best singers.' Tanya shifts in her chair, as if she is being personally flattered.

In the dining hall, with late-night tea and cake, I

theatre. First built in 1586, now entirely renovated. Aren't I a good guide, Giovanni?'

A large man with a sheaf of papers sweeps in behind us, followed by others racing to keep up with him. He flings his hat on the ground. 'We have been in here since January. We have decided on *La Pellegrina*. We have a *concetto*, for how it will all work. Why the fuck isn't it ready?'

Jacopo whispers: 'You are in luck. The great man himself. Emilio de Cavalieri, responsible for all the Medici arts. Spider-in-chief, you might say.'

A tall, stately man follows Cavalieri and his group.

'The theatre will be ready. You must have patience, my friend.'

'I am not your friend. Bloody provincials. In Rome, we would be ready.'

'Then, Signor Cavalieri, if you are not happy with the way things are here, please feel free to return to Rome.'

'I should remind you, Count Giovanni de' Bardi, that the Duke himself has commissioned me to oversee all expenditure, outlay, and the cost of workers. Every day's delay costs the Duke more.'

'I am fully aware of your responsibilities. And I should remind you, Count Emilio de' Cavalieri, that the Duke has entrusted me with overall responsibility for the music.'

'Ah, yes. When you hear my music, you will know what real music is. My music is the future.' Cavalieri gives a contemptuous toss of the head and goes to talk to some workmen.

Jacopo has a fit of the giggles and puts his hand over his mouth to contain the spluttering.

congratulate Roberto on his interesting talk. I don't tell him he's no great shakes as a historian. Then I remember listening to the viols playing that first evening. I remember the revelation of my first experience in the choir. I remember the sound of his breathing and the warmth of his hand as he guides my bow onto the viol.

Perhaps here, on this course, we are as close as we could ever get to Italian palaces, where ducal musicians joined the jobbing players, to perform in front of the court. Perhaps I am having a glimpse of the Golden Age, just by being here. No wonder people want to recreate it. Am I letting sentiment erode academic inquiry? If so, it is a wonderful feeling.

SEVENTEEN

❖

THE FOLLOWING AFTERNOON, I proudly show Roberto how I can put my fingers on the frets. He nods. 'Your finger must go behind the fret, not on it.' He places my forefinger and presses it down, so that I can feel the edge of the gut. Then he does the same thing with my other fingers, so that each one is behind its own fret. These are not very far apart, but the angle of my hand feels strange. I have to resist the impulse to lift my hand from the instrument and curl it into his.

'Now play,' he says, 'without moving your finger.' I try, and the sound is looser, fuller. 'That is because you

Bardi turns on his heel and stalks past us, throwing a wave in Jacopo's direction. Jacopo bows, and leads us out of the theatre, and along a dusty corridor.

'Is Bardi your friend?' I ask.

'Everyone is my friend, dear. I may not be an arse licker, but I make people laugh, so they like me.'

As we walk, the cacophonous sounds of a jungle of musical instruments increases in volume.

'Bitchy Bardi is composing *intermedi*. However, the Duke hates him, because he helped to arrange Ferdinando's first unsuccessful marriage.'

More confusion. 'So why – '

'Patience, dear. Bardi knows all the right people and has the best musical contacts. He is good friends with Strozzi, the poet, and with Caccini, who is keen on the new monody.'

I nod. Musical information I can understand.

'Bardi doesn't care whether people like him. He has composed some of our best music. Luckily, he loves my music, and that's enough for me. Between you, me and the lovely Giovanni, I think the Duke has deliberately brought Cavalieri here to rile Bardi. Art, eh. Who needs it?'

We have arrived at the open doors of a large room. The floor is strewn with straw, the windows covered with lengths of ragged linen. Bare wooden benches punctuate the space, crammed with musicians, unwrapping instruments, sitting or standing, the wind instruments vying for notes, the string instruments tuning in the midst of the cacophony.

A man in a grey cloak, strands of black hair hanging round his face, comes towards us. He is carrying a huge pile of papers. Jacopo throws an arm round him and says: 'My old teacher,

are stopping the string behind the fret – you are, in effect, creating another open string. We'll do a scale. Listen.'

He plays a sequence of notes on his viol.

'That's the scale of G major,' he says. 'Play it.' I fumble with my fingers, trying to listen and copy his mirror image fingers.

'Good,' he says. He hands me a piece of paper. 'This is the treble clef, the same as the clef from which you sing in the choir. A clef is the symbol at the beginning of the stave, and it shows you how to read the right note in the right place on the instrument. The first note you see is the G you have just played.'

'I do know how to read music,' I say – 'well, only basic stuff. I had cello lessons when I was little. But I don't know anything about scales.'

'Ah,' says Roberto. 'That explains a lot. I think you are a lady with many secrets.'

We begin together, very slowly. The scale goes from my middle finger on the second fret on the third string, to the open top string, and then carries on up there. Roberto plucks his viol, holding it across his knee, like a massive guitar. At the end, he puts another piece of paper on the stand. It has diagrams of all the strings, the note-name of each, and then another diagram with all the frets drawn in, and the note name of each fret. 'Play tunes you know. Find your way round the instrument, and then check to see what notes you are playing. Now. Try the bass.'

He hands me the instrument. It is gigantic. With Roberto's help, I manage to hold it still. My arms go round the world in order to move the bow across the

the best composer in Florence. Signor Malvezzi. Salamone Rossi and Giovanni Gastoldi. From Mantova.'

Malvezzi bows to us: 'Jacopo. Look. Final copies. Can you distribute these?'

Jacopo, Giovanni and I take batches of music, and we go first to the *piffari*, stereotypically drunk, their unhemmed cloaks little more than rough woollen blankets thrown over their shoulders, and doubled back to allow their arms free rein. The smaller instruments are already into their stride, fingers flying, tiny high notes skittering away.

The string players have cocooned their instruments in canvas, wool, and lovingly embroidered thick woollen blankets designed to keep the instruments dry. The inner hour-glass shape of each string instrument and the long neck coverings are padded with rough sheep's wool. At the back of each cloth case is a long pouch for the bow, also thickly padded with rough wool.

'Malvezzi was my teacher.' Jacopo leans close to me, to whisper through the noise. I smell jasmine, roses, something sweet and light. 'I call him *Male* because that was the only thing he ever said when I was a boy. *Male*, if I wasn't good enough.'

We find the Mantovan contingent, and Giovanni reunites me with my viol. Jacopo leaves us, to continue distributing music. How was the ghetto, they want to know. When they hear my description, they laugh, and say that sounds more comfortable than where they spent the night: in recently vacated stables, still smelling of horses and straw. They breakfasted in a damp, chilly outhouse, surrounded by hanging onions and garlic.

strings, but the sound is deep and thrilling. The lower strings resonate down through the earth.

'Good,' says Roberto, taking the bass and putting it into its case.

When the door closes behind him, I try to play 'Twinkle, twinkle, little star' on my little treble. I get through the first part – it sounds uncannily like 'Baa, baa, black sheep'. I stop for the day. I lift the bow, and there is a gentle, ringing sound, as the viol thanks me.

EIGHTEEN

❖

THIS BECOMES THE PATTERN for my days: breakfast, a walk and viol practice in the Servants' Room, lunch, lesson with Roberto, tea, dinner, choir and snippets of Xan in between. She lets me borrow her viol for the duration. I may not be playing with any groups, but feel I am part of the course. Now and again I ask Gabriel a question about his involvement with early music in order to look as if I am really researching. I even take notes, and then promptly forget what he has told me.

Of course, as a researcher, no-one minds me asking questions. I learn more about some of my fellow course members. Luther's real name is Gerald, but because he is a luthier (that is, he makes viols), everyone calls him Luther. Like Martin Luther, or Martin Luther King, I say. I can't tell if anyone gets the joke.

PRIMA PARTE

A brass fanfare at the door sounds. The clanging and twittering and trumpeting and strains of tuning quieten. Cavalieri enters, calm and noble, his entourage behind him. He mounts a small wooden platform, so that he is looking down at us, like an Emperor, surveying his army.

'Welcome, my friends. Welcome to everyone, from Pistoia, Arezzo, Siena, Ferrara, Mantova, Verona, and above all, from Rome. We are here to celebrate a marriage, a union which will perpetuate the Golden Age of the Medici in Florence, and herald a new Golden Age for us all. I am sure you all appreciate the honour bestowed on us.'

Some scattered applause.

'Duke Ferdinand has always been loyal to Rome. That is why I have been honoured with the responsibility of supervising this event. I am a gentle, but firm, taskmaster. Lateness will not be tolerated. Drunkenness will not be tolerated. Food and drink will be provided during rehearsals. I expect everyone to behave appropriately.'

Sounds of musicians shifting in the room, but no applause.

'I am delighted to tell you that our new Duchess is on her way down the Arno. She will arrive in Florence at the end of April. We must be ready. Beyond rehearsal. Perfect. Joyous in the honour of our celebrations.' Some of the sackbut players let out a ragged cheer.

'Above all, we celebrate the classic virtue of *magnificenza*.' The cheers are louder. Cavalieri holds up his hand for silence. 'I am sad to say that none of the singers are here with us today. They are saving their voices. Or so they say.'

Instrumentalists ganging up on the singers. That goes down well.

❖ SECUNDA PARTE ❖

Nora-Jane often loses her place, and Edison helps her get back. I suspect she loses her place on purpose, so that he can be momentarily superior. Ellen is an assistant headmistress in a private girls' school in North London; she never looks directly at anyone. Her bow often squeaks, because she moves it too slowly, as if it might break. They have come as a pre-formed group, and have been playing together in their various London houses for years.

On the last day, Gabriel announces at breakfast that any groups who would like to perform in the final concert, should let Netta know by lunchtime. Barton will rehearse the choir after tea. Xan flits in to breakfast, grabs some coffee and toast, and then she and Barton leave together. Tanya trips after them. She's wearing blue high heels.

I go to the Servants' Room. On impulse, I leave the room again, lock the door, lift the safety rope and go up the spiral staircase, as I did with Mrs Dean. I turn left almost at the top. The tapestry is gone. I pick my way across bits of plaster to the wall.

I can make out the familiar Tudor rose. Orange or yellow flowers, with small, fine petals. Marigolds, perhaps. The rough sketch of a man – grey outline, with yellow washes. He may be wearing armour. To one side nestles a dog, its tail curled round its paws. On the other side is a large animal, reddish-brown, a bear, or boar. Hard to tell. Its head is blurred. Its body is lumpy, slightly misshapen.

Higher up is a cherub, leaning on a semi-circular window-sill. Its chin rests on its hands, wings behind its head. Round the cherub's head is a circle of stars, on a faded blue background. To the right of the cherub, is

'We have been preparing for this occasion since last summer. Tailors, seamstresses, materials from all over Italy: Bologna, Naples, Venice, Mantova.'

Some wag shouts out: 'And Rome.' General laughter and applause.

'Precisely. From Rome. Our own Giulio Caccini studied in Rome. Jacopo Peri, one of our most exciting young singers, was born in Rome. He, at least, is here today.'

A cheer goes up from a group near the front, and Jacopo stands up, and plays a flourish of chords on his chitarrone, 'Some of us may have been born in Rome, but it is here, in Florence, that our talents can blossom.'

Another heckler: 'What about Buontalenti?'

'All in good time,' calls Cavalieri. 'There is an order for everything, and everything must be in order. Signor Giovanni de' Bardi is well known to you already. He is a leading member of the *Accademia della Crusca* and is a veteran – if I may put it that way – of Medici wedding celebrations. What he does not know about this event – its *concetto*, the themes and musical style, and even the costumes, is not worth knowing. He has been in close consultation with Bernardo Buontalenti – ' In the hall the chanting begins: 'Talenti, Talenti … ' Cavalieri waits for it to abate, continuing as if he hasn't been interrupted.

'We are, you might say, the organising trio – working in harmony and counterpoint with one another: Bardi, Buontalenti, and your humble servant, Cavalieri. We are supported by talented composers, Marenzio, Malvezzi. Beside them, I am merely a humble servant, in charge of expenditure. In that capacity, I will be everywhere, at all times, checking that there is no wastage.'

another figure; black, with a multi-coloured turban, and a long, red, yellow and blue cloak. The contrast between the black face, the still piercing blue eyes and the cherub's pink cheeks, is startling.

Can a wall like this be restored, without damaging it? Can someone find authentic pigment, for the colours? I hear footsteps below, and a man's voice. Damn. There is nowhere to hide in the room. I remember steps continuing upwards. I tiptoe up one more spiral, the noisy footsteps below covering my sound. I am at the top of the tower. There is a shallow niche at the top, and in it is a wooden chest. I brush my hand across the top, and it comes away, grey with dust. I crouch next to it, in the corner.

I hear Mrs Dean. 'Well, what do you think?'

'What a find.' The voice is male, very upper-class.

Mrs Dean again: 'The tapestry pretty well disintegrated when we took it down.'

'The Trust will be delighted. How very exciting. Thank you, Barbara. I'm sure we can restore the wall-painting. We will do our best.'

The footsteps move away, down the stairs. I stand. The edge of my skirt catches on a corner of the chest. I lift the lid, to make it easier to extricate the material. There is something at the bottom of the chest. My hands are already covered in dust and plaster, and my skirt is filthy. It can't get much worse. I open the lid fully and take out a package, wrapped in some greenish material. I stupidly blow off the dust. It powders into the air, makes me cough and gets into my eyes.

I go all the way back down the stairs to the Ladies, my heart thumping. I collect handfuls of paper towels and

There is a heckle from somewhere in the crowd: 'Getting rich on it, are you?'

Cavalieri is quick to reply: 'I do not have special privileges. My apartment in the Pitti Palace, and the gift of an excellent horse, are merely in the interests of helping me to carry out my duties.'

There is some applause mixing with a handful of boos.

'Bernardo Buontalenti has studied with the great master, Vasari, alas, no longer with us. Buontalenti conjures devils out of the trees, and angels from the skies. He is truly named Bernardo delle Girandole – a fire cracker, spinning round, sparkling in all directions and illuminating all our work. He is a true *ingegnere*, respected by crafts and guilds alike.'

Huge cheers.

'Finally, may I take this opportunity of welcoming our troupe of Jewish musicians from Mantova.'

Polite applause. Jacopo nudges us to stand and bow.

'As you all know, in appreciation of his talents, our Duke commissioned Buontalenti to design the ghetto, where our respected Jewish *universita'* live in our city, in comfort and security.'

'Has he ever visited the ghetto?' I whisper. Jacopo shakes his head.

'Signor Buontalenti has now completed our Uffizi building, so wonderfully begun by Giorgio Vasari, and he has redesigned the theatre here. I would like to invite Bernardo to tell you about these himself.'

Deafening applause, hooting, whistling and stamping. Jacopo snorts in frustration: 'I wish this pointless formality would stop, so that we can get on with the music.'

❖ SECUNDA PARTE ❖

wrap them round the package. I wash and dry my hands, the package lightly under my arm, replace the key on its hook in Reception. For a brief moment I wonder whether I should tell Mrs Dean, and then decide not. She'll be busy with lunch.

I go to my room and change into jeans and a clean T-shirt. I wrap another T-shirt round the package and put it at the bottom of my suitcase. At lunch, I join Xan's table. She puts a hand up to my cheek. 'You've got a smudge, Em,' she says, and wipes it away. I put my hand up to my face, and there is a dusty grey streak on my fingers.

Roberto arrives punctually at two in the Servants' Room. It is our last lesson. This time, instead of sitting with his bass, he hands it to me. The pitch of the strings (except for the seventh, bottom one) are the same as the treble, but much lower. He explains the bass clef to me, and once I have tried a line or two of music, it feels as though I have always known the clef. The clock strikes three. Something occurs to me. 'I'm sorry. I should have asked before. How much should I pay you – for these lessons?'

'Nothing. It's been a pleasure. I haven't exactly been fully occupied this week.'

'Are you sure?'

'Yes, yes. I'm sure.'

He clicks the clasps shut on his viol case. He slings it over his shoulder and then picks up the treble. Of course. To give it back to Xan. There is a silence; an abyss. No more to say, no lesson tomorrow. He holds the door open for me. Chivalry is clearly not dead in Italy or East Anglia. He fishes in his jacket pocket. 'Here.' He hands me a card.

133

Buontalenti shuffles up to the platform. He is stooped, dressed entirely in black. Compared with Cavalieri, his tone is calm, modest.

'Thank you. Well. I have designed something very new: a frame, a *proscenio*, which will hide the flying machines, and mechanisms. For example – Jacopo – Signor Peri – will appear as Arion in a boat, then disappear overboard, beneath the waves.' Gasps of simulated horror. 'But never fear, he will be rescued on the back of a dolphin.'

Cheers. Jacopo bows extravagantly.

'There are at least a thousand costumes, so some of you will be wearing more than one. Not at the same time, of course.' Appreciative laughter. 'So – our friend, Jacopo, will be a siren, a Delphian woman, and he will sing Arion in *intermedio* number five. The gentlemen, whether you have beards or not, will be called upon to play nymphs, angels and shepherdesses.'

Huge cheers and floor thumping. Buontalenti shuffles gratefully away, and Cavalieri returns.

'Friends. Music brings peace and harmony. Signor Malvezzi will lead you. Thirty voices, seven choirs – just the instruments today. *O fortunato giorno*. Primo choro, here.'

I take my place in the seventh choir, the lowest of three bass lines. I am the foundation of everything. Malvezzi, statuesque, proud, hair flowing round his shoulders over a black gown, stands before us. He raises his arms. His breathing gives us the pulse. The *choro secondo* begins. Then, miracle of miracles, comes the sound I have been waiting for all my short life so far, without even knowing.

O fortunato giorno.

'If you would like to get in touch. For more lessons, maybe. You have a talent.'

NINETEEN

❖

AFTER TEA, THE CHOIR gathers in the Great Hall for our last rehearsal before the concert. Barton claps his hands for silence and we warm into *Vieni Imeneo*. I have forgotten how full and exciting it is. We clamber through the faster section, with two soprano voices chasing each other: *'Lasciate i monte, Lasciate i fonti ... '* Barton flings his arms up in mock despair. 'Go from the mountains, go from the springs – go from my sight, you cacophonous spirits of the underworld. That last bit, by the way, was me, not Monteverdi. Once more, remembering everything we did once upon a time in the dim distant past at the beginning of the week. It's love and beauty and happiness. We should all be so lucky.'

We are better, more responsive. The silence is palpable when we finish. 'Please regroup for *ahi, caso acerbo*. A bitter blow. Apart from anyone who missed that rehearsal, that is.' Barton holds his arms up, and there is total silence. Then he drops his arms. 'I've changed my mind. We won't run through it now. Remember your cruel fate, your bitter future. Remember the brutality of the stars, and remember that a beautiful landscape hides dangerous rocks.'

PRIMA PARTE

And so it is. This spring day, with the sunlight creeping in through the stained and dusty windows. A tired, motley throng, far from comfortable homes, forgetting everything but their sound. The fifth choir answers:

O fortunato giorno.

The sixth and the third follow, with all seven rousing together in great choral instrumental triumph, the bass instruments sending vibrations through the building, under the Arno, reverberating down to the sea. The choirs move in waves round the room, from high to low, then all together, in the slow stately gathering of the end. Later, when I see the words, the word is appropriate. *Insieme* – together.

> *O fortunato giorno*
> *poi che di gioia e speme*
> *lieta canta la terra e' l ciel insieme:*
> *ma quanto farà' ritorno*
> *per Ferdinando ogni real costume*
> *e con eterne piume*
> *da l'uno e la'tro Polo*
> *la Fam'andrà' col suo gran nome a volo*

O fortunate day, when heaven and earth rejoice in joy and hope. Greater splendour will shine, when Ferdinando restores every royal custom. Fame will carry his name on eternal wings from one pole to the other.

As if on cue, as the last note dies away in stately triple time,

❖ SECUNDA PARTE ❖

TWENTY

❖

A LARGE SEMICIRCLE OF chairs for the instruments and a smaller semicircle for the choir in front of the Great Hall's large bay window. Catherine tunes the harpsichord in the window's curve, as everyone gathers. Xan and Roberto arrive, with their viols. Roberto wears black velvet trousers, a deep red smoking jacket, and a bright red ribbon secures his pony-tail, Xan with a blue and green kaftan sweeping the floor.

Barton wears a crisp white shirt and a black jacket. His dark hair is wet and plastered back, as if just washed. He puts his music on the high stand by the harpsichord, and claps his hands. The choir stands. The audience consists of house staff and their family members, sitting or standing by the walls.

Barton turns to the audience. 'We begin with Anna, who will sing 'La Musica', the prologue to Monteverdi's *Orfeo*.'

Xan's voice is pure and soaring, strong and clear, with Catherine her harpsichord orchestra. What she sings is almost like speech. Barton doesn't conduct; he listens, his head gently moving in rhythm. At the end, Catherine plays a dance-like piece, giving Xan time to return to her place in the choir. Barton raises his arms. Celebrations, a marriage, happiness, beauty and glory. We sing *Vieni Imeneo*.

After the applause, we sit. The five viols I heard the first night, play through the *Lachrimae*, with Xan's treble

the heavens open, and enormous drops of rain clatter down outside the building, bouncing in through the windows. The *cornetti* spontaneously repeat their last phrase, decorating with runs of notes. Malvezzi stands, arms still raised. The sound slides into the walls, out into the streets, fading, until there is only the smooth patter of rain.

Applause. We have united. *Insieme.*

Not for long. The celestial harmony is interrupted by a group of workmen clattering in with ladders and carrying chunks of wood, and flagons of wine.

Cavalieri's voice rises above the din. 'Thank you all. From tomorrow, we shall rehearse in the theatre – but only at night. There is still scenery to be painted. The workmen will use the temporary bridge between the theatre and the Palazzo Vecchio, to store their tools, so that we can take over from them in the evening.'

Jacopo and Giovanni find me. With them are three strangers. Jacopo is efficient: 'Claudio, Giulio, Alessandro. Salamone. Shall we go?'

Claudio and Giulio both carry violins. As we jostle our way through the crowd of musicians and workmen, I ask: 'Which choir were you playing in?'

'We weren't playing,' says Claudio. Jacopo and Alessandro walk ahead of us. I feel shy. 'Do you live in Florence?' I ask.

'Cremona,' says Giulio. 'We are visiting.' I nod. We arrive at an imposing house. Alessandro bows. 'Welcome to the Palazzo Strozzi.' A rash of small children comes running down the steps to embrace Alessandro. They grab and push the rest of us up into a great palazzo, through the courtyard, along a corridor to one side of a sweeping marble staircase, and into a

❖ SECUNDA PARTE ❖

full and sweet. There is a small silence between each version, the players' suspense holding the audience still. At the end, they stand and bow, following Roberto's lead. Xan returns to the choir. Roberto goes up to Gabriel, squats down and says something, to which Gabriel nods assent.

The viols are followed by two recorder groups. One plays a jaunty dance, a bit like a tango, and the other, a sonorous piece. Well, they try to play. After the second group has broken down and restarted twice, Catherine gets up from the harpsichord, counts them in and conducts them through. We applaud, they sort of bow and scurry back into the crowd.

Gabriel and Roberto stand up, the latter holding his viol. Gabriel addresses us: 'I'm delighted to say that we have an extra treat. Robert would like to give us a piece from his repertoire. Captain Hume's Pavan – is that right, Robert?'

'Yes,' says Roberto. 'Before I play, I would like to thank Gabriel, and everyone here for being so friendly and hospitable towards me. I am especially honoured to have met Barton and Catherine, both very fine musicians.'

He sits and checks his tuning; the sounds are like a whole orchestra, running and echoing into the corners of the room, swirling up into the ceiling. He begins to play, and speaks as he plays: 'The music has a rhapsodic melancholy ... there are tiny trills at cadences ... chords and melodic shapes hurry, are held back, catch the heart where there is an interrupted cadence ... first from A to b flat, then from D to e flat ... these sneak between the simple chord progressions of I ... IV ... V ... I ... excitement ... reassurance alternates in leaps across the instrument ... notes are displaced in different octaves ... double ...

kitchen. Servants cut, cook, roast, bake, chop. Alessandro shouts: 'Mamma. We are back. Mamma.'

A stout, grey-haired woman, her face and hands covered with flour, emerges through the steam.

'Mamma. More for supper. Is there enough?'

'Is there enough? Is there ever not enough? Get out of here, before I cook your violins!'

Alessandro drops a kiss on her cheek, and grabs a dish piled high with biscuits. His mother shakes her head and waves us away. 'I'll send in some wine.'

We go into a square hall, huge dark wooden cabinets lining the walls. We flop onto comfortable couches. Alessandro puts the biscuits on a long dining table.

'*Fiorentini*, almonds, sugar, the whites of eggs. You have never tasted anything like these. Please.'

Three women come in, one holding a large jug of white wine and a jug of water; another, with a plate of white cheese, hunks of coarse, white bread, and a large bowl of olives; a third carries a pile of wooden plates.

I have had nothing since breakfast. The wine, gentle and reassuring, warms me through from the top of my head down to my feet. The bread is dry, bland. Alessandro notices my expression.

'No salt in our bread,' he says. 'We prefer it like this. It is sweeter, and the olives are salty enough.' He is right. The soft cheese has an edge to it. '*Pecorino*,' explains Alessandro. 'We are lucky. We get the spring cheese early. *Marzolino*. And it isn't even March yet!'

Jacopo devours his food, refilling everyone's glasses as if he is in his own home. He brings out a handful of furry, light

❖ SECUNDA PARTE ❖

and triple-stopped chords ... juxtapose ... and resonate ... against single-note melodic phrases.'

It is mesmerising. Roberto's breathing holds every moment, even the occasional scratchy bow as he goes from the depths of the instrument to a high point, above the frets. The words weave into the music, each augmenting the other. At the end, there is complete silence in the hall, and then a great burst of applause. Roberto bows. The audience settles down, and Barton stands.

'Thank you, Robert,' he says. 'If Hume had wanted words for his music, I'm sure he would have written them himself.' A brief pause. 'To end our concert,' continues Barton, 'we are going to hear an extract from *Orfeo*. Tanya will sing the Messagiera, bringing the sad news of Eurydice's death, and I will sing the *pastori* and Orfeo.'

He nods to Catherine. Barton sings, sad, pleading, regretful, as if his soul is in the sound. Tanya interrupts with a long, plangent note: '*Ahi! Caso acerbo ...* ' Her voice is very different from Xan's. Where the latter seems to soar into a perspective above and around us all, Tanya's voice spreads into a perspective around and behind us. I don't know how else to describe it.

Contrasting with her everyday fluttery, flirty manner, Tanya's voice is strong and full, as she sings to the shepherds and Orfeo. Barton's low, pained farewell, as he sings Orfeo: '*a dio*', precedes his transformation back into our conductor, and the choir explodes into a final '*Ahi caso acerbo ...* ' We have witnessed revelation, shock, terror and pity.

Finally, Barton conducts choir and instruments into a

green oval shapes from his bag. handing them round. 'Walnuts,' he says. 'Fresh from the tree. The shell is still soft.' We break open the fruit, and eat the inner kernel, creamy and sweet.

Alessandro turns to me, his mouth full of bits of white almond. 'Is it true that the Jews in the north fatten their geese by feeding them millet?'

'I don't know,' I say. 'My mother keeps chickens.'

'Have you ever eaten melon, preserved in honey?' I shake my head.

'Well. Once, in Modena, someone leaves a melon on a bench, under which there are vats of honey. The bench collapses and the melon falls into the honey. After a few weeks, someone finds the melon, cuts it open – and it is perfectly preserved. Wonderful, isn't it?'

'You are obsessed with round things. Nuts, melons. Women. Alessandro, I shall have to have a word with your mother,' says Jacopo.

'My mother has taught me to love food. And now, my Jacopo, you must sing for your supper.'

Jacopo picks up his chitarrone, unwraps it and starts tuning as he speaks. 'An audience of three to four thousand people,' he says. 'Where are they all staying?'

'No idea,' says Alessandro. 'The really important people – probably in the Palazzo Vecchio, the Pitti, and the Palazzo Medici. Your Duke,' he says, pointing at me, 'is bound to be at the Pitti.'

Jacopo plucks chords: 'Guess how many socks and belts. Hundreds of pairs of shoes. Three visiting theatre companies. Temperament, temperament, temperament. Obedient, pliable, humble musicians.'

rousing *O fortunato giorno*. When it rings to its triumphant end, the whole room bursts into cheers and applause. Barton leads the tutors in a bow, Gabriel standing modestly at the end of the row.

TWENTY-ONE

❖

I PACK MY CASE before I go to bed. How will I manage away from this Golden Age? Without a viol. Without Roberto. I wake at five and wander along the silent corridor to the main house. The lights are on in the connecting corridor. The bar smells of crisps and wine. I stand at the top of the main staircase, looking down into the entrance hall. As I do, the front door opens. Two people come in, closing the door softly. Roberto and Xan. They stand for a moment at the bottom of the stairs. They kiss slowly, slowly. I draw back and walk quickly and quietly back to my room.

Xan isn't there at breakfast. Roberto comes to sit at my table, in jeans and a loose shirt, his pony-tail in a rubber band. He is as friendly as ever. Before I leave, I say goodbye to Gabriel and Netta. As she hugs me she says: 'Do let us know when the programmes are on. Anna has our address.'

Outside, a gardener is trimming the grass at the side of the gravel forecourt. Barton and Catherine come loping up the drive, in matching tracksuits. They wave at me as

We roar with laughter. Jacopo continues. 'Red silk, yellow taffeta, buttons, embroidery, garlands. Nuns making garlands. I love nuns. Feathers, ticklish feathers. I should have been a nun.'

Claudio has taken out a violin, rippling light chords across the strings. 'They won't be real feathers,' he says. 'They'll be painted on, won't they? Otherwise they might fly off in the middle of the performance and choke the Medici.'

'Be careful,' cautions Jacopo gently. 'Walls have ears.'

There is a loud knock at the front door. Alessandro's mother comes in. 'He's here,' she says. Alessandro pours another glass of wine. Count Giovanni de' Bardi strides in. He goes straight to Alessandro's proffered glass, drains it and sits down. 'Good God,' he says.

'Tell us,' says Alessandro.

Bardi jumps up. A fireball of fury, he paces round the room, gesturing as he talks, beating his breast.

'*Miseri abitor*. A miserable, wretched Florentine. That is all I am. The Duke has always hated me.'

'Rubbish.' Alessandro is emphatic. 'The Duke hasn't always hated you. You made a diplomatic slip-up.'

'Not my fucking fault his first wife was such a shrew.'

'You're shocking the provinces here.'

'Not at all,' I slur.

'You're pissed, my little northern boy.' Jacopo plants a wet, winy kiss on my cheek.

'You mark my words, that cavilling bastard so-called Roman shit will squeeze me out.'

'Cavalieri is a coward. You're paranoid, and hungry. Have some bread and cheese.'

they run round the side of the house. It is chilly, the sun just beginning to lighten the damp grass.

I put my case in the car. A motorcycle comes roaring up the drive, slewing to a stop on the gravel. As the driver begins to remove his helmet, I recognise him. It is Terry.

TWENTY-TWO

❖

O FORTUNATO GIORNO. In four. *Poi che di gioia.* In three. It was a struggle to get all those vowels in. The choir put the stress on the last *'o'* of *giorno*; Barton drilled the stress onto the diphthong *'ior'*. The penultimate syllable, the penultimate syllable. I sing the phrases out loud down the M11, stressing the last syllable wrongly, then sing again, correcting myself. I turn into my road, and brake suddenly as a squirrel runs across. *O fortunato squirrel.* An image of Xan and Roberto kissing in the early morning flashes through my head.

My flat is silent. Reproachful. I open all the windows. Kitchen. Kettle. It's nearly lunchtime. In a parallel universe everyone crowds into the dining hall, to chatter over music, tutors, plans for later in the day.

The fridge is empty. My local café has morphed from a traditional, grubby workmen's *(sic)* dive, into lowkey smartness: white brickwork and fresh flowers. Poached egg on toast and two mugs of hot strong tea. Smashed avocado on toast. *O fortunato giorno* can't

'What? Yes.' Bardi comes to sit down, takes two mouthfuls of bread and then bursts into tears. 'I've written the end. I've written your aria for the fifth *Intermezzo*, and all Cavalieri says is that the Duke may want to – quote – "change things around a bit".'

Jacopo looks up. 'Just a minute. You've written my aria?'

'Yes. Cavalieri told me to. And I obey the all-powerful *superindente* of everything on heaven and bloody earth.'

'But I want to write my own aria.'

'Take it up with the *maestro*. You'll see. I'll land up in hell with the rest of the dead in *Intermezzo* four. Who is responsible for *recitar cantando*?'

'Bardi.' Jacopo and Alessandro are in unison.

'Melody and rhythm following the stresses of spoken speech.'

'Sung speech.'

'Exactly. He gets a horse, and an apartment in the Pitti Palace. He is paid more than I am. He doesn't need a salary. He's a rich bastard. I'm talking to him about sirens. A thing of beauty. A celestial being. And he says: "It's just a character on a cloud." There is no magic in him. He doesn't pay anyone on time. The tailors have threatened not to deliver the costumes.'

Jacopo plays the ground bass to *Ruggiero*. Claudio joins him, also playing the ground. Giulio takes out his violin and hands it to me. I too play the ground, and Claudio begins to improvise. The dark, gaunt young man is transformed. He sways and smiles as he plays. Fire sparks from his violin as the bow hair teases the strings, the instrument held just below his collarbone. We circle round the table. Alessandro picks up my bass viol and bows the ground. I have no idea how long we

❖ SECUNDA PARTE ❖

compete with Elvis singing 'All Shook Up' over the rock cakes.

The rest of the day is pure domesticity. Shopping, stocking the fridge, hoovering, putting away shoes, cosmetics and washing bag. I take dirty clothes out of the case, leaving the clean clothes. I have one answerphone message. My mother. Where are you, how are you, why haven't you phoned? I have an impulse to phone Xan, lift the handset, and then change my mind.

I run a bath. Eucalyptus bathsalts. I am preparing for supper in the dining hall, choir rehearsal this evening. The water is hot, comforting. I lean back and close my eyes. The cold porcelain warms and I can feel Xan's fingers stroking along my collarbone, reaching down to ease tensions in my back. Her light jasmine scent mingles with the fresh eucalyptus. I shiver, sitting up suddenly. I must have dozed off. The bathroom is steamy, my skin chill. I wash quickly. I'm shivering. Suddenly, deathly tired.

I go to bed, closing the curtains to shut out the light, huddling under the duvet. I sleep fitfully. Each time I get up and check through the curtains to see whether it's dark. Eventually, it is. No moon. Just the nearby street lamp with a bloom round its light.

Something wakes me. A bang, like a door slamming, or a car backfiring. It's pitch dark. The street outside is quiet. No car idling. I open my front door. Just the dim light on the landing. Back in the bedroom, I notice that the wardrobe door is ajar. I close it and go back to bed. A bang. A sharp crack. I sit up. The wardrobe door is open again. There is a slim shaft of diagonal light, from the street lamp outside the window. I must have left the curtain open.

play for. First Alessandro drops out, then Jacopo, and then me. Claudio plays the ground for a last time. Giulio and Giovanni applaud gently.

Alessandro's mother comes in. She wears an elegant blue dress, her grey hair now braided in a twisted ribbon of green velvet. 'Enough,' she says. 'Dinner.'

It is dark. The sky is deep blue-black. The stars above us here in Florence are also shining above Mantova. I revive for long enough to eat and be taken to the comfort of a bed, where I fall asleep.

FIFTEEN

I WAKE UP WITH Jacopo curled around me. We are both naked. He drops a gentle kiss on my cheek and jumps up. 'You sleep soundly, my Mantovano,' he says. 'Get dressed. We have work to do.'

Somehow I am not embarrassed, or even curious. Here, in Florence, everything normal seems to have been put aside. Perhaps it is permanent *Carnevale* here, with everything upside down. Nothing is right and nothing is wrong.

In the cavernous kitchen, we breakfast on bread and raisins soaked in milk. Giulio, Alessandro and Giovanni have music to copy, and Jacopo invites me to go with him to try on his costume. 'Bernardo Buontalenti is well named,' he says. 'His

As I get out of bed, I notice two glittering points of light. Oh, my god. A rat. The wardrobe door creaks open a little wider, and something small jumps out. It's on its hind legs. It is remarkably like a small human figure. Large ears. A smile. Bright, white teeth. It's definitely not a rat. I am no longer scared, just curious. The figure stands in the shaft of light from the window. It is covered with soft, brown hair or fur. At first I think it is a long coat, then realise he is naked. It is a he. I can see. He bends to gather up something behind him. A long, thick, furry tail. He wraps it across his front, slowly, and loops it over his left arm, across his genitals, as if he has noticed me staring. Of course. It's the devil.

He bows. A small cloud of grey dust flips out around him. He bows again. I yawn, closing my eyes. I wake up in bright sunlight. The wardrobe door is ajar. I laugh out loud. I have seen the devil. *O fortunato giorno.* The church bells in the square opposite are clanging away. It is Sunday. I get out of bed, and see some grey dust by the wardrobe. Must hoover better.

TWENTY-THREE

❖

DURING THE NEXT FEW days I am acutely aware of everyday sounds. Doors opening and closing, lights switched on and off, lavatory flushing, taps on and off. I exchange only necessary words in shops. I phone my

costumes fly off the page. Later, you and Claudio must come and listen to my aria. It is almost finished.'

'Has Bardi given you the music?' asks Claudio.

Jacopo shakes his head. 'No. I've written my own.'

'Won't Bardi mind?' asks Claudio.

'Bardi,' says Jacopo, 'is my friend and mentor. I love him as I love my father. But when it comes to art, I will write my own words and sing my own music. Giulio, can Salamone borrow your violin?' Giulio nods. 'Claudio, come with us – I want your opinion.'

We emerge into the street, dwarfed by the vast wooden studded doors of the palazzo. We wind through *piazze*, under arches, into a courtyard lined with tables. Some are covered with piles of multi-coloured clothes; groups of women and girls sit round others, sewing materials, which float and ripple. Nuns walk from table to table.

Jacopo goes up to one of the tables. 'My breasts,' he says, 'where are my breasts?' The nun laughs and says: 'Good morning, Jacopo. I'll find your breasts.'

'Graziella is my cousin,' explains Jacopo. 'She shouldn't be a nun. She should have eloped with a prince.'

'Some of us have a calling,' says Graziella.

She takes us into a large tent. A hive of human sewing bees. Graziella stops at a table. Jacopo unstraps the chitarrone and seizes two paper-padded half-moons. He holds them against his chest and prances round the room. The tent erupts into laughter.

'Take smaller steps,' I say, 'otherwise you look like a man pretending to be a woman.'

'In spite of his funny accent, my friend is right,' says Jacopo.

mother, apologising for my silence (!). I was busy working. 'I'm glad you're getting back to work,' she says. 'You must be lonely, away from your friends and your teaching.'

I'm not. I love the silence. I need it to stay with Catchpole. The dining hall. Gabriel. The choir. Barton. I dream my way back through the lessons with Roberto. One night I wake up, frantic. My skirt is caught in a nail. I tug and tug and tug at it. In the morning, my duvet is on the floor, my wardrobe door open. Over breakfast I think about Xan. She hasn't phoned. I am angry. She has my viol. I could phone her, perhaps borrow it. But I don't.

TWENTY-FOUR

❖

THE DAY I STRUGGLE to remember the opening phrase from *O fortunato giorno* is the day I finish unpacking my suitcase. A couple of unworn T-shirts on the top. Underneath, some underwear. Sandals, unworn, because it was never warm enough. And then, at the bottom of the case, a package wrapped in a T-shirt.

I take it to my desk in the living room and unwrap the T-shirt. Inside is some sort of matted fabric, the edges ragged, chewed or eaten away by mice or insects. It has a faded green bloom on it. Velvet, perhaps. Carefully, I peel back a section of fabric. Underneath is paper, also ragged round the edges. The top sheet is loose, with faint lines

He minces exaggeratedly round the room. 'Have you ever seen anything like it? Breasts and a beard.'

Graziella brings a green and yellow costume. 'Your sea nymph, Jacopo. It will fit over your other clothes. Do you want to try the mask?'

Jacopo is transformed into an exquisite woman, with flowing locks painted on the mask. Below it, his beard sticks out.

'Unlike some,' he says, 'I will have the grace to trim my beard so that it doesn't show. The *castrati* won't have that problem.'

One of the nuns calls out: 'But they have other problems.' Everyone laughs, then they stop abruptly. Graziella turns to the door.

'Good morning, Signor Buontalenti.'

The women return to their sewing and Jacopo, still with breasts and mask, hugs the great man. 'Don't I look wonderful? Is my harp ready?'

'Not yet. I haven't decided. Either *cartone* – cardboard, or *carta pesta* – papier mache, painted in silver or gold.'

'Gold,' says Jacopo decisively. 'And cardboard, rather than papier mache. Remember the weight. I need my arms free to play the chitarrone behind the harp. Oh, where are my manners? Salamone Rossi, from Mantova.'

'Ah,' says Buontalenti. 'I have read your de Sommi on staging. He says that velvet and silk are suited to aristocratic characters. However, I am using them for divine, supernatural characters. So, for example, Doric Harmony, in the first *intermedio* will be in dark green velvet, to represent the virtues of virility and strength.' He indicates a length of deep green velvet on one of the tables.

on it. I switch on the desk lamp. The lines come into focus.

There is fine grey dust on the paper, a darker streak waving across the page, almost like a tail. I touch the paper; it is warm. My hand slides and the dust disperses, a cloud in the air. I cough and move the top sheet to one side. The next page has clear, strong lines ruled across. A stave, slightly uneven, as if drawn by hand. There are faint words underneath.

My heart beats fast. I should phone Catchpole Manor and say – what? That I found some weird papers in my case by accident? How did they get there? Should I ask someone what to do – Xan? Roberto? They will ask the same questions. I wrap the package back in the T-shirt, and put it at the bottom of the wardrobe.

I go to my computer and Google Luther, luthier.

TWENTY-FIVE

❖

LUTHER LIVES IN A bow-fronted, semi-detached suburban house in North London, just inside the A1. He opens the door, wearing a huge pair of plaid felt slippers, with bunny rabbit pompoms on the fronts. He flings open his arms: 'Ah, the lovely Emilia. Come in, come in.'

He takes me to the top of the house, a room under the eaves. Sweet smells of wood shavings, varnish and cedar. Sections of viol, like anatomically dissected wooden

'*Velluto verde*. Cavallieri says the best green velvet comes from Rome. Jacopo: you'll have a laurel wreath – painted paper – to cover your curls. A loose jacket, long sleeves, with a flounced upper arm. Soft leather boots and a short skirt, just above the knee. A cardboard harp, with a buxom woman – apologies, Graziella – as the neckpiece, behind which you can conceal your chitarrone. Here is the final drawing. You will have to trim your beard.'

'Of course,' says Jacopo, bowing.

'Good. I have just had an almighty argument with the nymphs in the first *intermedio*. None of them is prepared to trim their beards, so the masks will have to be longer.'

'Half of them are singing *basso* anyway,' says Jacopo. 'On the other hand, you could have them castrated as well. That would teach them a lesson.'

There is laughter and the atmosphere is easy again. Jacopo picks up fabrics and decorations. 'What else is there for our *intermedio*? The Mantovani are playing.'

'Pearl, mother of pearl, shells and coral branches made of cardboard, to fit over the front of the instruments. Marine motifs throughout. Wait till you see the dolphins and the waves!'

Jacopo, Claudio and I walk back to the Palazzo Vecchio. The surrounding streets are mayhem. Worse than yesterday. We pass a group of chanting, dancing people in animal costumes.

Outside the Palazzo Vecchio, there is a burst of shouting and screaming. Two men are carried out and laid on the ground. Someone shouts for water. A fire, in the theatre. No-one badly hurt, but a terrible mess. As the men recover, coughing, their faces and hands blackened with smoke, Cavalieri comes

animals, lie on two high benches, set at right angles to each other.

He goes to a black case in the corner of the room, its lid open. It is lined with deep rose pink plush, and cradles a light golden bass viol. He lifts the viol and hands it to me. I support the viol between my calves. It feels comfortable. He hands me a bow.

My feet are slightly turned out, like a ballet dancer; my knees splayed outwards in a wide V. I lift the bow and put it on the strings. I fumble for the G fret on the third string down. I move the bow across the string, slowly, then faster, to get a clear, deepening contact with the string, the sound locked within, waiting patiently to be released. My legs are quivering with tension. I love it. 'Wow,' I say.

I turn the viol round carefully, and stroke the shiny, flat back. Luther points to a thin strip of wood winding round the outside of the back. 'This is called purfling. Inlaid wood.' I turn the viol back. On the front is a stylised red and brown flower. 'This is a rose. The belly – the front, as you'd expect – is made in the same way as early seventeenth-century English viols. A bent front – that is, five – or, in this case, three – pieces of wood, warmed up and curved. I've taken other elements from a later, French viol maker, a man called Michel Colichon.'

'How much is it? Can I take it home today?'

Luther smiles. 'I'm sure we can come to some arrangement.' He puts the viol back in the case and carries it downstairs. The doorbell rings, and he welcomes Edison and Nora-Jane. No wispy Ellen, thank goodness. Luther feeds us with a hearty, home-made steak and kidney pie and rhubarb crumble, tart and sweet.

storming out of the building. The square falls silent, as he stands on the steps. He shouts, his voice cracking with fury.

'Some stupid bastard left a bloody candle on some bloody wood. Fire burns wood. You think these peasants would know.'

One of the injured men shouts: 'If we have to work at night, candles are the only option. Unless you can order the moon to come and light us.'

'Very funny. If you had finished the job on time – '

'And if you didn't keep changing your mind – this is the third lot of scenery we've had to build.'

'We shall rehearse in the theatre, for six hours after sunset. You will work by candlelight when we have finished. From now on, wine is banned.'

Cavalieri marches away, out of the square. Jacopo leads us up, past the heavy black and gold doors of the theatre, and then to the floor above. At the end of a long corridor, is a horse-shoe bend which winds round the building, to the west wing and through half-open doors. We glimpse marble busts, paintings. Jacopo says an earlier Medici Duke converted the building for his collection of art treasures.

We arrive at a large, roughly painted screen between two elaborately carved wooden doors. Jacopo heaves the screen aside, and instead of the pile of rubble I was expecting, there is a plain, white door. No lock or handle. Jacopo pushes it open, and we go through.

We are at the top of two wide, shallow flights of stairs. Jacopo runs down, his shoes softly slapping against the stone. At the bottom, a corridor slopes downhill. It is littered with fragments of plaster, bits of discarded wood, and all kinds of furniture: tables, chairs. At the end of the corridor we turn right, following

❖ SECUNDA PARTE ❖

After supper, we play. Luther gives me the bass viol, and says: 'Emilia is thinking of buying this', to approving responses. We tune to a little machine Luther puts on his music stand. They are impressed that I can read bass clef, and, apart from a few glitches, I manage the four-part Byrd. The conversation is to the point: how to play this or that note; how to arrive at a cadence. After an hour we stop for coffee and cake. Luther says I can take the viol home. I arrange to pay him in monthly instalments. It is not cheap, but then it is hand-made, and you couldn't buy it in a shop. I can afford it. I am still receiving my fulltime academic salary.

Edison and Nora-Jane offer to drive me (and the bass) back to my flat. As we are saying goodbye to Luther, I realise something: 'How am I going to tune at home?' Luther disappears into the back room, where we have been playing and brings the tuning machine. 'It's alright,' he says. 'I have at least two more.'

The session at Luther's house introduces me to a network of amateur viol players, meeting weekly or fortnightly at each others' houses. These sessions are referred to as 'rehearsals', though we are never rehearsing for anything. Edison and Nora-Jane live in a higgledy-piggledy two-up two-down in Tooting.

It is fun: dinner parties without the pressure. Making our own entertainment. The Victorian experience. We are recreating the drawing room ambience of the middle and gentry classes, where everyone (supposedly) played an instrument or sang. Another Golden Age of music making. Acton and Ealing; leafy Enfield and urban Tooting Bec are not, after all, art-free zones. This Golden Age is free from open sewers, rotting vegetables and

the north bank of the river. Jacopo explains that the corridor was designed and built in a hasty five months by Giorgio Vasari, as a safe and secure retreat from the Palazzo Vecchio, through the Uffizi, ending in the Pitti Palace, on the south side of the Arno. It will be used during the celebrations by all the important guests, but for now, it is a useful storeroom.

The Vasari corridor crosses above the Ponte Vecchio, with its shops on both sides. I stoop down to the tiny windows. The Arno stretches away into the distance. Ahead of us, Jacopo stops. Light haloes his red-gold curls. He points through a heavy iron railing. Below is a small church, lit by candles.

'This is Santa Felicita, where the Medici come to pray. We'll rehearse here.'

'Won't someone hear us?'

Jacopo shakes his head. 'If they do, they will think we are preparing music for the service.'

We unwrap the instruments, and tune. We play a warm-up round of *Ruggiero*. We sit, leaning against the wall opposite the iron railing, golden from the glow from the candles below.

'The *quinto intermedio* is the story of Arion,' says Jacopo. 'I appear, sailing back to Corinth. I am kidnapped by sailors, I jump into the sea, and am saved by dolphins. My aria must be full of anguish, and yet carry within it the seeds of my survival. No problem, eh? Except I have no words yet.'

'But,' I say, remembering yesterday, 'hasn't Bardi written words for you?'

'I will sing my own words and compose my own music.'

He sings, accompanying himself. A slow, wordless song, the first phrase ending with a small flourish. Claudio lifts his violin and echoes the flourish. I follow suit on Giulio's violin.

❖ SECUNDA PARTE ❖

plague. It is a Golden Age with fridges and hospitals and drugs, central heating and microwaves. We are the Dukes and Duchesses of suburbia.

One experience sours the glitter. A whole day in a large, Hollywood-style house, on the edge of a village in the Cotswolds. Owner-architect, George Taylor, tells us over coffee and biscuits on arrival, that he also owns the local abattoir. Solar energy, piped speakers in every room, remote control panels everywhere, and sliding walls and doors change the shapes of rooms at will. The TV series, 'Grand Designs', has made a programme about the house.

George has organised three groups for the day. He slides two walls across the floor of the open-plan living room to make separate sections, each full of light from the outside, glass, walls. Sound proofing ensures we do not disturb each other. His wife, the Honourable Cecilia, greets us, and then leaves, to run the local Bring and Buy Sale for the homeless.

At lunchtime, the room dividers slide back. We gather round a long table at one end of the room. Everyone opens up aluminium foil packages and Tupperware boxes. Nora-Jane, seeing I have nothing with me, says: 'We bring our own lunch.' I am mortified. 'I didn't know.' Nora-Jane collects sandwiches and fruit from the others. I have enough to eat.

At the other end of the room, the Honourable lady wife has popped back in. She and George eat salad from a large wooden bowl, with a selection of cold meats, cheeses and hardboiled eggs. I can smell the oven-warmed bread. This really is the Golden Age. I am close to asking for some salt, so that we can properly sit below

Jacopo is our God, Arion, candlelight haloes his hair, his profile fine and intent, his body bent round the chitarrone as if it is the boat in which he sails to safety.

We continue in a free, meandering improvisation, each phrase ending with a tiny flourish, or a longer sequence of divided notes, echoed first by Claudio, and then me, whispering on my violin, as if I am far away. The echoes overlap. Jacopo's voice is like honey, silking decorations on a single vowel, a *melisma* which goes on for ever, while Claudio and I are there to catch the notes and pass them to each other.

A final extended flourish could signify a dying breath, or the celebration of a return to life. We play through again – sometimes remembering what we have played before, sometimes inventing anew. As Jacopo's voice leads us, words float into my head and I speak them below Jacopo's wordless notes, as we play. Jacopo picks them up and sings them. The aria falls into place. Words. Music. Voice. Instruments.

The sun is setting over the river when we eventually stop, bathed in sweat. We stand, stiff and cramped, and hug each other. We wrap our instruments, and continue along the corridor, down a slope, to come out through a small, unobtrusive door at the back of the Pitti Palace, into the gardens.

Alessandro's house is a long walk, back across the river and through the town. When we get there, Jacopo finds paper, pen and ink, and between us the words and music arrive on paper.

One Sunday, when we have some precious free time, I take Jacopo to visit the ghetto. I feel guilty, that I have deserted my hospitable friends. They welcome me with no hint of censure for my neglect. We coincide with a ghetto wedding. At the

it. After lunch, the aroma of freshly brewed coffee drifts across to us. My fellow musicians fish out thermos flasks of tea and bottles of water, and share them with me.

At the end of the afternoon, the Honourable passes round a fruitcake from her Bring and Buy. I suppose she hasn't Brought them herself, but Bought them from another lady. She regales us with a string of unfunny viola jokes. I can't wait to leave.

TWENTY-SIX

❖

DESPITE THE FRIENDLINESS AND generosity of these amateur musicians, there is something missing. I am not sure what it is. As I practise Luther's bass (I still think of it as Luther's bass), I take pleasure in the tuning; the moment when my sound and the pitch of the machine merge. It often takes a long time, but I persist to get the best sound I can. I play 'Happy Birthday', and I want it to sound pure and beautiful. Why?

I have a boiled egg for supper and take down my copy of Henry James's *The Bostonians*. I read and marvel at the way he makes a work of art out of words. That is it. Gabriel's words come back to me: music is a civilising experience; it helps create harmony in the world. 'No, it bloody doesn't,' I say out loud. 'Not if it sounds like rubbish.' I remember Barton's passion in moulding the choir's sound; I remember Roberto's

end of the ceremony, a glass is broken, as is the custom, but unlike what I am used to, it isn't broken underfoot by the groom. It is placed in a bowl, lined with rough cloth, and broken with a small silver hammer. Jacopo is fascinated, and we return the following week, this time for a circumcision. Jacopo observes afterwards that it is just like a christening, but more painful. The baby wears a long, white lace christening robe, threaded with pink ribbon. Reuben and his family embrace and feed us.

SIXTEEN

THE PLAY, *LA PELLEGRINA*, round which the *intermedi* are grouped, is being presented by the Sienese *Accademia degli Intronati*, an all-male troupe of young patrician Sienese. The day before the first complete run-through, Jacopo and I peer into the theatre. Buontalenti stands in the middle of the stage. Above and around him is a whirl of machinery, painted canvas backdrops, wooden trusses and beams overhead, winches. pulleys and catwalks. He beckons us into the centre of the auditorium.

'Stop there,' he calls. 'Perfect. The sightlines from the stage converge to the point in the middle of the room where you are standing, and that's where the Duke will sit. He is the vanishing point of our perspective, the beginning and end. Perfect.'

❖ SECUNDA PARTE ❖

attentive teaching, and the piece he played at the course concert. The devil is in the detail, he said. That is what makes a work of art.

It has never occurred to me before that I might want to make a work of art. My profession has been predicated on commenting on other people's works of art (literature), exercising my critical faculties. For the first time in my life I want to make a work of art, and here I am, frustrated because the playing I do doesn't feel like a work of art.

Is music an art? Is the written music or the performance the work of art? I am steeped in literary and cultural theory, and yet asking old questions feels fresh. Perhaps it's because I am asking from the inside, not from the outside. It isn't the theory of the thing, it is the doing of it.

It's getting cold. I close the curtains in the living room and go into the bedroom. The wardrobe door is open. Something is preventing the door from closing. The package. I'd forgotten about it. I take it out and put it on the desk. The wardrobe door closes with a tiny puff of grey dust. I wonder if I have woodworm.

On the desk, I unwrap the package quickly, moving aside the blank top sheet and the second sheet with the empty staves. On the third sheet are some words and music. I can just make out something which looks like '*Questi i campi ...*' and then it gets very faint again.

The next sheet has four bars of five-part music. At the top it says '*Ritornello*'. I put the two sheets on my music stand and try to play from them. The first, two-line one is very confusing. It has long, tied notes in the bass, and then a not very tuneful melody on the top

In early April, when the *Intronati* and Malvezzi almost come to blows about rehearsal time in the theatre, Cavalieri announces that the Duke will come to a run-through of everything, warts and all. Food and drink are sent, rations following rank: apprentice manual workers get a loaf of bread, one piece of cheese, and a flask of wine between every five men. Carpenters get the same, and share one flask between four men. Senior technicians also get meat. The *Intronati* and musicians all receive meat and cheese. The women share ten pounds of luxury almonds; men and women eat in separate rooms; I notice that some women smuggle almonds in their sleeves for their male friends.

The run-through is a chaotic stagger-through. We break after the third *intermedio* for bread and wine. There is panic when clouds refuse to behave, and rise and fall either too quickly or too slowly. Cavalieri fires one of the technicians. We are there for hours. There will be another full rehearsal later in April, announces the Duke, and this must be faultless.

We rehearse and re-rehearse our sections. I see little of Jacopo, who is on call for other *intermedi*. I dream that I am in Vasari's secret corridor, where Leonora meets me by the church railings. We make love by candlelight. The dream comes to an unpleasant end, when Emilia arrives and finds us together.

At the end of April, the Duchess Cristina (as she is now officially called) enters Florence. I join the crowds. In the distance I see the Duke and Duchess of Mantova, tiny figures in an exotic painting. I tell Jacopo about Leonora. He puts his arm round me. 'Loving women is a mistake,' he says. 'No, it isn't,' I say, and then I tell him about Emilia. He bursts into raucous laughter.

line. I play the two top lines of the other piece, one after the other. It's short and sweet. I repack the music, leaving it on my desk.

TWENTY-SEVEN

❖

NEXT MORNING, AS I wash up my breakfast things, there is a swirl of grey dust on the marble draining board. I sweep it into my hand, and a thrill goes up my arm and down my spine, like a tiny electric shock.

The package, in its ragged once-green wrapping, is still on my desk. I sneeze – there may be mould on the package. I empty my bag to get a tissue. A card, with Roberto's phone number on it.

Two rings and a smart female voice says: 'Gwyn School of Music.' Wrong number. I try again. Same answer. Turns out the number is right, and Roberto teaches there. I leave a message. While I'm waiting, I Google it. The Gwyn School of Early Music, Nr High Holborn. It's just behind Russell Square, and the building was lived in by Nell Gwyn, before she moved to the further reaches of North London. It was originally a Tudor manor house, and the oldest surviving part is a large oak-panelled Dining Hall, with a spectacular stone fireplace, which was possibly once a priests' hiding hole.

In the 1960s, the Gwyn School was bought by an anonymous benefactor, and, unique among music

'I am amazed,' he says. 'You do nothing, and two beautiful women chase you. There must be something about you.'

'Passivity.'

'Rubbish. No-one is passive. Perhaps it's vulnerability. Perhaps you have something they want.'

I laugh. 'What could I possibly have that a Duchess could want?'

'Apart from your body?'

'I don't think about my body.'

'Then that's it. You don't think about your body and that makes you desirable. You are all music, Salamone. Anyone can see that.'

Walking along the river, we sing, without instruments. I take the bass line, and Jacopo pirouettes round my voice.

Dunque fra torbide onde
Gli ultimi miei sospir mandero' fore,
Ecco gentilcon tuoi suavi accenti:
Radoppia i miei tormenti;
Hai, lacrime, hai dolore,
Hai morte troppo acerba e troppo dura.

Ma deh chi n'assicura:
O di Terra o di Cielo
S'a torto io mi querelo:
E s'a ragion mi doglio;
Movetevi a pieta' del mio cordoglio.

I shall breathe my last in these murky waters, in double torment, with tears and sorrow. Death is too bitter, too harsh.

colleges, it specialises in early music. It takes in only thirty students each year. I get no further than this, when the phone rings: Roberto is delighted and when would I like to come for a lesson?

The School nestles at the end of an easily missable alley. A high metal gate opens into an oasis of peace. Between benches in the courtyard are small bay trees in terracotta pots. A handful of students loll around. The receptionist directs me up the once grand staircase, to the King Charles Room.

A large square room. An intermittent frieze of fruit and plants runs round the top of the walls, below the cornice. Perfect bloomed peaches, red, green and yellow apples cuddling on a plate, dusky lime-green-brown pears, fronds of ivy and other green leaves wind among them. A harpsichord stands at one end of the room. Roberto sits at it; his hair curls round his ears, strands of grey showing through the blue-black. He comes to take my bass, putting one arm round me in a greeting.

'I see you have ambition,' he says. I'm not quite sure what he means. 'It's really good to see you,' I say. He takes the bass from its case, pings a note on the harpsichord and tunes the instrument rapidly, then tries it out. He nods approval. 'Good tone. The bridge may be a little high.'

He starts me on a *Fantaisie*. No composer. A photocopy. It looks handwritten – wavy lines joining the quavers. At first, it seems straightforward. By the eighth bar, the music is climbing above the frets, enough to make me sweat with anxiety. At a couple of points I have to play two strings at the same time, and this brings me to a halt.

No-one on earth or in heaven can blame me for lamenting. Have pity on my anguish.

'Could you love a man?' asks Jacopo. 'Of course,' I say. 'I love you.' Jacopo puts his arms round me and kisses me lightly on the lips.

SEVENTEEN

THERE IS ONE FINAL rumpus. Bardi inevitably discovers that Jacopo has written his own aria. Cavalieri says the Duke prefers Jacopo's music. Bardi refuses to talk to Jacopo. Cavalieri tells Bardi that the Duke wants him, Cavalieri, to write the closing ceremonial number, where the gods send rhythm and harmony to earth.

Bardi protests. He has already written the words and music. Cavalieri delivers the ultimate insult. A woman, Laura Lucchesini, from Lucca, is writing the words for him to set. Cavalieri hides behind his title of *intendente generale delle belle arti*. Bardi needs a great deal of wine and comfort before he is persuaded to remain at all involved in the production.

During rehearsals, Bardi and Cavalieri sit well away from each other. Bardi is stony calm, the only sign of unhappiness showing in the fact that whenever he speaks to anyone, he refers to himself in the third person, as if he were not personally present.

'Double stopping,' says Roberto. 'Notes on more than one string. Chords. Look at the last bar. Four notes, a D major chord, characteristic of solo French viol music.'

'French viol music?'

'Stop asking questions,' he says. 'Just play.'

'But I want to know,' I say.

He doesn't answer; he takes me through the piece, softens a note here, finds a legato phrase there, staccato notes for jumps across strings. He writes in pencil on the music, showing phrasing and articulation. When I put my viol away, he says: 'Same time next week.' No question mark. I haven't even asked him how much to pay.

In a small music shop off the Marylebone Road, I buy a guitar stand for my viol. Real viol players lay their instruments sideways on the floor. That is too precarious for me. A casual touch on the neck with a foot could set the instrument spinning. I can't be bothered to keep the instrument in its case, and keep taking it out. Besides, I want it as my companion, visible all the time. The instrument sits proudly, the neck held safely between two foam-covered prongs. The bow hangs on a rounded protuberance at the back.

As the weeks pass, I devour Roberto's vocabulary. The terms are 'technical', not emotional: changing the dynamic, the intensity, decisions about how the beginning of each note is articulated, the shape of groups of notes – phrases. I don't understand the rationale, but that is because I don't understand the basics, whatever they are, and I don't know how to ask about what I don't know. My facility belies my ignorance. I am groping towards an aesthetic, but I don't know what words to use. How to understand what it is I am trying to understand. One

In early May, we are ready. The final run-through is deceptively smooth. A few creaking machines leave nymphs stranded in the air, or caught behind bits of scenery, but we get through it. There is little space at the back of the stage. It's a military operation for the play's cast to alternate with the musicians and singers in the *intermedi*. There is no chance that any of us will be able to see the play or the other *intermedi*.

Jacopo surreptitiously takes me behind one of the scenery flats, to see the theatre fill. The floor slopes towards the stage. My Duke and Duchess are there, among the most honoured guests. Leonora is plumper than when I last saw her. I wonder if she is pregnant again. She looks sulky, uncomfortable. Ladies sit along the side walls, in six *gradi*, carpeted tiers, and men, grouped by rank, sit on the sloping floor below them. The *galleria* above, is crammed with faces.

Between the dais and the stage there are twenty-four pyramids. On the apex of each is an urn, with white wax tapers brightening the auditorium. Scattered through the hall are ten fountains, painted to look like marble, and ornamented in gold.

Baskets with flowers and plants hang below the gallery. As the guests take their seats, live birds are released from the baskets, which then catch the wax from the chandeliers; each basket holds some three hundred torches. Jacopo points out coloured spotlights; a legacy of Vasari's invention. Torches are shone through glass jars filled with coloured water. Backstage, there are hundreds of lamps, positioned to glow between painted holes in the sky, which is attached to the walls of the painted houses on the backdrop of Pisa, where the play is set. Moveable shutters open and shut for day and night, revealing stars or sun.

Ferdinando and Cristina arrive last. She is in white, dressed

day I say: 'I want to do scales.' Roberto ignores the question.

He stands behind me sometimes, adjusting a finger, a soft, jasmine scent wafting from him. Shafts of warm air move between us. He is punctilious. He doesn't see me. He sees only the music. Straight down to work, always on the dot of the hour, ending at five to the next hour.

We work on each piece for two or three weeks, then move on to another. I never play anything through, as if 'complete'. I begin to think I am no good at it. But since I don't know what I am doing, how can I be any good? Roberto is asking me for the immediacy of performance without the conditions of performance. I plough on, hoping it will make sense if I work hard enough.

I ask questions: Is music an art? Are scales a kind of alphabet? Out of which you make phrases, sentences, structurally, like a language? Is there a grammar? Am I better off not knowing? He points to a place on the page. 'Go back to measure fifty-four.'

Annoyed, I correct him: 'Bar fifty-four. "Measure" is American.' But I obey. I play bar fifty-four. I am none the wiser. I decide to provoke him further. I blurt out that I want to be a professional musician. He says nothing. As soon as I say it, I know that it is true. I have signed up to an athletics training course, and to Roberto's aesthetic.

I give in, and enter the time of courtly love. My medieval English studies make new sense. In the conventions of courtly love, the lover is always abject. The lover is obedient to the other's lightest wish, however whimsical. The lover must be politely addressed, for the other is superior, whether the other is lord or lady. Only the courteous can love, and only love makes them

in the Florentine fashion, Jacopo whispers. They sit on gilded chairs, on a central dais, covered in dark red velvet. As soon as they are seated, sixteen candelabra burst into flame from invisible wicks – Buontalenti has invented a way to create an artificial twilight, with hundreds of candles twinkling on the jewels the ladies are wearing.

The Duke raises his right hand, to signal the beginning of the performance. The red velvet curtain drops, and there is a painted Rome. The world is a theatre and the theatre is the world. *Theatrum mundi.* The first *intermedio* begins, with one of the leading singers, Vittoria Archilei, descending elegantly on her cloud. The stage crews' sinews stand out as they struggle to keep the cloud steady. She sings a prologue of harmony and peace.

The heavenly scenes disappear, and the main set takes its place. Pisa, with real smoking chimneys, perfumed with rosemary and lavender. The Pisan cast jostle into the wings, ready for their first act, shouldered aside by sweating musicians and singers.

Jacopo prepares to become a siren, and I join my fellow musicians. Performers return to report the growing stench of perspiration in the hall, scarcely disguised by fountains full of rose petals and lavender. More than one aristocratic spectator falls asleep, not afraid to snore.

Finally, it is our turn. *Quinto intermedio.* Amphitrite, queen of the sea, sails in a mother-of-pearl shell, pulled by dolphins. It is Vittoria again, in a seamless, flesh-coloured sheath, a blue cape embroidered with snails, shells and fish, a headdress of coral branches, a mother-of-pearl crown. Pearls are draped round her neck and on her ears, strings of coral hang from her

courteous. Courtly love is despairing and tragic. The lover despairs and is in despair. From the moment I first saw you, from the moment I first beheld you, I wanted to hold you close in my arms. My love was not blind. I was merely dazzled. Through it all runs desire. The desire for performance, and the conditions of performance.

When I practise at home, the rosin on my bow leaves tiny traces on my hands. I imagine that it is the devil, his gently twitching tail flicking my thumb. Sometimes he perches on top of the bridge, facing me, watching the bow as it sleeks right-left-right.

Eventually Roberto answers my questions: 'Music has nothing to do with words.'

'Yes, it does,' I say. 'Or it should. Musicians are the most inarticulate people I have ever met.'

There is a silence. Then Roberto says in a more gentle tone: 'Would you like to sit in on some of the classes here, in the college?'

'What? Do you mean it? What will I need to pay?'

Roberto shakes his head. 'I've spoken to the Principal, and she is happy to have you. She has heard of you. You won't need to pay.'

At the end of the lesson, Roberto hands me a piece of paper. 'I've underlined the lectures you might find interesting,' he says.

arms. Tritons wear sedge garlands in their blue hair. Their tails are made of turquoise satin, edged with silver scales. Nymphs, so sheerly clothed that they appear naked, prophesy fertility for the Ducal couple. Sea gods carry instruments. I am a sea god, draped in a green, blue and brown cloak of seaweed, beneath which my bass viol is concealed.

Arion's giant ship glides onto the stage, greeted by gasps of amazement. Jacopo stands on the gilded poop with his cardboard harp, behind which his chitarrone is concealed. He sings his aria, and two of the seagods sing the echoes with him. It is exquisite. At the end of the aria, Jacopo jumps into the waves, throwing his laurel wreath across to me. I catch it and put it on my head, hoping that no-one will notice. Spray fills the air, and Jacopo emerges again, riding on the back of a dolphin covered in silver foil, which ducks and scoops its way through the waves.

The whole thing takes about seven hours. Behind the stage are scores of toilet buckets, stinking, despite the scurrying young servants who carry them out of the building at the back, empty and bring them back lined with fresh straw. Servants pass through the hall, distributing water and wine to as many of the audience as possible. Buontalenti supervises everything from an observation desk underneath the tiered seats, with a small door cut in the side, so that he can emerge backstage without being seen.

Finally, we must all become nymphs and shepherds, to prepare for the thirty voices of *O fortunato giorno*; with instruments and voices doubling, there are sixty voices. It is Malvezzi's triumph. The sound rings magnificently. Everyone in the hall is bright with attention, despite the wax dripping

❖ SECUNDA PARTE ❖

TWENTY-EIGHT

❖

ON TWO DAYS A week, I go into the college. A choral conductor, in charge of music at one of the royal chapels, Dr Marshall, lectures us. He is tall, with lightly waved, greying hair. He looks like a distinguished aristocrat. Neat, straight nose, a well-formed mouth. He wears suits with brashly coloured ties. He catches my eye more than once during the lectures. I am, by far, the oldest person in the room, apart from himself.

We learn about the history of printed music. The development of printed type, the early laborious metal setting of printed music. The history of musical notation. Cantillation signs in Hebrew texts. A huge church choir-book, round which the choristers could stand and sing. He gets us to try it. We jostle, peer and laugh. Medieval neumes, longs (a noun, not an adjective), breves and semi-breves (from the Latin *brevis, semi brevis*). No barlines. Musical notation develops.

Dr Marshall talks about the magic of the perfect circle, the single large note, the breve, which is then divided into two or three. A vertical line bisects the large C, the broken and imperfect part of the circle. The perfect O is the perfect circle, the trinity, the truly Christian pulse.

One day, after the lecture, I wander into nearby Waterstones. I go into the coffee bar area. Dr Marshall is sitting at one of the tables, reading a newspaper. He smiles at me.

on the floor, the smells and the heat. The applause at the end is deafening.

There are post-production celebrations which pass in a haze. Jacopo disappears in the middle of a large group of young men and women. They dance with rowdy energy, singing songs of unbelievable vulgarity. Another kind of harmony.

After it is all over, I sneak in for a last look. The dragon from the *terzo intermedio* lies forlornly on the floor. Two broken clouds lie near it. Next to them is a pile of ragged green velvet. I scoop up a length, fold it and tuck it under my cloak. No-one sees.

EIGHTEEN

BEFORE WE LEAVE FLORENCE, Claudio and I climb to the top of the Duomo. We count the steps, in unison, in perfect rhythm, alternating between triple and duple time. After four hundred steps, we stop counting, our feet clattering, our breath laboured. At the final ladders we slow. The space is smaller, claustrophobic. No question of turning back. By the time we reach the top, Claudio and I are exhausted.

We arrive at a narrow terrace, running round the inside of the dome. I push open a loosely fastened wooden shutter at waist height. A glimmer of sky above. We burst out laughing, light-headed with the height and effort. The wind takes our

❖ SECUNDA PARTE ❖

'Your lectures are really interesting,' I say. 'Thank you for letting me sit in.'

'Roberto brooks no refusal. It's a pleasure,' he adds. 'What's your connection with him?'

'He's my viol teacher.' Dr Marshall nods. 'It's a bit of a long story.' He follows my lead. 'Are you free for lunch after the lecture next week?'

'I'd love to.' He stands. Checks his watch. Waves. Walks away. Neat, efficient stride. Slightly nervy. Attractive.

The following week the class looks at facsimiles of fourteenth- and fifteenth-century music. No barlines. Rhythm and phrasing is contained in the way long and shorter notes create elongated shapes along the lines of the undivided stave. 'Proportional mensuration,' says Dr Marshall. The students giggle. Black and white notation signify changes in rhythm. You have to be able to tell where a black note is the shorter note in a triple rhythm, and where it is just a shorter note in a duple (or quadruple) rhythm. Along with the absence of barlines, this means you have to take in longer phrases with the eye, to see where the stresses lie, and to feel as you play and/or sing. Mostly, these are the empty, hollow notes, the Os, or the squares in ligatures (more than one note 'stuck' against another note, again, indicative of particular rhythms, very often at the end of a section or piece). It is complicated, and enormously exciting.

Dr Marshall and I have lunch in an old-fashioned Italian café round the corner from the college. Students troop in and out, buying sandwiches and snacks. I give Dr Marshall a quick potted history of my dive into early music, with only a passing reference to my academic history. Then it's his turn. A choral scholar at Kings

breath away. We stand, side by side, our arms round each other. In the distance, the sun lights up the hills. Below us, red roofs swirl and undulate in higgledy-piggledy patterns.

'I am a blackbird,' says Claudio. 'I shall fly across the hills, into the sky, into the heavenly spheres.'

'Don't you dare,' I say. 'We need you here.' I hug him. His shoulders are firm, thin, tense. 'Let's spend the rest of our lives up here.'

'Not very practical,' says Claudio. 'What would we eat?'

'The heavenly spheres are bound to have servants. They can bring us food.'

'And where would we shit?'

I point to the terrace behind us. 'Not a good idea,' says Claudio. 'We would be trapped here, with a pile of ever rising human dung.'

There is a sharp gust of wind. 'Quite right,' I say. 'It's a terrible idea. We're not birds and we're not angels. Come on. Let's go down.'

I go first. No counting this time. We rest briefly on the small standing places. Oddly, as each phase of the descent brings us onto wider platforms, I panic that the walls will close in and squeeze the breath out of me. Our echoing footsteps make the feeling worse. I almost dash down the last few steps. My legs are quivering. I sink onto the cold marble floor.

Claudio nudges me with his foot. 'Up you get, little one.'

I look up. 'Who are you calling little one?'

'I'm older than you,' says Claudio, 'and don't you forget it.'

'Not by much,' I call after him. He walks rapidly into the middle of the space. I scramble to my feet. 'Wait for me.'

'Stay there,' he calls. He is tiny, far away. This must be what

College, Cambridge, straight into an organist's job at Canterbury Cathedral, now in charge of music in one of the royal chapels. He enjoys his outings to Gwyn, and contact with what he calls the 'raw side of life'. I may call him John.

He offers, chivalrously, to pay. I allow him. I allow him to open the café door for me when we leave. The old-fashioned bell on the door tinkles.

'Would you like to learn some music theory?' he asks.

'Oh, yes. But there aren't any college classes in the basics. The kids have done all that.'

'We could do half an hour after my lecture, if you like.'

John takes me through the keys and each key signature. He shows me on the piano how basic harmony works. It is too three-dimensional for me. I have a logical, but not a mathematical brain. John suggests I should memorise and practise a small number of keys and scales, for the music I am likely to be playing. C major and its related a minor. G major, B flat. F major.

When I practise the scales, the rosin deposit on the bow builds up on the strings. As I wipe it off carefully with a piece of bright pink silk, some lands on the wood of the viol. A curved shape, like the devil's tail. I'm sure the devil approves of my scale practice. It couldn't be any more detailed.

Practising is tiring. One evening, I don't even undress before I fall into bed. In the middle of the night, my bedroom door opens, and Xan comes in, wearing a long-sleeved, white flowing nightdress and a mobcap on her head. She comes towards the bed, and I see it isn't Xan. It is a man, with a beard and moustache, a soft, green velvet helmet on his head, long curling tresses over his

heaven is like. Stone and soaring. Perhaps the Catholics are right. Perhaps they are the only ones who know what heaven is. Perhaps they are the only ones who can build heaven on earth.

Claudio stands by the vast entrance door, under Uccello's clock. White petals radiate out from the clock's centre, each holding a gold Roman numeral. A cluster of golden spikes bursts from the middle, one longer hand indicating the hour. Light from above shines on the spikes. The hours move anti-clockwise, with 1 at the bottom, the first hour at sunset, when the Ave Maria is sung. Sunset launches the new night, and following it, the new day. Until sunset again.

A voice sings. Two short phrases, long, sweeping notes wing their way up and across the space, playing round my ears. Claudio repeats the phrases. Then silence. He begins again. I join the opening note. Claudio rises a tone, and I remain where I am, our voices clashing and jangling. I bow to the harmonic inevitable and go down a semi-tone. The clash thrills; there is harmony in the cosmos.

I walk forward. Claudio puts his arm round my shoulders and he continues to lead. I echo. He repeats, decorating, with *passagi* and *groppi*. I imitate.

Claudio holds up his right hand and sings slowly and clearly.
Duo seraphim clamabant alter ad alterum
Two angels, one calling to the other.

Claudio begins again. I imitate, held by Claudio's soaring voice. My twin, the other half of my sound.

We feel the end together. Tiny, silken slivers of sound slide like salamanders into the walls. I hug him. His body quivers with the intensity of his breath. The great door behind him

shoulders, and what looks like a flesh-coloured suit of armour, with firm, domed breasts, the nipples clearly outlined.

I sleep late next morning. The light on my answer machine flickers. I listen to my messages. My parents, then another message, bright and friendly and urgent. Frank wants to know how my research is going, and can I give him a date to deliver something.

I go to the wardrobe. I pick up the Catchpole package and put it on the bed. I fold back the thinning velvet, and there, on top of the paper is more fine grey dust. Perhaps the paper is crumbling. If I don't look through it, the whole lot may crumble into an untidy heap. I will be late for my lesson if I don't hurry.

TWENTY-NINE

❖

WHEN I ARRIVE AT college, Roberto is by the window, talking to a student in jeans. The student has his back to me. I unpack my viol. Music on the stand. Test the open strings, ready for tuning. Roberto and the student turn to face me.

It isn't a student and it isn't a boy. It's Xan. Her hair is cut short, close. Tight, smooth curls embrace her head. She waves at me. 'Today,' she says, 'I am a castrato.' She bows, an extravagant, courtly bow, like a dancer, the right leg outstretched, before the left, which bends at the knee.

opens, and a figure stands, red hair haloed in bright sunlight.

Claudio and I repeat the last phrase, and Jacopo joins in on the last note. We move round each other in a huge circle, Jacopo's sweet soaring voice following our slow opening phrases with long, high melismatic elegance. We echo and chase and lead. We end on a major chord. We are three laughing angels playing truant from heaven.

Giulio is waiting outside the cathedral. He folds a cloak solicitously round Claudio. A stab of something hot and angry. Jealousy. I want to look after Claudio. I watch them walk away together, Claudio describing the view from the top of the Duomo, I relax. They are brothers. I am lucky to have had Claudio to myself for the afternoon.

NINETEEN

GIOVANNI IS BY MY side. We share warmth and bread. Olives. Wine. Goats' cheese, slimy and yellowing at the edges. We are so hungry that we ignore the signs of decay. Sharp salty *pancetta*, water and wine, and the treat of Alessandro's mother's almond biscuits, carefully packed for the journey. We are exhausted. Any extra energy holds the instruments firm, to prevent them from being jolted and broken. Wet roads run with shining streaks bubbling out from the edges of the wheels. The wind blows my hair across my face.

The atmosphere is jaunty, expectant. Xan holds a butter-yellow A4 folder.

Roberto picks up a similar book, and puts it on my music stand. Two lines of music. Words under the top line, in between the staves. A bass line with not much written on it. A series of long notes, some tied together. Plain. Bare.

'Monteverdi. Published 1609. Here it is. Listen first, Emilia,' says Roberto.

I sit back, my viol across my knees, the strings facing outwards, like a giant guitar. My left hand steadies it, my right hand supports the bow.

Roberto begins with a delicate flurry of harpsichord notes, and then Xan takes off. Clear, impeccable, neat vowels and consonants. A beautiful plangent tone. It tugs at my shoulders, at my heart. Xan and Roberto are completely out of time, and yet completely together. I can't tell what the beat or rhythm is. Sometimes the bass notes sound alone, delicate and poignant. At other times, there is a sudden chord, a cluster of notes. At yet other times, often at the beginning, announcing a new section after a short rest, there is a flurry, over which Xan's voice dances. As she ends, a chilling male voice cries out in anguish. I look round and realise Roberto is singing.

'There is a translation into English at the end. Act Two. The Messenger. Sylvia,' he says.

I find the place. Sylvia, Eurydice's close friend, and the Messenger, sings of Eurydice's tragic death. In a meadow, she was picking flowers to make a garland, when a sly snake, hidden in the grass, bit her. Her companions could do nothing. She called to Orfeo in anguish, and then expired with a sigh in my arms. Thus sings the friend,

Back through chill night winds, into bright spring morning sun. Music sings in rhythm with the rivers' wash and jolting carts.

O fortunato giorno.
Duo seraphim clamabant alter ad alterum

'What's that?' Giovanni's voice startles me. I must have been singing out loud.

I repeat the phrase. My voice is rocky, hoarse. The cart bumps and jumps. We rumble onto the bridge. On both sides, shutters are going up. Lanterns wave. The shops are closing their eyes at dusk. The lake is choppy. Steam rises, carrying the stench of foul mud. Ahead is the Castello di San Giorgio. Giovanni begins to sing Arion's lament.

Dunque fra torbido onde
Then from these murky waters
Gli ultimi mieie sospir mandero' fore
My last breath will go forth

There is no last breath here, only the breath with which we sing. My left-hand fingers imaginary divisions on an invisible violin. My right hand holds an invisible overhand bow for my violin, now an invisible underhand bow for my viol. The cart, packed with musicians, clatters off the bridge and up the steep bank to the road by the side of the castle walls. We rock gently on the hard-packed earth.

'Home,' says Giovanni.

The cart stops. The musicians pile out, too tired to do more

❖ SECUNDA PARTE ❖

the Messenger. I turn back to the music. The vocal line has sharps, flats, naturals, changing the pitch of the relevant note up or down by a semitone.

'Emilia.' Roberto is poised by the harpsichord, Xan standing beside him. I put the viol between my legs, my bow ready. Roberto takes Xan and me into the span of his attention.

I begin confidently enough. A long D. Followed by a longer D, tied across bar after bar. I try to follow Xan's voice, but the rhythm seems to be too free, too jagged. Roberto calls out bar numbers. Thirty bars are a lifetime.

'Good,' says Roberto. He stands up. 'Perhaps the two of you can get together. We are giving a concert performance of *Orfeo* as this year's college production. It will celebrate the launch of my new edition.'

On her way out Xan says: 'I'll come over tomorrow night.'

'Roberto,' I say. 'I have a question. I'm playing the same notes as the keyboard.' Roberto plays a note.

'The harpsichord plucks the note.' He plays again, and a tiny stick jumps up. 'A quill plucks the string. But the sound dies. Your bass sustains the note, continues it, if you like. *Basso Continuo*. That's what you are playing.'

'So what have you been playing?'

His fingers possess the keyboard, hurrying from top to bottom and back to the middle. 'In the original, there are just notes in the bass. With numbers. It's called "figured bass".'

'You're improvising, then.'

'It is a kind of improvisation, yes.'

He picks up the music folder from the keyboard stand and shows it to me. It's in neat handwriting, not printed.

than wave to each other. Giovanni and I walk. Ahead of us, in my street, doors and windows are open. People lean out, welcoming us back, waving blankets, lengths of coloured material.

Two figures in Pierrot costumes run towards me and fling their arms around me. Menahem and Esther. My mother and father wait in the doorway. I unload everything, hug and kiss them, smelling my own dirt and sweat. Everyone is laughing. We go inside, and my mother beckons Giovanni. 'Come in, come in. Come and eat with us.'

He shakes his head. 'No, no. We are all tired.' He looks at me. 'Tomorrow afternoon. Santa Barbara.' We hug. This is my true brother. I have tears in my eyes. My mother wipes them away. 'Come. You must be hungry.' Smells of chicken, rice and pungent tomato mix with sweet apple and almonds. My stomach shouts and everyone laughs. Inside, Zio Leone is at the table, his red woollen blanket wrapped round his shoulders.

I am so happy to be home. I have never eaten food so fresh. So delicious. Everyone watches. I talk myself to a whisper in response to the tumbling questions. I burp loudly and everyone applauds. I yawn.

'Enough for today,' says my mother.

I kiss everyone. My father's face is wet. Leone's face feels like paper. My mother shoos my brother and sister out of the bedroom and I am alone. My spirits sink with my body. I am happy to be home. But I want to be back in the wide open spaces of Florence, walking in dangerous, dark night-time alleys. I want to soar up into the Duomo and touch Vasari's angels. I want to fly up and move the pointed golden dagger

He points to numbers under the bass line. The music is thick with notes.

'I don't understand. All the music you're playing is written out.'

'I'm playing what is called a realisation of the harmony implied by the figures under the bass notes. Do you understand that?'

'Sort of. So you improvise, and then write it down, so that you know what to play?'

'Not exactly.' There is a slight pause. 'The figures are authentic. The realisation is authentic.'

'I don't understand.'

'The realisation is by Monteverdi.'

There is a small silence. 'But the music you gave me just has two lines.'

'Yes.' Another small silence. 'So where does your – the extra music by Monteverdi – where does that come from?'

'That, Emilia, is my discovery.'

Pennies drop fast. 'Your new edition – '

'Exactly. My new edition of *Orfeo* is an authentic early seventeenth-century realisation. It is the only one of its kind. It must be by Monteverdi. You can see how important it is.'

'You will have to have it authenticated.'

'Of course. Please – it is a secret. You are the first person I have told.'

'I won't say anything – it sounds really exciting.'

'It is. Believe me.'

hands of Uccello's clock. Jacopo was right. I am provincial. He spotted my dissembling, my pretence that I was a sophisticated musician, a cosmopolitan artist. I feel guilty that I tried to con them. I feel guilty that I cannot just be happy to be home, here in Mantova. This is where I was born.

The next day there is a curtain of mist over everything. My bedroom window trickles with water. Figures ghost the streets. The mules' hooves are softened on the cobbles. Menahem and Esther are already out.

My mother drops a kiss on the top of my head. 'Good to have you home,' she says. 'I have something to tell you. Leone is getting weaker,' she says. 'I want him to come and stay here, with us. I can look after him properly. Will you help me persuade him?'

My heart jumps. I left here a boy. Eager. Talented. Ignorant. I have come back with something of the world. I don't need to yearn for Florence. I have brought Florence back home with me. *O fortunato giorno.* I know what my mother is asking. I nod. 'Of course,' I say. 'He can have my room.' My mother kisses and hugs me, and goes to tell Zio Leone.

I tread the familiar streets to Santa Barbara for rehearsal. The church is chill. The sacristy soon warms up with the heat of our bodies. Giovanni hands us copies of his new *balleti a cinque voci*. Songs and dances. Voices and instruments alternate. My bass takes a while to settle in the damp. The strings are unstable, temperamentally sharpening at the top and flattening at the bottom. I retune constantly, fast, accurate. Finally, with the pleasure of harmony, they settle. The air inside the instrument is warmed, just as our lungs and voices have warmed. Each string finds its sound place.

❖ SECUNDA PARTE ❖

THIRTY

❖

I'VE JUST GOT HOME, when the phone rings. It's Frank.

'Emilia. How are you?'

'Fine. Everything is going really well.'

'I have some news. Not very good, I'm afraid. We have just heard that our research funding has been slashed next year.'

I'm puzzled. 'How does that affect me – us?'

'Well.' Frank pauses. 'It will have a knock-on effect on current projects. Damage limitation, I think it's called. Can you finish this summer?'

'I – I don't know.'

'There is another option. If you don't publish.' A pause. 'Voluntary redundancy. You can finish your research at your leisure. We might be able to take you back part-time later.'

'Might?' I've known Frank a long time. I don't want him treating me to corporate-speak.

'I'm sorry. Really. It's not up to me. The Dean is breathing down my neck. The Vice-Chancellor is breathing down his neck. The government – '

'I get the point.' I am thinking on my feet. 'Look. I have an idea. One of my research contacts is an Italian colleague from America, on a guest Professorship for a year. He's doing a concert performance of an early opera by Monteverdi. Not quite the Jacobean masque, but he is planning a performance to launch his new edition of

◈ PRIMA PARTE ◈

We play through the *balletti*. Giovanni nods, scribbles on his copy. We know his style, his aesthetic. First voices sing, then instruments play. We repeat each section, and on the repeat, I hear something as familiar to me as my own heartbeat. A soaring, sizzling rippling decoration and divisions. I smile. I don't need to look round. At the end, everyone bursts into spontaneous applause.

A familiar thin figure in black comes towards us. Giovanni puts his arm round Claudio's shoulders and draws him into our circle.

'This, my friends,' he says, 'is the new addition to our forces. Claudio Monteverdi. From Cremona, via Florence. And with him, his brother, Giulio Cesare.'

Claudio embraces me. I cannot speak for delight. 'To finish for today,' says Giovanni, 'we shall perform *Vien Himeneo, deh vieni*. Five voices, Claudio. Written a few years ago in tribute to Duke Vincenzo, on his second marriage. Today we shall celebrate the marriage between Mantova and Florence, where we first met.'

Claudio and Giulio join us, both soaring over the top with divisions. We play it twice, and the second time my bass runs away with its own divisions. High and low join as one.

By the time we leave, the day's mist is mingling with dusk. Everyone disperses. Giovanni, Claudio, Giulio and I wind our way out into the Piazza di San Pietro, across the cobbles, avoiding the horse dung left by the weekly visit of wild mountain horses. Pairs of old women, in their widow black, shovel the steaming piles into small carts, pulled by mules, to fertilise their gardens. They each have a section marked out, and woe betide anyone who invades someone else's territory.

the opera. Perhaps there could be another performance at Lavenham?'

'A piece of practice-based research. Excellent. A concert performance means no set and no costumes, doesn't it?'

'Yes. No further expense. Perhaps some slides from documentary records.'

'Great. How soon can you write the proposal for the committee?'

'Give me a couple of weeks.'

'Thanks, Emilia.'

The phone is dark with sweat from my hand. Damn. I lie down. A faint, musky, almost pleasant smell comes from the package. I move it from my bed to the desk. I sleep for a while. I wake, exhausted. In my doze I have been running in and out of the kitchen, supplying tea and coffee to a group of angels with musical instruments: viols, harps and lutes. The kitchen is neat and tidy. Must have been female angels.

I go on the internet. Wikipedia tells me the one thing I already know: the legend of Orpheus and Eurydice. The latter dies, the desolate former goes down to Hades to bring her back, is successful, on condition that he doesn't look back at her until he is back in the earthly world. But Orpheus can't resist looking back, and Eurydice subsides into Hades. Gone forever. *L'Orfeo, favola in musica*, was written by Claudio Monteverdi, and first performed in 1607, in Mantua, in northern Italy. The opera was published in 1609.

The package is next to my computer on my desk. The top page is dusty. I brush it and feel a pin-prick on the side of my right hand. I blink. Something small and black slides round the side of the page. A fly. A small spider.

PRIMA PARTE

Through the small door at the back of the town cathedral. We are in a higgledy-piggledy group of rooms which Giovanni shares with the higher clergy. Claudio and Giulio are staying here. The housekeeper serves us with bean soup, rice and wine.

'You kept your secrets very well,' I say, a little accusingly to the other three. Giovanni throws out his hands. 'I couldn't tell you before it was properly settled,' he says. 'I am Duke Vincenzo's pimp, after all. That's what I was doing in Florence, in between rehearsals and performances. Pimping. Do you want the story?'

'Of course,' I say.

'You're in charge of the wine, then. Well. Vincenzo wants Marenzio. Vincenzo wants Palestrina. Palestrina hates Marenzio, so we can't have both here in Mantova. Besides, as I keep telling Vincenzo, Palestrina is the past, and we must look to the future, to *le nuove musicche*, as Caccini might say. Besides which, I know that if Palestrina comes, he will want de Wert's job. And I'm not having that, am I? Because I want de Wert's job when he dies. I love him, but I want his job.'

'Nothing wrong with that,' says Claudio, his mouth full.

'But I don't tell Vincenzo that. So, says Vincenzo, forget about Palestrina, and go for Marenzio. But Marenzio doesn't want to come to the cold north. He is happier in Rome. He has a better life in Rome. So he asks for impossible money. Vincenzo wants everything on the cheap. So Marenzio is out.'

I refill our glasses. 'Meanwhile, I have been talking to Vincenzo about the Monteverdi brothers.'

'And both of us together are cheaper than either Marenzio or Palestrina,' says Claudio.

'So,' continues Giovanni, 'we have the best result. I love

SECUNDA PARTE

The devil. There is a tiny spot of blood on my hand. I lick it away.

The next page has music on it. Sixteen staves, made up of tiny, uneven lines, placed side by side, in slightly broken lines. At the top it says *Atto Quinto*. I remember Dr Marshall's description of tiny, moveable pieces of metal type, out of which the horizontal lines were constructed. The notes, black and open, are all diamond-shaped. Semibreves, minims and crotchets. The second eight staves end with a double bar at the end of each line. Barlines. No words.

The next sheet is handwritten: Italian and English. It starts with a song sung by Orfeo. There are choruses. I can make out the odd word here and there – the name Bacchus, the word heaven – the rest is hard to read. A date at the bottom of the page; 160 – something. Not clear.

There is something else hastily scrawled at the bottom of the page. My front doorbell rings. I bundle the package back into the wardrobe.

Xan is enormously patient. We go over her conversational phrases, until I can remember and feel where I need to punctuate her, adding passion and stress with my notes. Afterwards, we go out to the pizza restaurant at the end of my road.

Over pasta, salad and cheap red wine, I ask Xan when she cut her hair? 'Oh,' she says airily, 'I got tired of brushing it every day. It was the right moment.'

'What do you mean, the right moment?'

'I finished with Terry.'

'What about Roberto?' I want to ask: how long have you known him? Are you sleeping with him?

Marenzio, but Claudio is the real future. You don't mind my saying that?'

Claudio smiles. 'You are only telling the truth,' he says.

'My brother is known for his modesty,' says Giulio.

'Never too modest,' says Claudio. 'I know what I want.'

'Good. You can give Salamone some new ideas.'

Claudio nods towards me. 'I think the exchange of ideas will be mutual,' he says. I blush. Claudio yawns. Giovanni jumps up. 'You must be tired.' He takes the brothers into another room. When he returns, we sit in silence, then: 'I need somewhere to stay,' I say finally. 'Zio Leone is ill. My mother wants to look after him. Can I stay here?'

'A Jew, living in the Palazzo Ducale?'

I shrug. 'I spend most of my time here already,' I say. 'And my brother, Menahem – Emmanuele – works here, with the financial administration. Why should anyone mind?'

'Stay. There is room here. If anyone asks, you have to work into the night.'

'Thank you, slave driver.'

The following morning, with a bundle of clothes and my bass viol, I go to Giovanni's door, behind the cathedral. No guards here. A dull wooden door with a large brass handle. Inside, someone sits at the table. It is Emilia. She stands when I come in. She comes close. I smell cloves. I smell cinnamon. 'You have put on weight,' I say. She laughs. 'Silly,' she says. 'Would you like a boy or a girl?'

'What?'

'I don't mind which it is,' she says. 'It won't be long now. Come and see me when you can.'

'He's brilliant, isn't he?' The bill arrives. 'Let's go back and give Sylvia another go.'

As I pay the bill, Xan says: 'There is something.'

'What?'

'I've got to move out. My house is being underpinned. It's just a few weeks.' She pauses.

'You can stay with me if you like,' I say. 'Makes it easier to rehearse.'

'Really? Have you got room?'

'Well, you'd have to sleep on the couch.'

'Just a couple of nights a week. I'm dividing myself between friends.'

'No problem. I can give you a key. Come and go as you want. Do you want to stay tonight?'

I make up a bed for Xan on the couch. She sings as she gets ready for bed, and her voice follows me to sleep. I wake, bewildered. Xan and Roberto, their arms intertwined are leaving the room. I jump out of bed, looking for my clothes, desperate to follow them. My clothes are on the chair by the window. I go to pick them up, and they fold in upon each other. Shirt into skirt into sweater into the cushion on the chair.

A jumble of colour rises to the ceiling, swirling and shiny, like rainbow colours in a pool of spilled oil. I raise my arms, to chase my clothes, pin them down, put them on. I rise into the air. Success. The clothes tease me, until I am up against the painted ceiling, my arms and legs flailing, hitting plaster, which flakes off and drops past me onto the floor.

I look down. My room is painted, walls and ceiling, a deep, azure blue. Signs of the zodiac swirl around. I am swimming in the sky. Diana waves to me from her chariot,

TWENTY

LIFE IN MANTOVA RESUMES, now infinitely enhanced by the presence of the Monteverdi brothers. Giulio is six years younger than Claudio. He is gentle and kind, always putting his brother's welfare first. He and my mother become firm friends.

Giulio confides that Claudio is more secure here in his composing than he has ever been. He writes new, exciting madrigals. *Lumi, miei cari lumi* – light of my dearest eyes. Five voices, beginning with a single voice, then building as the others arrive, passing each other, and coming to rest together, with lightning contrasts between fast and slow. Each time we sing, I see Emilia's eyes in the candlelight.

I decide to write my own version for her: simpler and plainer than Claudio's, and with one important difference. Mine has a basso continuo with the five voices. The music from Florence still comes easily to mind, with Jacopo's thrilling melodies and improvisations, over a sound and secure bass line which continues reliably all the way. An equal, and yet underpinning voice. Claudio is delighted at my work, always encouraging, never in competition, even as we continue to set the same texts. His version of *Lumi* appears in his third book of madrigals, mine in my second book, in 1602.

Giovanni observes that I have a new confidence since Florence. He is right. I know that my place in the world is in my control. Living with, and surrounded by, music makes the

❖ SECUNDA PARTE ❖

drawn by two dogs. I float round a lion, crouching over a crab. A fat angel points at me and laughs. A dark-skinned woman in a turban pushes me away.

A serpent with a bird on its back twines round me, like a ribbon. The bird flies, the tips of its wings brushing my hands and face. The serpent uncoils, its skin smooth and warm. Xan leans against the door. Casual. Suntanned. Smooth and cool. Her hair is wound round her head into a dark crown. Behind her stands Roberto, his mouth nuzzling her neck. She hunches her shoulders up and laughs. He looks up at me, then at Xan, and puts his arm round her waist. She leans her head on his shoulder and they walk away from me, out of the room.

I fall back onto the bed. I am drenched in sweat. I strip and put on my dressing gown. Xan is already in the kitchen, pouring hot water into the cafetière. 'Did you sleep well?' I ask her.

'Like a log. Last night was good,' she says. 'You are a natural.' She is already dressed. She leaves her coffee half-drunk. She mustn't be late. She has a part-time job in a gastro-pub. Before she goes, I take a spare key out of the kitchen drawer and give it to her. Afterwards I see she has forgotten her stripey bag.

days flow. Rehearsals, participation in Santa Barbara, writing my own music, and copying Claudio's music as fast as he writes it. Giulio and I are the only two Claudio will trust. We love his aesthetic and are loyal to it.

I still have time for my *universita* responsibilities. I compose music for psalms and other Hebrew texts. We sing in Daniele Norsa's synagogue, at the top of his house. Some days I can't tell the difference between the synagogue and Santa Barbara. Latin in one, Hebrew in the other, and in between, my Italian *canzone* and *canzonette*. It's all one. It's all music. I am happy.

Until one day, when my father, Azariah, asks me to come to a meeting at home. The *masari*, the leaders of the *universita*, will be there. When I ask what it is about, he shakes his head and insists gently: 'You must come.'

It is a sombre group of men. Rabbi David Provenzal sits at the head of the table. Zio Leone sits in his usual chair by the fire, wrapped in his red and yellow woollen cloak.

The rabbi waits for our full attention. 'Salamone is a clever and talented young man. I am sorry he has not seen fit to continue with his Hebrew studies. I am sorry he spends so much time singing in Latin. I am sorry that he lives among the gentiles. I am sorry that he helps to celebrate a non-religion.'

I look round. My father is looking at the floor.

'What is this?' I ask. I am annoyed. 'Why have you called me here? Am I on trial?'

'No,' says the Rabbi. 'You are not on trial.'

'Good,' I say. 'Please remember that I am no different from our other musicians and performers. We provide plays, entertainments, dances for the Duke. We provide performers and musicians, dancing masters.' Provenzal tries to silence

❖ SECUNDA PARTE ❖

THIRTY-ONE

❖

ACT FIVE. *ATTO QUINTO.* Roberto will sing the role of Orfeo. There is an instrumental opening. Out of the final note, Roberto's pure light voice sings sadness, with rising urgency. *Dolore.* I dip in and out of the bass line, as I feel his summons from voice and keyboard. *Lagrimero.* I notice there is an English translation at the bottom of the page. I don't need to understand the words. I can feel the meaning.

Roberto decorates the final note of each phrase. He and I come to rest again and again, before taking flight once more. A low, melancholy *Sinfonia* follows. We have not played this before. Roberto conducts us from the keyboard, one finger across his lips, to indicate *piano*. The door bursts open. A young man with peroxide golden hair, roots proudly showing, in jeans and check T-shirt, begins singing, as if on cue. He looks very like the young man who sang in my first Wigmore Hall concert.

Roberto nods to me, and I find my way into the music and join them, my bass line angry, strong. Roberto leaves the keyboard, to sing a duet with the boy. I am alone on the bass line, a long, slow G while they dart above. I falter a couple of times, and Roberto runs and points at my music, not dropping a note himself.

'Excellent,' says Roberto. 'Thank you. Apollo. Thank you, everyone. We shall have the chorus with us next time, and the other soloists.'

This is not music I can practise alone. I need Roberto,

me. I ignore him. 'We perform at carnival. We invite the Duke and his guests to visit our synagogues. What is the problem?'

'One day you'll displease the Duke and the whole community will be punished. Some monk will accuse the Jews of polluting the Catholic church; of killing Catholic babies.'

'If I hear about any unpleasant monks, I will come straight home.'

My father is stern. 'This is not a joke, Salamone.'

'Of course not. Look. In times of real persecution, we stand together. Think of it another way. Perhaps the palace is the best place for me to be. We hear everything first. I can forewarn the community if there is any danger.'

'You sing in church. In Latin.'

'I am a professional musician. I don't mind what language I use. I set Italian texts by Guarini and Tasso. Their poems are about desperate, courtly, unrequited love. The lover dies of the agony of unrequited love. I do not believe those texts any more than I believe the Latin texts about fathers and sons and holy ghosts.'

'Does that mean that you don't believe in our religion either?'

'Oh, now I understand.'

My father intervenes. 'Whatever Salamone thinks and believes, he is honest. He is my son. I trust him.' Zio Leone speaks for the first time: 'Rabbi, you have never said anything to me about my role in the *Academia degli Invaghiti*. I wrote *intermedi* for the Duke's first and second marriages, in 1581 and 1584. You know that.'

'And I played for the second marriage,' I add. 'Isaac Massarano wrote dances. In between banquets and fireworks, Vincenzo

his flying fingers. When we play together, it's his hands which keep me tethered to the right place. His hands play over the keyboard, over my viol and over me. There is rhythm and no rhythm. It is sung, it is spoken. It may be religion. It may be sex. Now you see it, now you don't.

I glance at the music, as I prepare supper. Some words stand out in the music: *immortal vita*; *cielo*; *virtu*, and in that last elaborate duet, *saliam cantand'al Cielo*. I read the translation, running across the bottom of the pages.

Orfeo has returned to the fields of Thrace, where he lost Eurydice. He is desperate with sorrow, despair, and anger. Neither heaven nor earth have reunited him with his love. Echo laments with him. Finally, Orfeo praises Eurydice's goodness and beauty, while all other women are fickle and wicked. He will never love again.

Apollo appears. He has come to save Orfeo, to remind him that all earthly experience is transient. Orfeo bows to his will, and Apollo invites him to rise to heaven, where eternal life awaits him. A chorus reinforces Orfeo's passage to heaven, and it all ends in a celebratory dance. A *moresco*. Happy ever after.

It's a hasty ending. Orfeo's anguish is overwhelmed by Apollo's persuasive voice. The triumphant musical finale is absolute. Except, of course, for Eurydice, who is left to moulder in the underworld, forgotten by everyone.

As I eat, I wonder which is the more important: the words or the music? I must ask the devil, next time I see him. I realise I have spoken out loud. It makes me laugh. I mean, of course, that I must ask Roberto. I have been spending too much time on my own. Too much time with music.

I look again at the translation. Something nags at me.

chose Jews to accompany his succession to the Dukedom in 1587. What would have happened if we had refused?'

The Rabbi looks a little uncomfortable. 'The *Accademia* refused to accept Leone as a member.'

'Of course. Only the nobility are members of the *Accademia*. A Jew cannot be a member of the nobility. Ergo. They are not stupid. As the *Accademia*'s scribe, I am as good as any other member. There are ways round everything. And,' adds Leone, 'Duke Vincenzo came to Isaac Massarano's birthday party.'

The Rabbi sniffs. 'He must have some ulterior motive.'

'Yes,' says my father sharply. 'Isaac is his dancing teacher. Isaac plays the harp and sings like an angel. That is the Duke's ulterior motive. He cannot understand how it is that a Jew, who is not a castrato, can sing so high and pure. Rabbi, when any Jew finds favour in the Duke's eyes, the whole community benefits.'

'Oh, yes. The Duke has a great deal of respect for us. So much respect that we must advertise our honourable Jew-ness with a yellow badge of dishonour.'

'Good Lord,' says Father. 'I quite overlooked your yellow badge, Rabbi. Now, where are you hiding it?'

The Rabbi opens his cloak. Just inside is a small piece of yellow cloth. We laugh and similarly open our cloaks and jackets.

'Very visible,' says Father.

'The Duke has given me a special dispensation, so that I do not need to display the badge in public,' retorts the Rabbi.

'Then,' I say, 'you are the same as I am. I have a special dispensation to move freely about the Palazzo Ducale without wearing my badge. No-one has ever challenged me.'

❖ SECUNDA PARTE ❖

I bring the Catchpole package into the kitchen. I am quick, meticulous. On the top sheet is some familiar grey dust and something I haven't noticed before: there is a Star of David at the top of the page, followed by parallel Italian and English texts, in hasty, untidy handwriting.

I put the music from which I have been playing next to the Catchpole page, and compare the Italian in the two. The texts begin with the same two lines and then diverge:

Quinci non fia giamai che per vil femina
Amor con aureo strale il cor trafiggami.

The god of love should never again send his dart with the love of a vile woman into my heart,

Where Apollo and Orfeo sang about heaven this afternoon, the Catchpole text announces the arrival of a horde of drunken women: the Bacchantes. They sing in ones and twos, and then in chorus, of Bacchus's glory, and of a divine fury which they will mete out to Orfeo, in punishment for his contempt for women. My heart speeds. On the next page there is music.

A *ritornello*, identical to the one we have been playing, is followed by a rapid, triple time chorus, then brief solos, then the *ritornello* again. It ends with the same *moresco*, the wild Moorish dance which we played this afternoon. At the bottom of the last page is a word, in different handwriting. It looks like a name: 'Torin'. There are a handful of pages left. No more music. A series of dates and what could be diary or journal entries. They are in Italian. The same hurried handwriting. No translation.

I am freezing cold. I must show this to Roberto, I think.

My father joins me. 'We are fortunate. We are not in Florence. We are not in Venice. We do not live in a ghetto.'

'It's only a matter of time,' says the Rabbi.

'Then we should enjoy our time while we can,' says my father firmly.

As if on cue, Mother brings wine and cakes. Rabbi Provenzal says a blessing and we eat and drink. The atmosphere relaxes. 'Forgive me, everyone. I am just doing my duty. There have been complaints from some people.' He turns to me: 'Remember, Salamone, there is only one God.'

I nod, and am relieved that he has not asked me to commit myself to belief in this one God. On my way back to the palazzo, I remember that Zio Leone had no appetite, and could only hold his glass with my mother's help. I think about my role at Santa Barbara. I am at ease with the rituals. I am at home with the music. I don't need to believe anything to play and sing. This is my job. It takes no belief, except in the music.

That evening, I ask Giovanni whether the Duke knows I am a permanent member of the church's *cappella*.

'Of course. Each year, at carnival, I ask his permission for you to continue with us. Each year, he agrees.'

'I didn't know that.'

'You didn't need to know it,' he replies. 'We need you, Salamone. Unlike Claudio, you are a stable genius. You and he make a good team. Vincenzo is a realist. He values his Jewish community. When it suits him, he ignores papal edicts. You are as safe here as anywhere. And it is in my interest to have the best people round me. De Wert is ill again.'

I have never had much contact with de Wert, a shadowy figure, an elder in my musical world, just as Zio Leone is an

❖ SECUNDA PARTE ❖

Then – no. I can't show it to Roberto until I know what I have found. I go onto the Internet. I trawl from site to site. In my university work, I warn students against over-reliance on the internet. Now I read again about Monteverdi, Mantua, the Gonzaga court, early opera.

Orfeo was first performed in 1607. The libretto was printed for the audience to follow in 1609. So Act Five from that has survived. There was another edition in 1615. Only a handful of these editions survive. On one of the sites there is a reference to a fire in a library in Turin, in 1904, where a lot of manuscripts from the Mantuan archive were stored. Turin. 'Torin.'

For the first time for months, I long for days of careful reading, notes, organising and categorising information. I don't know what to think. The phone rings. It's Frank again. 'Any more news?' he asks. Damn. 'Hang on, I say, I must turn off the bath.' I put my hand over the phone, to buy a little time.

'Yes,' I say. 'Has Professor Castelli rung you?'

'No. We need to get some publicity together. Dates. Can you get something from your Professor? This is an academic event, so we may need a lecture – something.' I can hear impatience at the back of Frank's voice.

'Well. There is a new discovery. There is – an original manuscript, newly discovered. Part of the original opera.' At least that is true. 'I can't say any more at the moment.'

'Can you give me a provisional title?'

'How about *Monteverdi's Orfeo: Back From the Underworld*. Oh. My doorbell's just gone. I must go.'

I check the last page again. It could be 'Torino'. That would explain the ragged dark crumbling edges of some of the pages. Fire. The grey dust could be ash. Does ash

elder in the Jewish and dramatic world. Like Zio Leone, he is often ill, as he ages. He retires in 1592, and from that year, Giovanni's life changes. He is appointed *maestro di canto*, *maestro di contrappunto*, teaches musical theory. He deserves the responsibility of *maestro di cappella* at Santa Barbara. He is firm and a stickler for musical precision, without de Wert's temperament and unreliability.

That year, a light goes out of my life, when Zio Leone dies. The community is in shock. There are few people so widely creative, so widely loved, so justifiably arrogant. When the period of mourning is over, my mother asks me if I would like to come home. There is room. Menahem and Esther are married, with their own homes. I am afraid she might mind when I refuse gently, saying that I need to stay near Giovanni. Work is going well, and, considering that I am only occasionally paid, I have somewhere warm to sleep, and good food. My mother nods. She understands.

What I don't say is that I can't leave Emilia and the children. Each day after my return from Florence, she waited for me. The first day, she took me into a small, walled garden. Small orange trees shelter a seat. A marble cupid spouts clean water into a fountain.

One of Leonora's secret gardens, which she never visits, has become our haven of peace. It leads to three plain white rooms. The largest room is brightened by a vivid Turkish carpet. A small iron brazier keeps the chill out. In the corner is a large, soft couch, tousled with embroidered cushions.

As Leonora's closest maidservant, Emilia has a servant of her own, from the Mantovano. Maria is gentle, kind, and has a harelip. She will never marry, and she has no dowry to admit

stay around for nearly five hundred years? I go back to the top. A handful of blank sheets. No drawing. No sneaky devilish tail disappearing. No more grey dust.

THIRTY-TWO

❖

I LEAVE THE COLLEGE after the next rehearsal, I hear rapid footsteps behind me.

'Glad I caught you.' John is slightly out of breath. 'How is *Orfeo* going?'

'Very well. I think.' We stand a little awkwardly.

'Look,' he says. 'Are you busy this evening?'

'No. No, actually I'm not.'

'Good. Come to supper.' He takes out a card. 'About eight.'

I dress carefully. I find a green silk shirt I haven't worn for ages. I stare at the package for a long time, before putting it carefully into Xan's stripey bag. She won't mind me borrowing it.

her to a convent. She looks after our children. They are light skinned, a boy and a girl. We have invented names for them. Listizia and Perlo. We don't want their names to announce where they 'belong'.

After Perlo's birth, Emilia nearly died. Since her recovery, we have had no more children. Perhaps her illness had something to do with it, but we are happy enough with our two. We are spared the anguish and grief of our babies dying before they are born, or when they are very small. Gradually, the other rooms round the garden have filled with children, born to the household's other servants. It is a wonderful place. I brought Menahem here once, and swore him to secrecy. One day I will tell my parents.

Emilia was still delirious with fever when I accompanied the Duke to one of his battles. Countering the threat of Turkish invasion, a Duke must recuperate after a day of fighting. What better than entertainment provided by musicians, who form part of the ducal retinue? There was little to recommend the experience, except that we were always at the rear of the ragged army, and the first to escape or retreat.

Vincenzo ordered Claudio to come as well, since he had been appointed a temporary *maestro di cappella*. We had to raise money ourselves to pay the other musicians, who included a little Carmelite priest. Girolamo Bacchini, a castrato, couldn't hold a candle to Jacopo, but he has proved to be a lovable, mischievous musician, singer and friend.

The Duke marches into our tent one freezing day. Claudio is shivering with a terrible cold. No matter. A fanfare for the sackbuts, says Vincenzo. The soldiers are cold and wet. They need to have their spirits raised. By tomorrow.

❖ SECUNDA PARTE ❖

THIRTY-THREE

❖

JOHN MARSHALL LIVES IN a huge house at the back of Notting Hill. There is one bell. He comes to the door wearing a striped apron, his shirt sleeves rolled up. He kisses me on the cheek, as if I am an old friend, and leads me to the back of the house. A huge open kitchen has a conservatory roof at the back. Gentle plainchant fills the room. The table is laid for two. He takes a bottle of white wine from the fridge, opens it, and pours two glasses. He indicates the bag. 'Are you going somewhere after dinner?'

'Just home. Actually, I've brought something with me. I'd like you to look at it. Sorry. It's work, I suppose.'

'Shall we have dinner first?'

I nod. I'm already a little light-headed.

John brings an earthenware dish from the oven; a flat dish of vegetables: bright yellow carrots, strong green spinach leaves and paler green peas. He whips off his apron and ladles a fragrant stew onto our plates. 'Lamb. Help yourself to vegetables.'

As we eat, he asks me more questions. Am I married? He's a good listener. Anyone important now?

I shrug. 'No-one. I'm a workaholic. A celibate workaholic.'

'So am I.' We drink to that. And then we drink some more.

Dessert is a very alcoholic lemony, fluffed up something. To follow the wine, we get through some

Claudio has to be held back from attacking the Duke, and, since he is in no condition to do so, I produce a short, bright fanfare. Claudio sneezes his way across the mud to deliver it. Vincenzo is delighted with his apparently lightning recovery.

When I arrive back in Mantova, my hair matted and tangled, my skin weathered and wind-swept, everyone wants to know what other countries are like. How do the languages sound? What are Southern Hungary, Innsbruck, Prague, Vienna like? I shrug.

TWENTY-ONE

CLAUDIO HAS PERMISSION TO marry Claudia Cattaneo. He and Giulio leave the palace, to live with the Cattaneo family, also musicians. The Duke announces that he is reducing Claudio's salary, on the grounds that his father-in-law should support him. We all agree that the Duke is a mean bastard.

Claudio and Claudia marry in 1599. The choice of year is ominous. The end of another century. *Mutazione di secolo*. The sky floods the Po valley. Walking anywhere is like wading through swampy marshland. We are never warm. We are never dry. Stagnant waste haunts the winter, dragging into summer humidity. Malaria and swamp fever are rampant.

cherry brandy. 'What about you?' I look round the impeccable room. 'Are you married?

'I was. Divorced. No children. I'm a loner. Much happier that way. Marriage is not my thing. Do you want to see the rest of the house?'

I am a little unsteady going up the stairs. The whole of the first floor is one vast bedroom suite. Breathtaking. Kitsch. A huge, canopied double bed with velvet drapes. A soft white carpet. John puts an arm round my shoulders. I am a student being seduced by an older, wiser, infinitely attractive teacher. Celibates? Do me a favour.

In bed, with the lights off, I reclaim intimacy. John is agile, adept with his fingers and every part of his body. The warmth and intensity is scarcely interrupted as he reaches for something on the bedside cabinet. Such wordless tact gives me licence to enjoy a wonderful end to a luxurious evening. I sleep soundly and dreamlessly.

When I wake next morning, John is dressed. On a table is a tray with coffee, croissants and orange juice. 'Sorry we didn't get round to coffee last night,' he says. I dress quickly, and we have breakfast like an old married couple.

John pours the last vestiges of coffee. 'You said last night you wanted to show me something?'

We laugh at the unintended double entendre. 'Yes. I nearly forgot. You distracted me.'

'I'll make some more coffee.'

In the kitchen I take the package out of Xan's bag. There is more fine grey dust on the top sheet. John goes to a cupboard and takes out a pair of fine white gloves. He puts them on and takes over. Fast. Neat. He nods. He

TWENTY-TWO

THE FOLLOWING YEAR JACOPO writes to me from Florence. He has written a new dramatic piece, mixing madrigal and *intermedii*. *Stile rappresentativo*. 'Don't you remember, my friend? It is just more of everything we did together when you came to Florence. How I miss you.' The piece is performed at the Pitti Palace, in October 1600.

Vincenzo summons us to a meeting in the Rotonda, the small round medieval church by the main market square. Inside, palace guards line the bare walls, shoulder to shoulder. Vincenzo paces backwards and forwards. He begins by making a speech about the hardships this year. Bad floods have seriously affected the harvest.

Then he turns on us. Giovanni, Claudio, Giulio and I are accused of laziness, of not caring about Mantova's reputation, of letting him down. Perhaps the Rabbi was right. I may never get out of here alive.

'How will you make amends?' shouts the Duke, staring at Giovanni. 'Sir.' Giovanni's voice is low and calm, but I can see his hands shaking. 'We are always anxious to please you. Our Claudio Monteverdi is Italy's leading composer. He is revolutionising our music. He is the envy of Ferrara, Venice and Florence. His madrigals are mature and tasty fruit. The masses he writes for us are exquisite. Mantova – and you – can take all the credit.'

'Oh? And where is his – whatever this new music is called?

whistles. He holds up the first sheet with music on it against the light.

'Well?' I ask.

'Where did you get this?'

'Do you know what it is?'

John leans back in his chair. 'It looks as if it is Act Five, the last Act of Monteverdi's *Orfeo*. I don't recognise the music. It looks like the same libretto – at least the first couple of lines. Where did it come from?'

'I can't tell you.'

John nods. 'Do you know why this is – could be – so important?' I shake my head. 'Well. The first version of the last Act of *Orfeo* had the Bacchantes tearing Orfeo limb from limb – if you'll pardon the expression. The Gonzaga Duke didn't like that, and wanted a happy ending, where Apollo takes Orfeo up to heaven. That's the version which has come down to us. It looks here as if you have the first version – which seems to have been written, not by Monteverdi, but by someone else – from the star of David it is most likely Salamone Rossi, a Jewish musician and composer who worked with Monteverdi in Mantua. Much of his music has been found, and some is played today. But not this.'

This is breathtaking. I don't know what to say. My father's words come to mind: beating the *goyim* at their own game.

John continues: 'Has Roberto seen it?'

I shake my head. 'I haven't told him. He has found some other original material connected with *Orfeo*. I don't know what it is. His concert performance will – he says – highlight his discovery.'

'Yes. Gwyn College is very excited.'

How can it happen that Florence leads musical fashion? Monteverdi? What have you to say for yourself?'

Claudio steps forward and bows. 'I am at your service, Duke Vincenzo. With all due modesty, I would like to reassure you that my music is at the forefront of the most exciting musical developments of our time.'

Giovanni adds: 'Claudio Monteverdi is too modest. His music has prompted enormous controversy everywhere in Italy. This has directed attention to your courage and enterprise in so generously employing him here, in Mantova.'

'Good. I am glad to hear it. Now. I want you to beat Florence at their own game.'

Claudio steps forward. 'I have something – very original in mind. A drama. Music and – '

Vincenzo waves him to silence. 'Good. Get on with it.' Then he sweeps out, followed by his thugs.

When the soldiers have left, I realise my hands are clenched, my palms wet with sweat. In Giovanni's rooms, we fall into our chairs. 'The bastard will forget about it,' says Giovanni.

'No, no,' says Claudio. 'This is a real opportunity for me. Salamone. I shall need your help.'

Claudio and I walk by the lake. We talk about Florence, and the *intermedi*. This is how he wants to write. Not a play with musical interludes, but a powerful drama, which is sung, from beginning to end. There will be short musical *ritornelli*, like choruses, and sung recitations to punctuate the action. I am excited. I know exactly what he means. But who will write the words?

'Alessandro Striggio,' says Claudio. 'He is a poet. I shall ask him to write a drama – about Orfeo and Euridice.' I join in.

❖ SECUNDA PARTE ❖

'There's an added complication,' I say.

I tell him about Lavenham, Frank and my job. 'I've promised him a second performance of *Orfeo*. I haven't asked Roberto yet.'

'He won't refuse, I'm sure,' says John. 'Everyone knows that Barton Kemp's has been the definitive edition of *Orfeo*. Until now.'

'Yes, but if you're right, and this really is the original ending – '

John waves me silent. He wraps the package carefully, and puts it back in the bag.

'Well,' he says. 'This manuscript will have to be properly authenticated.' I nod. 'I would guess that this discovery has come too late to make any difference to Roberto's edition. I suggest you tell Roberto about the performance at Lavenham – I'm sure he'll agree – and we can decide what to do about this later. What do you think?'

I note the 'We'. I am relieved to have found someone who thinks so clearly. 'A good idea,' I say.

'When you're ready,' he adds, 'I can suggest some names for authentication. Unless you already – ?'

'No, no,' I say. 'I don't know people in the musicology world – apart from you and Roberto, of course.'

John stands up. 'Good. And you must tell me sometime where you found it.' At the front door he kisses me on the lips.

'Yes. The underworld. About music. About – well, love, everything. The gods.'

Alessandro is as excited as we are, and together we plot out the first four Acts of the story. Before we can go any further, Mantova is distracted. One morning, Giovanni and I go to Santa Barbara, to find the courtyard packed with servants and people from the town. Giovanni goes into the church, to find out what is happening. Then he hurries back to me.

'Go home, Salamone, and tell your family and friends to stay in their houses. A monk has come from Siena. I don't know who he is. He is blaming the floods and the bad harvest on the Jews. Please. Go.'

I hurry home. My parents have already heard. The monk chooses cities where there are Jews and the reins of authority are relatively relaxed. Mantova is ideal. No ghetto, and he knows the Duke and Duchess are relatively easy-going.

There is a loud banging on the door, and we hear screams from the street. My father lets in a neighbour. Blood runs down his face from a cut on his head. My father slams the door and pushes our heavy table against it. Apparently, a mob has broken into one of the more dilapidated houses at the end of the street. A group of elderly Jews live here, cared for by the community.

The crowd drags them into the Piazza di San Pietro. Three men and an old woman. Judita Franchetta, they say, is a witch, who has cast spells on the countryside to damage the harvest, and bewitched the nuns in one of the Mantovan convents. Luckily, our neighbour gasps, she is old and frail, and not very aware of her surroundings. There is nothing we can do.

Later that evening, when the streets are quiet, a distraught Giovanni comes to tell us what happened. A massive pile of

❖ SECUNDA PARTE ❖

THIRTY-FOUR

❖

A NOTE ON MY kitchen table says Xan is going away for a few days. She will be back in time for the concert. Can I tell Roberto?

The final week of rehearsal is hectic. The English National Opera makes an emergency demand for student singers for their chorus. Roberto argues, but to no avail. Gwyn needs the money. Streaky, from Catchpole days, arrives, to sing Proserpina. Her hair alternates bright red and white streaks. Deep blue eyeshadow. Shiny, teetering pink high heels. Black tights, as good as their name, hugging legs and bum, with a loose jersey top barely covering her hips. The male students can hardly keep their eyes off her. She is put out to find that Xan will be singing both La Musica and Sylvia.

Terry arrives, to replace a chitarrone player. His head is shaved, and he has silver ear-studs along both earlobes. The tension is palpable. I am the last to leave rehearsals. Roberto is still at the harpsichord, his head bowed. I hear a sob. I put my arm round him.

'I am very Italian, you see,' he says, wiping his tears. I give him a tissue and he blows his nose. 'But perhaps I am becoming English. I apologise for making a fuss.'

'Don't be silly. It's been a strain.' I put my viol away. He closes the harpsichord lid. He still looks miserable, so I say: 'Come and have supper with me.'

In my flat, it all comes tumbling out. He has applied for tenure in America, which would establish him at his

wood was built in the square. The old woman, bent and barely conscious, is bound to the top of it. They force three of the old men to light the fire. They try to comfort her. As the flames take hold, one tries to climb up to release her. The others pull him away, and the crowd lets them escape, hastening their steps with a shower of stones.

The ropes round the old woman burn, and she holds her hands in front of her face to protect herself. The flames flare up and she falls into them. There is no sound. The Duke returns and orders the Jews to clean the square. He sends the monk away and offers the Jewish *universita* absolution, in return for a heavy tax. The three old men are taken in by other families. The community is in shock.

Then a group of young Jewish men celebrate the birthday of one of them in synagogue, on Sunday. The windows are wide open. They sing and shout and carry each other round the room, shoulder high. There are complaints. A group of worthy Mantovan citizens invade the synagogue and take the young men to prison, where they are all strangled for polluting the Catholic Sabbath.

Their bodies are dragged through the streets, and hung by the feet. Even the Duke thinks this goes too far, and orders us to take the bodies down and bury them. One of the seven is Moses Fano, one of our talented theatre performers. We are graciously granted absolution again, with another tax imposed, and the Duke finally orders the Christian citizens to leave us alone. In return, he promises to listen to their demands for a ghetto in the city.

Our hearts sink. Not at the principle of living near each other – after all, most of the Jewish *universita* is already gathered in a university. If this production, and his new edition, don't produce the goods, there are enough people in the musical world who would like to see him fail. And where is Xan? She isn't answering his calls.

As I cook and he drinks wine, I tell him about Frank and a possible follow-up performance at Lavenham. Like him, my job may depend on it. We may need an accompanying lecture. Perhaps along the lines of the talk he gave at Catchpole? Roberto is overjoyed. Supper is fun. Roberto talks, and I punctuate with questions. He is an impressive and amusing mimic. Ancient family members from the south of Italy; pretentious American colleagues. He even does a passable imitation of Gabriel's shuffle, and a wickedly caricatured version of Barton's conducting style.

Over coffee, I ring Frank at home. I introduce them and hand the receiver to Roberto. There is laughter, what sounds like man-to-man bonhomie, and finally a 'Ciao, ciao' from Roberto. He is buoyant. 'He will pay expenses for me, and he would like my talk. Thank you, Emilia.'

I open another bottle of wine to celebrate. We clear the table and I wash up. Each time he brings dishes to the sink, he passes closer to me. Then, one hand on my shoulder, he spins me round, and still with a wet cloth in my hand and a tea-towel in his, we kiss. It is wordless and long and exploratory. When our mouths part we are holding each other.

'Would you like to stay? I can sleep on the couch.'

'Nonsense,' he says. 'I can't let you sleep on the couch.' We laugh.

'I didn't mean it anyway,' I say.

We leave the washing up and go to bed, all the lights

handful of neighbouring streets. It's the idea of walls and gates and guards. Vincenzo announces that there will be stricter observance of the requirement to display the yellow badge on our clothes, in the streets and squares.

My parents and I agree that it is probably better if I return to live with Giovanni.

TWENTY-THREE

VINCENZO SUMMONS US TO the Camera degli Sposi. Soldiers surround us. Giovanni, Claudio and Giulio, Alessandro and I bow. Vincenzo and Eleonora sit in ornately carved and gilded chairs, in front of the window. She is heavily pregnant. A fire burns. I am relieved to see there is no bed.

A table is set with wine and sugared cakes. Vincenzo invites us to drink and eat. He sweeps his arm round the walls in a large gesture.

'These are my ancestors.' Vincenzo points to a small boy, near a large dog and an enormous horse. 'That is one of my grandfathers. Just an ordinary child. The Gonzaga worked their way up in the world, just as you have all done. Isabella d'Este married Francesco, and their son, Federigo, was the first Duke. I owe him everything. Now. Next week is carnival.'

I wonder what is coming. 'Next year will be carnival again.'

❖ SECUNDA PARTE ❖

on. He doesn't mention contraception. He is determined, dynamic and insistent. It is turbulent and thrilling, and as soon as it is over for him, it is over.

He sleeps with a deep snore, and I lie awake, warm and unsatisfied. Eventually, I get up, open the wardrobe, take down the spare duvet and go to sleep on the couch. As I take the duvet out, there is a spray of grey dust. I must do something about the moths.

Roberto leaves early the following morning. He has to collect proofs from the publishers. Everything is done electronically, he says, but he likes to go through it on the page. Would I like to come and have dinner with him this evening? He can cook artichokes. His mother's recipe.

In the afternoon we work on the final Act. Orfeo confides his desperation to Echo. Without his beloved Eurydice, he will never love again. All women are fickle and faithless. Apollo descends from heaven. Come to heaven with me, he sings, and you will be reunited with your beloved. Off they go, to a mad, frantic, exhilarating *moresco*. All instruments at full stretch, recorders trilling and warbling in unending virtuosity. I feel like a traitor. Everything in me cries out to say no, no, this isn't the right ending.

I go home to change for dinner. I take the Catchpole manuscript out of the bag. I remember John's white gloves and feel guilty that I am not being scholarly and responsible. I look at the last pages. Unlike the heavenly ending of this afternoon, here, in clear English at the end, is a stage direction: 'The Bacchantes tear Orfeo to pieces.' Below that are two signatures. A. Striggio. S. Rossi. Under these: Mantova, 160 – the last digit is blurred.

I breathe more easily. 'I want to know whether you have finished the work of which we spoke some time ago?'

Alessandro bows. 'It is nearly finished. The *Accademia degli Invaghiti* will be honoured to present the new work. It will be the most heavenly entertainment in Italy.'

Claudio and I flash a glance at each other. We have written nothing since our walk by the lake.

'Well,' says Vincenzo. 'You are known, I believe, as *Il Ritenuto*. I would like you behave without your customary reserve, and get on with it. That applies to you all.' We bow our heads.

Vincenzo stands, and we all follow suit. 'That is all. For carnival next year. 1607 will be the year Florence finally bows to the genius of Mantova.'

'It will be a pleasure,' says Alessandro.

Vincenzo gives his hand to Eleonora, and they leave, followed by all but two of the soldiers. The soldiers close the door and join us at the table. 'No rush,' says one. 'We may as well finish this lot. The Duke always leaves wine and plenty of cakes.'

'Bastard,' says Claudio. I look warningly at him. The soldiers laugh. 'You're not the first,' says one, his mouth caked with white sugar.

'He expects me to add this new thing to everything else I have to do. Do you know how far in arrears my salary is?'

'You're not the first,' repeats the soldier.

'He'll pay you eventually,' says Alessandro reassuringly, making inroads on the food.

Claudio coughs. 'He promised Claudia an allowance. Then he cancelled it. I am owed months of salary.'

❖ SECUNDA PARTE ❖

My impulse is to take this to Roberto. I must talk to John first. I put the manuscript back in the bag, and the bag in the bedroom.

THIRTY-FIVE

❖

ROBERTO LIVES IN A STUDENT block belonging to the University of London. Reception phones his room, and I sign in. Once in his room, I am in another world. A small double bed along one wall is neat, with a yellow and black striped velvet cover. On the wall above the bed is a small wooden cross. A desk under the window, with papers and pens lined up. A small table with two chairs. A bookcase, with a handful of books, a couple of wine glasses and mugs. Next to it, a small fridge. A sink in one corner, and a two-burner gas cooker on a small stand. Two saucepans, and a delicious smell.

'Not much room, I'm afraid.'

'It's fine.' I sink onto the bed. It is firm. Comfortable.

He opens one of the desk drawers. Crockery, cutlery, serviettes. He stirs one saucepan, turns the other one off and then opens the fridge.

'I can't believe it,' he says. 'I forgot to buy milk.'

'Shall I go and get some?'

'No, no,' he says. 'There's a machine downstairs.'

'I could lay the table.'

'Yes. Yes. That would be nice.'

'I bet he fobbed you off with some old clothes,' says the second soldier.

'Of course,' says Claudio. His voice is strong again. 'Cheap silk, no overcoat, no silk lining for the cloak. No stockings. I had to buy the rest with my own money.'

'You'll still write wonderful music,' says Giovanni.

'*Dramma per musica*,' says Claudio, his mouth full of crumbs.

Giulio takes the glass away from Claudio. 'Don't overdo it. You'll get a headache.'

TWENTY-FOUR

I TAKE SOME CAKES to Emilia and the children. We cut the cakes into small pieces, so there is enough for everyone in the courtyard. Emilia tells me that things are bad between Vincenzo and Eleonora. He spends most of his time with his mistresses, and who knows how many other women. Of course Eleonora knows. Everyone knows. I hug Emilia to me, and whisper: 'I want to tell my parents about us.'

'Not yet, my love.'

'I want us to be together all the time.'

She sends the children off to play. 'We'll never be together all the time. Mistress Music needs you as much as we do. Anyway, where could a black woman and a Jewish man go? I

When he is gone, I open the wardrobe door, out of sheer nosiness. As I expected. Shirts arranged by colour. Neatly folded T-shirts and underwear on the shallow shelves at one side. No grey dust in sight, I find myself thinking: the devil wouldn't dare.

I open the desk drawer to look for cutlery. I open the wrong one. It is crammed with music manuscript paper. The staves are littered with notes. Bars are crossed out. It's in a mixture of pencil, and blue and black biro.

I lift a page out of the drawer. It looks very like the realisation Roberto showed me, with crossings out and scribbles. The writing has Roberto's characteristic slant; I know it from the writing on my music. The top sheet is headed 'Prologue'. There is an elaborate keyboard part. Under it are a series of signatures: Claudio Monteverdi, Alessandro Striggio. Over and over again. Tiny differences in each version. I am chilled. I recognise something. Somewhere in my filing cabinet I still have sheets of paper on which I practised my Henry James' handwriting.

Footsteps in the corridor stop outside the door. I am setting knives and forks when Roberto returns with milk. Conversation over the excellent dinner is about Italian food. Different ways of cooking artichokes in different regions. Roberto's mother's wonderful dishes.

'You must visit my home. You would like my parents.' I am touched.

Dessert is a bit stodgy, and so are my thoughts. Roberto has composed the realisations himself. Clearly, he is very clever. But he has, no doubt, forged what he is claiming as the rediscovered 'original' manuscript. I have a sneaking admiration for him. Great minds think alike, I

couldn't live in the Jewish *universita*. You can't live here. We see each other every day, anyway.'

She kisses me. 'Here come the *putti*.'

The children run and climb all over us. Emilia whispers to me: '*Nigra sum*.' I whisper back: '*Pulchra es*.' I kiss them all and leave.

TWENTY-FIVE

CLAUDIO IS SITTING AT the table in Giovanni's room. Giulio holds a cold cloth to his brother's forehead.

'I can't do it. I won't have time.'

'You'll do it brilliantly. You always do.'

'Claudia is ill. The air here is bad for her. The air is bad for me. I wake up every morning with a headache. Look.'

He lifts his shirt. His body is covered with angry red spots. 'It itches like crazy.'

'I'll make you a poultice,' says Giulio. 'You need rest, Claudio.'

Claudio jumps up. 'Very funny. How can I rest?'

'I've got the opening,' I say.

Claudio brightens. 'What?'

'Remember my fanfare? The Turks. The battle.'

'Of course I do.' Claudio imitates a trumpet.

'War is the inspiration for peace. Waste not, want not.'

think. And yet, do I want to be complicit in another academic fraud?

I stay the night as if it were the most natural thing. The bed is narrow. Cosy. The sex is less frantic, less thrilling and more satisfying. We both get to the same place together.

We breakfast in Roberto's local café. 'When do you go back to America?'

'After the performance. Cara, you can visit me.'

'That would be great.'

'And you? You go back to your university?'

'I suppose so. I'm not sure I want to.'

'How do you mean?'

I have become fond of Roberto. After all, he has taught me to play music. He is passionate about music. That's not the problem. It's the career structure which has pushed him into being unethical. Perhaps I can help him avoid the same mistake.

'Have you heard of Henry James?' He nods. 'I'm a Henry James specialist. Years ago, I discovered an unpublished story, and that made my academic reputation.'

'An original discovery. Like me,' he says eagerly.

'Except,' I say, 'I didn't actually discover the story. I wrote it.' I watch Roberto's face. He gives nothing away. 'Really?'

'Towards the end of Henry James' life, his handwriting became more wayward, irregular. At first, it was an academic exercise. I wanted to see whether imitating his handwriting would help me understand his compositional processes better. I have a good eye.'

'And a good ear!'

∽ PRIMA PARTE ∾

I pick up one of the recorders lying on the table. I play a sharp, dotted fanfare. Claudio joins in, his voice harmonising.

'The opening *toccata*. Trumpets. Sackbuts. Recorders. The organ, a sustained fifth lower. Followed by a sweet, short *ritornello*.'

I play a fragment. Claudio picks up another recorder, harmonising a third below me, then, clashing, leading me on. Giulio finds a chitarrone. By the time Claudio and I have played it through twice, he has tuned, and joins us in a stately duple rhythm. Giovanni applauds.

'We could use the fanfare as a *ritornello*,' I suggest. 'Or — perhaps have words over it?'

Claudio shakes his head. 'No, no. We'll open the *dramma* with it. I've had another idea. I'll also use it under plainchant, for Santa Barbara. I must go to bed. I'm exhausted.'

When he and Giulio have gone, I pace round the room. 'I wrote the fanfare. In that damn muddy tent.'

'Do you mind Claudio using it?'

'No. Of course not. But I would like, for once, to be able to write some sacred music, as Claudio does. I want to hear my work in bigger spaces. I want it revered. I want to be acknowledged. Appreciated.'

Giovani smiles. 'You are appreciated, Salamone.'

'You and I know that there is something — special about sacred music. It is what people remember best.'

'Salamone. Your frustration is understandable. But you know, as well as I, that you will never write music for the church.'

There is a brief silence. 'Yes. I know. Still, it is a shock to hear it said.'

'Do you really mean that you actually want to write for the

❖ SECUNDA PARTE ❖

'Thank you, Roberto. Then I thought – what if I try to imitate his writing – well, to see if I can write a story in the style of Henry James. I put imagination and handwriting together. I became a Professor on the strength of it.'

Roberto's eyes are intense. He puts his hand on mine. The pressure is strong.

'Was it authenticated?'

'Of course. I knew what I was doing.'

'Well. I think that is very clever.'

'It's not very ethical.'

He looks at his watch. 'We all do things under pressure. I'm sure you still helped scholarship. Thank you so much for connecting me with your university. Full run-through at two. Don't be late.'

THIRTY-SIX

❖

I WAS NAÏVE TO think that if I confessed to Roberto, he would see the error of his ways. Why should he? Perhaps I am displacing historic guilt: wishing that someone, way back, had pointed out my 'sin', so that I could have stopped in time? Perhaps I am still feeling guilty? Guilt and confession. I am so damn steeped in all this Catholic music that my own Jewish guilt monitor has tripped into overload. Perhaps I am losing my marbles because, after years of celibacy, I have slept with – had sex with – made

church? Or do you just want to write – bigger music? There is nothing to stop you from writing sacred music. For the synagogue.'

'Giovanni, you know that the Hebrew texts I have set for the synagogue have caused arguments in my community. There are many who think it is wrong to have music as part of the service. It is, they say, a Catholic habit. It is not what Jews do.'

Giovanni gestures. 'I don't know what else to suggest.'

'You're really telling me I must stay in the ghetto.'

'No, I'm not. Don't be stupid.'

'My sacred music goes to Venice to be played and sung properly. Double choir. Antiphonal. Exactly the kind of thing Claudio writes. Leone da Modena performs my music in the Spanish synagogue in Venice. Leone says there is nothing wrong in using the human voice to sing God's praises. There is no blasphemy in pronouncing the name of God in song. Words and music joined together pose no threat to the integrity of the Jewish faith. But I want to hear my music here, where I live.'

'I don't understand why this suddenly matters to you.'

'Because I want to belong. Fully belong.'

My discontent doesn't leave me, but I have little time to give to it. The regular work for Santa Barbara, teaching, writing, and my work with Claudio, take up every moment. I copy everything from his chaotic hand. I organise rehearsals so that he can correct and revise.

Alessandro has written a prologue, *La Musica*, which is to be sung by a new singer, poached from Florence, to Vincenzo's pleasure. Claudio is delighted with her, until she says she is love to – (I really don't know what to call it) – two different men, within a short space of time.

The light is on in the kitchen. I don't remember leaving it on. I go into the bedroom. Xan is lying in my bed. I sit next to her. She turns towards me, sits up and sobs. I put my arm round her. I stroke her face. She is sweating. 'It's ok, Xan.'

'It's not ok. It's burning. I can smell the wood burning. There's too much fire. Too much smoke.'

I hold her still. 'Xan. Xan. Wake up, Xan. It's ok. Nothing is burning.'

She opens her eyes. 'Sorry. I dreamt I was on fire.'

'I'll make you some tea.'

She gets out of bed. She's fully dressed.

'When did you get here?' I ask. She shrugs. 'I don't know. Late. I rang you. You weren't here.'

'What's happened? Where have you been?'

She bursts into tears again. 'I've had an abortion,' she says. 'I'm alright. I just feel terrible.'

'Why didn't you tell me?'

'I haven't told anyone. It's nothing to do with anyone.'

'Is it Terry?' I don't really know why I'm asking. It's not really my business. She laughs. 'Good God, no. Bloody Roberto.'

I put some bread in the toaster. It gives me a chance to turn away from her. 'Does he know?'

'I told you. No-one knows. Please don't say anything.'

'Are you sure you should be singing?'

'Oh, yes. I'm fine. Just tired.' She looks sharply at me. 'This is professional. I know I'm not being paid. But I want people to hear me sing. Of course it's a good idea.'

pregnant, the baby is due in Lent, and she will not be able to sing in the performance. She is sorry. Claudio spends the next day in bed, in darkness, with a raging headache.

That Friday evening, at home, we are all sitting round the table. Menahem and his family, Esther and her family. As the children run round the room, and crawl under the table, on impulse I decide to tell them about Emilia. My mother hands round slices of fresh *mandorle*, then she puts her arms round me. My father has tears in his eyes. Menahem and Esther whoop and run round the table. 'Bring her and the children here next Friday,' says my mother.

TWENTY-SIX

I WRITE A TWO-CHOIR piece. Eight voices. *Eftach shir bisfatai*. My lips open with a song. *Cori spezzati*. I write fast. Giovanni looks over my shoulder.

'A little old-fashioned for Claudio,' he comments, then he laughs. 'Sorry. I forget that the modern is confined to the Gonzaga court, while the ancient is sustained in the Jewish community. Shall we get the boys to try it out?'

'I have a favour to ask,' I say. 'I want Emilia and the children to hear it. I want my family to hear it.'

'Of course.'

I take his hand. 'Giovanni, you are a saint. In the secular

'I'm sorry, Xan.' She yawns. 'Do you want to sleep a bit longer? Rehearsal isn't till two.'

She nods. We go into the bedroom and she gets into bed. I'm about to pull the duvet over her, when on impulse, I get into bed as well, shoes and all. She curls into my arms.

I am in a room painted a bright, deep blue. There are stars on the ceiling and the walls. In one corner a bear paws at a centaur. In another corner, a woman drives a chariot drawn by dogs through clouds. Her dress swirls round a swelling stomach. I look up and she winks at me, her eyes intense, dark.

Xan and I arrive together in the Tudor Hall on the ground floor of Gwyn College for the run-through. Over greetings and chatter, Xan goes up to Roberto. I can't hear what she says.

We are in a semicircle, the soloists distributed among the instruments, the chorus to one side. At the opening fanfare, Xan stands, her music open. We glide into the delicate *ritornello*. La Musica soars, punctuated by strings. Her voice is glorious. Tiny, sweet ornaments on notes and cadences. A final *ritornello* completes the prologue, and the story begins.

There are blips and hiccups along the way, but we get through. At the end, there is a smattering of applause. The principal and a handful of staff have been listening. After some work on the rough corners, Roberto wishes us all a restful weekend. 'We have two more days of rehearsals, and then performances on Wednesday and Thursday. Tell your friends. We need an audience.'

Roberto covers the harpsichord and takes my viol. On

sense, of course. You understand me. I owe everything to you. Why?'

'Salamone, my mother died when I was born. My music is my life. The men I work with are my mothers. I have never loved in any worldly sense, and I am free of the emotions which destroy most people. Emilia and the children can sit in the organ gallery, together with your family. We will sing in Hebrew.'

And so the incredible happens. The choir and instruments rehearse. I coach them in the Hebrew, making sure the word and music stresses cohere as much as possible. Giovanni suggests that if in doubt, they should sing whatever Latin phrases came to mind. 'Spirito Sancto is always a good one,' he says.

And so, my Hebrew wedding music is sung to a mixture of Hebrew and Latin, in the church of Santa Barbara. As promised, Giovanni guides my two families into the gallery. Not a note is out of place. Afterwards I take my family to see our courtyard, and then Emilia and the children come home to taste my mother's cooking for the first time.

TWENTY-SEVEN

ALESSANDRO AND CLAUDIO HAVE finished the fourth Act of *Orfeo*. This is Orfeo's last chance. Proserpina pleads for him, and Euridice is released to follow him back to earth from

the way downstairs, he says: 'Shall I come round for dinner tomorrow?'

'Of course. I'll cook.'

'I bring wine.'

He hands me my viol, and is gone. Neat, rapid steps. It reminds me of the first time I saw him walk away from me, at Catchpole.

THIRTY-SEVEN

❖

THE FLAT STILL SMELLS faintly of Xan's lily-of-the-valley. She has left her key on the kitchen table. Her perfume gives way to the memory of Roberto's body, his jasmine savour. My pulses remember his. I am in turmoil.

If Roberto and I are to have a relationship, he must understand. I will honour his secret, as he honours mine. Perhaps he could even come clean, gain accolades because of his authenticist construction of a notated improvisation. After all, that's what dalla Casa and Bassano and van Eyck did. John Marshall has taught me well. I know there are precedents.

Roberto arrives with two bottles of wine. We toast *Orfeo*, and he nuzzles my neck as I heat the soup. We gossip about the rehearsals. He talks and I listen. We take coffee into the living room. We sit close together on the couch. His hand runs over my shoulders. I tingle.

'Emilia. I have been thinking.'

Hades, on condition that he does not look back at her. He can't resist the temptation – he looks round, and she is taken away from him forever. His despair is complete. The chorus sings the moral to the story. Orfeo has learned his lesson.

The following day, we play through the fourth Act for Vincenzo. He waits. 'Well?'

'That is the end of the story,' says Claudio.

'It may be the end of the story,' says Vincenzo, 'but it isn't the end of the piece. This is – a damp squib. Dull. We must have an exhilarating, exciting ending. Please provide a Fifth Act.'

Back in the sacristy, to my surprise, it is not Claudio who flips, but Alessandro. Normally calm, conciliatory, thoughtful Alessandro. He throws the music on the floor and shouts: 'The man is a philistine. He understands nothing.'

Claudio, his face red with scratching, a line creased in the middle of his forehead, his shoulders raised with tension, waves him silent. 'We'll write a Fifth Act. I don't care.'

'Well, I'm not writing any more.' I have never seen Alessandro like this.

'You'll have to. I need words.'

The tension in the room is dreadful. 'I'll do it,' I say. 'I'll write a Fifth Act. Will that shut both of you up?'

They are surprised at my vehemence. 'We want this to be good,' I say. 'Let's give him what he wants.'

'He's an idiot,' says Claudio. 'He doesn't know what he wants.'

'Exactly. As long as there is a spectacular ending, he doesn't care what it says or how. Well?'

The room is calmer. Claudio sighs. 'Why not.'

I am thrilled. My ploy has worked. I won't have to collude in two academic frauds.

He takes my hand. 'It would be fantastic to be able to publish a facsimile of the keyboard realisation,' he says. 'Some of it is – almost impossible to decipher. It was very hard for me. But you have a good eye. You could help.'

For a moment I wonder whether the drafts of music I saw were attempts to transcribe a faint original. Then I remember the repeated signatures. I take my hand away.

'Are you asking me to – help you with forging the – manuscript – the facsimile?' He doesn't answer. 'No. I can't. I'm sorry.'

'Do you want money?'

'Good God, no. It's not about money.'

The doorbell rings. Roberto makes a sound of frustration. 'I must answer it,' I say.

It's John Marshall. 'I'm sorry to turn up like this. I got your address from college. I need to talk to you.'

I precede him into the living room. The two men seem surprised to see each other, but nevertheless exchange a strong handshake. I pour some wine for John. He asks polite questions about rehearsals, and how much he is looking forward to the performance

A silence. Then John says: 'Emilia, could I have a glass of water?'

He follows me into the kitchen. He notices the remains of dinner. He turns on the cold water tap. He speaks fast, softly: 'Have you told him?' For a moment I wonder whether he means 'about us'.

'About the manuscript?' He nods. 'Of course not. We agreed.'

'I've been thinking. You must tell Roberto.'

I play a sequence of chords on my violin. *Ruggiero*. Claudio takes his violin, and Giovanni picks up his chitarrone. The room is filled with round after round of improvisation. Slow and stately, then a few coy runs, then we are racing as fast as we can over the steady, repeated bass line. Finally, Giovanni soothes us into silence with a simple, slow series of peaceful chords.

'Alessandro,' I say. 'Will you write the words? I'll write the music.'

In the Fifth Act, Orfeo, despairing, vows never to love again. Women are faithless and fickle. Bacchus, the god of wine and ecstasy, sends his followers, the Bacchantes, to punish Orfeo. Bacchanalian celebrations were secret, attended only by women. Not unnaturally, says Alessandro, the Bacchantes are furious at Orfeo's behaviour and his attitude towards women. They tear him to pieces.

'There, Salamone,' says Alessandro. 'A jolly *moresca* to round it all off. Note my not-so-subtle symbolism. Orfeo represents Vincenzo, of course.'

'Good,' says Claudio. 'Neglects his wife. Keeps two public mistresses, and heaven knows how many private ones. We are the Bacchantes. We tear him to pieces. He deserves everything he gets.'

'We'll use the *moresco* from our last Purim play,' I say. 'Will Vincenzo realise?'

'Of course not,' says Alessandro. 'You don't think he'll be listening, do you?'

Vincenzo has decided he must have singers from Florence. It's his way of making sure that everyone knows what we are planning. After our initial irritation, we realise it could be the best solution. An agent is sent, to secure Giovanni Gualberto,

❖ SECUNDA PARTE ❖

'I don't want to discuss it now, John.'

We go back into the living room. I'm racking my brains, trying to think of a way to get rid of both of them.

'Are you doing the original ending to *Orfeo*?' asks John.

'But of course,' says Roberto.

'I mean the authentic original ending? The first version of the end of *Orfeo*?' I can't believe my ears.

'There is an alternative libretto. Everyone knows that. But no music for the original ending survives.'

'I see. Actually, it does,' says John. 'Emilia has found the original last Act of *Orfeo*.'

Roberto looks at me in amazed shock. 'What?'

John has no right to take this into his own hands. I am in a complete double bind. Damned if I tell the truth and damned if I don't. I say nothing.

Roberto snaps. 'Ah. So, Emilia, you have written the original ending with the Bacchantes, and not Apollo, and copied it out on old paper so that it would look authentic?'

'That's bullshit, Roberto,' I say. 'You know I couldn't write music if I tried. I don't understand music. I can play it but I don't understand it. That's part of the joy for me. To be able to do something well which I don't understand. But then, I doubt whether either of you would understand that, because you both do understand music. Too many understands, I know. John knows how ignorant I am. I could not possibly forge a musical manuscript.'

'But you do understand literature, don't you?' says Roberto. 'You forged a short story and claimed it was original. Emilia, our quiet, talented and respectable middle-aged lady here, has based her whole academic career on a lie. A forgery.'

one of Giulio Caccini's pupils. Vincenzo insists that Florence must pay his salary and his travel expenses. They agree.

Vincenzo is triumphant. 'We just have to make sure he doesn't eat and drink too much.' We smile dutifully. 'What will he sing?'

Claudio thinks. 'La Musica. Proserpina, perhaps. And there is the Messenger.'

Gualberto arrives a week before the performance, on the boat. He refuses to speak until he is in Giovanni's house, near the fire. He drinks only hot water with lemon juice, and insists on wearing a length of red woollen cloth round his head, wound twice round his neck. Once a chill gets into his ears, it goes straight to his nose and throat. If he hears anyone cough or sneeze, he walks quickly to the other side of the room. He's a stocky man, fussier than any woman. He washes his hands in rose water to keep them soft. The Duchess and all the ladies of the court love him.

He has learned La Musica but not Proserpina. There are too many notes, he says. Claudio is insistent. Alessandro throws a tantrum. I watch and Giovanni smooths the way. Once Gualberto stops complaining and learns the music properly, he is, indeed a genius.

❖ SECUNDA PARTE ❖

I am almost more furious at the 'middle-aged' than at anything else.

'Well, Roberto, while we are at revelations, I know that your so-called authentic keyboard realisation is all your own work. The difference between these two discoveries of authentic music manuscripts is that mine is real and yours is a forgery.' My back is cold with sweat.

John looks at me. He speaks calmly. 'Emilia has shown me part of a manuscript. If it is authentic, it is, indeed, the words and music of the first version of the Fifth Act of *Orfeo*. It looks genuine to me.' He turns to Roberto, and says gently: 'You won't be able to publish your edition, Roberto.'

Roberto is furious. 'How dare you, Emilia? When did you show him this – this – thing?'

Roberto may be professionally threatened, but I can see he is also jealous. That pleases me.

'I would advise you not to publish.' John is very firm.

'Or else what?'

'I am not bargaining with you,' said John. 'What you are proposing to do is not ethical.'

'And what she did was ethical?'

'Could you please not discuss me as if I wasn't here?'

'There is a solution, from which we could all benefit.'

My competitive scholarly drive kicks in. 'I found it, John,' I say. 'I don't like to say finders keepers – but I did find it.'

'I can't believe you didn't tell me.' Roberto is cold.

'I was going to tell you this evening. Before our good friend John arrived.'

'I don't believe you.'

John proposes a compromise. Roberto will delay his

◆§ PRIMA PARTE §◆

TWENTY-EIGHT

◆§

THE PERFORMANCE IS SPECTACULAR. We crowd into a room so freshly painted that it has not yet acquired a nickname. Walls and ceiling are a deep bright blue. Golden stars twinkle. The floor is tiled in Pesaro marble, and covered with Turkish carpets. Our instrumentalists fill half the room, with the singers standing or sitting in front, the chorus to one side.

The Duke and Duchess sit on a raised dais opposite us, surrounded by children and carefully selected members of the court, including some Florentine visitors. The candles cast a soft glow, and braziers with lavender and rosemary sweeten the air.

We play without a break. No-one shifts or shuffles. Glasses of wine and water, prepared for the audience, are left untouched. The deafening *moresca* is followed by thunderous applause. The Duke stops it by raising his hand: 'We shall schedule a further, public, performance, for the city dignitaries. For that, you will compose a new ending, with new words and music. This one is far too brutal. We want a hopeful happy ending, appropriate for our court. The *moresca* is a delight. Keep that.'

'Damn,' says Claudio. 'The bastard was listening, after all.'

edition and change the introduction, admitting to his realisation and explaining the rationale for it. A superb pastiche, he will argue, can be accurate, enjoyable and educational. After all the scholarly discoveries of the historical performance practice movement, now is the time to show how much we have learned about what might really have been played.

After authoritative authentication of my find, we would announce the discovery of the original Fifth Act, and Roberto would put on a full performance of the original opera, with this newly found original ending. We would all share the credit for this collaborative discovery.

It sounds as if there is nothing to lose. Roberto and I nod. 'Now,' he says. 'I would like to see this discovery. And I would like to know where you found it.'

I go into the bedroom. I can't see the bag. It's not in the wardrobe. Nothing under the bed, in drawers or cupboards. I brush a little grey dust off my fingers. I feel sick.

I go back into the living room. Roberto and John are laughing. Two men having a friendly time.

'I can't find it,' I say.

'No, no,' says John. 'That won't do.'

Xan must have picked up her bag the other day, thinking she had left it here weeks ago. I wasn't going to tell them.

'I think I know where it is. Look, I am telling the truth. I have no reason not to. I will find it. Alright?'

PRIMA PARTE

TWENTY-NINE

AT THE END OF the first performance of *Orfeo*, Giovanni and I clear up the litter in the room. Discarded music, crumbs, empty glasses. I collect the music scattered on the floor by the musicians. I sit for a few moments, putting the Acts back into the right order. I am the last to leave. As I carry my viol along the corridor, I hear soft, rapid footsteps behind me. Leonora puts a hand on my arm. She looks tired. Servants hurry past us, carrying chairs and boxes with flowers. She draws me away, and up a familiar staircase, into the Camera degli Sposi. She closes the door, and sinks onto the wooden chest by the fire, out of breath.

'Vincenzo. He should not have ordered you to compose a new final Act. I am sorry.'

'Thank you,' I say. 'There's no need for you to apologise. You're not responsible for his whims.'

She smiles. 'No. I hope you will have a chance to play your version again sometime. I enjoyed the last Act.'

On impulse, I take out Act Five, and hand it to her. 'Here,' I say. 'Keep this for me. We will have to compose another final Act. Please. Keep it. One day we may perform it in a private concert for you.'

Leonora smiles. She takes her green velvet shawl, swiftly wraps the manuscript, and puts it inside the chest. She comes to me, and cups my face in her hands, and kisses me lightly on the mouth. 'I am so pleased Emilia is happy with you,' she says.

❖ SECUNDA PARTE ❖

THIRTY-EIGHT

❖

ROBERTO LOOKS MAGNIFICENT IN his tailcoat, with a bright green silk scarf round his neck. His hair is neatly secured with a green ribbon. He addresses the audience.

'For many years we thought that the first performance of *Orfeo* took place in a room called the Hall of Mirrors, in the Palazzo Ducale, in Mantova. However, the room concerned – lined, as you might expect, with mirrors, only received its name in the eighteenth century: the *Sala degli Specchi*.' His Italian accent is crisp and bouncy. 'Recent scholarship suggests that the first performance – like ours, a concert performance, not a fully staged event – took place in a different room. Since no-one knows where for sure, let us imagine that this is the room, and this is the very first performance.'

Rustles of interest. 'This is also the first performance celebrating my new edition of the opera, with my realisation of the figured bass, derived from authentic evidence of historical performance. The edition is currently at the publishers, and will be available soon to the musical world, in a complete, new edition. I would like to thank Gwyn College, and all my musical colleagues for their enthusiasm and support. I hope you enjoy this evening's performance.'

I have time to look round the packed audience. Gabriel and Netta sit at the back, with Catherine and Barton. In the middle, at the edge of a row, is John. Frank left a message on my phone to say he was sorry, he couldn't

THIRTY

THE SECOND PERFORMANCE OF *Orfeo*, before an audience of local dignitaries, and more visitors, is as great a success as the first. Alessandro writes a new ending, and Claudio and I find some unused music, in order not to have to compose anything new. Apollo arrives, consoles Orfeo and carries him to heaven, where he is reunited with the silent and invisible Euridice. The closing *moresca* remains. We musicians agree that the first version of the final Act is much better.

Claudio is completely exhausted. Claudia is ill. He, his family and doctors blame it on the Mantovan air. His salary is accumulating – in the Gonzaga coffers. The treasurer takes a particular dislike to Claudio and has never paid him properly.

THIRTY-ONE

CLAUDIA DIES LATER THAT same year – 1607. Claudio pleads to be released from his obligations. Vincenzo won't hear of it. Now he knows he has Italy's most important composer at his court, he is not going to let him go. Claudio rebels, and

make it after all, and looks forward to the performance at Lavenham.

I am tense with concentration until the very end. As the last notes of the wild *moresca* die away, my bowing arm is numb. When I stand for the applause, my legs are quivering. By the time I can move properly, Xan has disappeared. Everyone crowds round to congratulate Roberto. Barton hugs him and shakes his hand warmly. They might be the very best of friends. The glow carries us into the nearby pub and off into closing time.

When I get home, there is an answerphone message from Xan. Well played. I have gone to Catchpole.

THIRTY-NINE

❖

THERE ARE TWO WEEKS before the concert at Lavenham. I field phone calls from Roberto and John. Have I found the music? I put them off, saying a friend has borrowed the bag in which I put it, and I'm going to get it back as soon as I can. That, at least, is true, but I can tell that neither believes me.

I phone Catchpole. The number has been changed. No, no-one has heard of any Xan. Or a Mrs Dean. I get in the car and find my way in the East Anglian countryside with ease. It's a hot summer's day. I remember the daffodils along the drive. This time there are small rose bushes, alternating red and white blooms. On the gravel

returns to Cremona with his two sons. Even the publication of *Orfeo*, in its final version, two years later, is little consolation. Vincenzo continues to demand music, and since he is still officially employed at the Gonzaga court, Claudio has to oblige.

Finally, Venice makes serious overtures to Claudio. Together we visit La Serenissima, Claudio to San Marco to see the Doge, and I visit my second lion friend, Leone da Modena.

THIRTY-TWO

FROM THEN ON, LIFE in Mantova becomes even more insecure for us. Vincenzo listens to those who clamour for the Jews to be confined in a ghetto, like other Italian cities. My father volunteers to be an intermediary, in discussions between the Jews and the Duke.

I am no longer comfortable in the palace. There are whispers when I walk round the courtyards where I have felt at home. Hostile looks, when my new instrumental music is played at the weekly palace concerts. One day Giovanni, embarrassed and apologetic, says I am no longer required for work during the Santa Barbara services. He has argued on my behalf, he says, but there is nothing he could do. I move back home, to live with my parents, visiting Emilia and the children only at night.

Leonora and Vincenzo die within a few months of each other.

are huge wooden tubs, full of summer flowers. Over the front door is a sign, silver on white: 'Catchpole Manor Spa.'

The hall has been transformed. The oak panelling is still there, and the staircase sweeps majestically upwards. But to the right is a smart, ultra-modern desk, with a 'Reception' sign hanging from two gold chains. Above the desk is a huge screen, with a constantly changing panorama of bedrooms, dining room, ballroom, and the pride and joy, the spa complex. Behind the desk are two young women in smart blue and white suits, and 'Can I Help You' smiles.

'I'm looking for Mrs Dean,' I say.

'Is she a guest here?'

'No,' I say. 'She used to work here. Barbara Dean.'

One young woman checks something on the computer. 'I'm afraid there's no-one here of that name.'

'We opened last month,' says the other young woman. 'The building has been completely refurbished. Would you like a brochure?'

'Thank you.' I accept a thick multi-coloured booklet from an impeccably manicured hand. 'I think most of the former staff still live in the village. You could ask there. If you go back down the drive,' she says, 'and turn left, ask in one of the cottages.'

The cottages have thatched roofs. The last one is like a traditional picture-postcard, with a rose trellis winding round the door. I knock, and Mrs Dean appears. She looks older, greyer, wearing a floral apron. She has a dishcloth in one hand.

'Mrs Dean?'

'Yes. What a surprise. Come in, dear.'

PRIMA PARTE

Their eldest son promptly fires Claudio and Giulio. Some might have felt this as an insult, but for the Monteverdi brothers it is a release. Claudio leaves for Venice, with his sons. I travel with him, to witness the celebrations and respect with which he is welcomed at San Marco. I am able to arrange for Emilia to become his housekeeper, and she takes the children with her.

THIRTY-THREE

THE YEAR AFTER *ORFEO*, I have a chance encounter with an English traveller, dressed in strange foreign clothes. On my way home one night, I hear a battery of sneezes. Thomas Coryat, he is called. His Italian is dreadful, but we manage to understand one another. I invite him home with me. My mother's best rice and chicken do the trick. He looks at my music, and says he recognises some of it. He has seen it in a collection of Italian pieces which English musicians are eagerly copying and imitating.

I should go to London, he says. I might be able to find work there. I can take my wife and children. He gives me the names and addresses of English musicians. A Mr Weelkes and a Mr Morley. He warns me that Jews are not supposed to live in England, but he believes there are some Jewish musicians in London, and he tells me where to find a Mr Lupo.

Before I leave for London, I return to Mantova. I arrive at

She leads me along the hall into a bright kitchen. Xan is drinking a glass of orange juice. She flings her arms round me. Instead of feeling pleased to see her, I feel angry and impatient. I cut to the chase.

'Have you got your bag?'

'Which bag?'

'Your bag – the stripey bag. The one you left in my flat.'

'How did you know?' she asks, surprised. 'Have you found it?'

'Know what? Found what?'

'Would you like a cup of tea?' Mrs Dean is filling the kettle.

'No, thank you.' I want to get this sorted. 'Xan, you left your bag in my flat. I put something important in it. Maybe I shouldn't have, but I need it.'

'I'm really sorry,' she says. 'I thought you'd come to tell me you had the bag.'

'Haven't you got it?'

'Emmy, I'm really sorry. I left the bloody bag on the train. I've reported it, but so far it hasn't been found.'

'Oh, my God.'

'What did you put in the bag?'

Mrs Dean puts a teapot on the table, and a plate of biscuits. I take one.

'Are you staying here till the Lavenham concert?'

'I'm not doing the concert,' says Xan.

'Why not? Have you told Roberto?' I ask.

'I'll write to him. Laura can sing La Musica and Sylvia. She'll be brilliant. I promise I'll let you know if someone finds the bag.'

night; the mist and the mud have waited for me. It is the habitation I miss the most, and it is the habitation to which I will never return again. Amidst the destruction of so many armies, the Camera degli Sposi has survived, and in it the chest with the final Act of *Orfeo*.

In London I stay with the Lupo family for a few days. They pray behind tightly closed curtains. This is worse than the ghetto; a life, doubly hemmed in by secrecy. I don't want to be a burden to them, and so when I hear about a post as tutor to one of the wealthy East Anglian houses, I decide to apply for it.

England is dull, dirty grey, misty and damp. I should be used to mist and damp. England has wide open spaces. Flat, windy stretches of countryside. I should be used to that. But the air quality is different. There is always a chill here, even on the warmest day. I almost wish for the humidity which brings malaria. At least Catchpole Manor is on a small hill.

I have with me a small bundle of clothes, some of my music, and the green velvet package with *Orfeo*. As I walk up the drive, overgrown with weeds, I guess that the family has fallen on hard times. I learn from Lady Catchpole that the local cows and sheep have been hit by a mysterious disease. Lord Catchpole has speculated in the East or West Indies (I never understand which) and has lost a great deal of money. Most of the servants have already left and much of the house is slowly falling into majestic ruin. Great timbers from a nearby abbey were brought here after Henry VIII abolished the monasteries. Apart from a dozen habitable rooms, the rest is vast, draughty.

A few days after I arrived, I wandered round the deserted rooms. Dirt, dust and dead leaves driven in by the wind lay in

❖ SECUNDA PARTE ❖

FORTY

❖

BACK IN THE FLAT, I drink my way through half a bottle of rum and coke. Then I phone Roberto and John. The manuscript is safe, I lie. I suggest we should all meet at my London flat after the Lavenham concert, and decide what to do next. They are not happy about the delay, but they agree.

We meet on campus for a rehearsal. Roberto and I are staying in the local luxury hotel, while the rest stay on campus. Roberto is charming and professional. Tanya is faultless as La Musica and Sylvia. No-one mentions Xan.

Frank takes us all out to dinner, commandeering the local pizza joint. Roberto is seductive and Italian, his hair newly shined, his elegant suit impeccable. I find the rehearsal curiously empty. I know what to do, I am attentive and responsive. But there is no thrill. Roberto congratulates me after the run-through. 'You have settled into the music, Emilia. Congratulations.'

The afternoon of the concert, Roberto tops and tails sections, and runs through choruses and instrumental *ritornelli*. There is excitement everywhere. Posters advertising the concert, colleagues greeting me. The students are all in smart-casual suits and brightly coloured dresses.

The hall hushes as we process onstage and take our places. Frank welcomes us. He runs through Roberto's credentials, and then announces that Signor Castelli is to be offered a Visiting Professorship for next year, in the

piles in the corners. In one room were the rotting remnants of fleeces, prepared, so Lady Catchpole told me, to be sent to Flanders to be woven into cloth and then sent back to England. A great number of Dutchmen have settled in Norwich to set up the trades of carding, spinning and weaving wool. Catchpole has had to sell so much of its land that there are no farmers left to tend sheep.

Lady Catchpole sits ramrod straight in the grand hall, which reaches up to the huge rafters. The oak fireplace sports carvings of a dragon and a greyhound. She has a small, sweet voice, and no technique at all on the lute. Nevertheless, she works hard at her music. I wonder why it is that she still wishes to hire a music tutor. She says standards must be maintained. And so, for the time being, with my hastily packed bundle, I have a room in the single remaining tower. It's a tiny, dusty space. I sneeze every night.

THIRTY-FOUR

I HAVE BEEN AT Catchpole for a few weeks now. In the evenings, the family and the remaining servants gather behind the heavy oak door in the kitchen. Blocks of wood in the fireplace support the end of a log stretching ten feet across the floor. As it burns, it is pushed up into the fireplace. A copper

Faculty of Music. Everyone applauds, and Roberto bows, shakes Frank's hand, and, to everyone's delight, kisses him on both cheeks.

Frank turns to me. He reminds everyone of my importance. He stresses how exciting this event is, not least because it demonstrates the merits of research based on a free-flowing sense of adventure and investigation. A project which began as a conventional exploration of the Jacobean masque, has led us to the unexpected.

I can see the Vice Chancellor in the audience, and I know that this speech is phrased in order to stress the importance of the university as a centre for research. Frank has great pleasure in introducing Professor Emilia Constantine.

I am confident. I tell the audience how I am the epitome of current thinking about 'life-long' learning. Here I am, established in my own field (applause), fortunate to have been able to acquire a new professional skill (applause).

'You will be the best judges of that in a short while,' I say. (Sympathetic amusement.) 'I wish to challenge the myths of talent which can only bloom if it is spotted in the early years of a child's life.' I speak highly of Roberto's talents and commitment as performer and scholar. And 'You will be the best judges of that tonight.' (Loud applause.)

Frank returns to the auditorium, and Roberto takes his place. He gives the same talk he gave at Catchpole, lauding the Golden Age and its culture. Then he takes his place at the harpsichord. The thrill of performance has returned. At the end, after bows and cheers, as we jostle backstage Roberto rewards me with a hug. 'Emilia, that was truly professional. You will go a long way.'

cauldron hangs by a chain over a fire. At the other end of the kitchen is a smaller fire, with an oven and roasting spit built over part of it.

These evenings do away with social divisions. I play and sing. The children dance. Lord Catchpole indulges us and enjoys the entertainment. The food is adequate. Vegetables are for the peasants, the cook tells me one day. We are lucky to have meat in these times.

At night, I climb up the winding stairs to my room at the top of the one habitable tower. Apart from my straw mattress, it is crowded with pieces of wood, chunks of plaster, a couple of broken chairs, and a bench with rough streaks of paint over it. An old piece of canvas covers the open window, shielding the room from the worst of the wind. Before I go to sleep, I practise my English, by translating the words of the final Act of *Orfeo*.

One night is particularly chilly. The canvas over the window has come loose. At the end of the room is a narrow gallery, overlooking the dilapidated hall. A low chest stands by the rails. On the wall behind it is a piece of tapestry. It comes away easily, and I secure it over the window. When I turn round, I see a pure white wall.

The next day I ask Lady Catchpole if I may have some coloured paints. Just to keep me busy during the day, and at the weekend. She is happy to indulge her mad foreign musician, and the gardener is instructed to give me whatever I want.

For the next few weeks, I look forward to my tower retreat. I don't have much talent for painting, but I have a good memory. I paint small orange flowers. Marigolds. Then a Tudor rose. There are plenty of those in this house. I draw a man

❖ SECUNDA PARTE ❖

The phone rings as I come through the door of my flat. It's Frank. People couldn't stop talking about *Orfeo*. The singing. The instruments. How amazing I was. Roberto's energy and charisma. Frank is looking forward to my return at the beginning of the academic year. He is looking forward to Roberto's edition. He is looking forward to my next research project.

Roberto and John arrive together. I make coffee. I tell them about my journey to Catchpole. I tell them about Xan and the bag. About Xan picking it up without realising. About Xan leaving it on the train. No, I haven't heard from her.

They look at me with a mixture of anger and disbelief. 'You can search the flat,' I say.

'I'll speak to Xan,' says Roberto.

'Xan doesn't know about the manuscript,' I say.

John bursts out laughing. 'Well,' he says. 'Let that be a lesson to us all.' He looks at Roberto. 'What are you going to do?'

'I am going to tell the publishers to go ahead with my edition,' says Robert. They leave together.

FORTY-ONE

❖

I SPEND THE REST of the summer cleaning the kitchen. Painting the flat. Buying new curtains and cushion covers. I take clothes to the cleaners. I reline a chest of drawers.

lying down. A dog beside him. I begin to paint a bear, and it turns out lopsided and a little lumpy. I paint as much as I can remember from the circle of sky from the *Camera Dipinta*. I enjoy the fat *putti*. I draw a black face, the face of my Emilia. I paint a servant in a turban and a peacock. I paint more flowers.

One evening Lady Catchpole looks uncomfortable. I wonder if she is ill. After supper she apologises to me. Unfortunately, they will be unable to pay me. I have been living there free, with plenty to eat. I am angry, but I am also puzzled. The cook explains. There have been stories of witch burnings. Someone has reported the presence of Jews in London. The cook thinks Lady Catchpole would like me to leave, but is too embarrassed to tell me herself.

That night, I am woken by banging at the heavy main door. From far below, I can hear shouting and tramping feet. I pile up furniture against the door. I crawl across to the end of the room, by the gallery. I stuff my bundle into the chest, and crouch down behind it, covering myself with as much canvas as I can find. Through the sound of my heartbeat I hear steps come up the staircase, then turn round and go down again.

When I come out, the house is silent. My straw mattress has been cut to pieces.

I leave England the next day. Lady Catchpole allows me to ride in a farm cart, covered with straw and bags of dung, to the nearest coast. I take a boat across a rough sea to somewhere in the Netherlands, and make my way back to Venice. I shake with fear and fever. Rather the ghetto I know, I think, than persecution in a foreign country.

When I take my shoes out of the wardrobe, I find a layer of grey dust all over them. My viol stays in its case. I fold up the guitar stand and put it in the wardrobe.

Late in August, at Frank's invitation, I drive up to the university for a meeting. He welcomes me with his firm handshake, gets coffee from his secretary and then stands with his cup in front of the window.

'I have had a letter from Roberto Castelli,' he says. He picks up a piece of paper. 'He makes a very serious accusation. He claims you told him that you forged the James short story. He suggests that we should subject the paper and ink to further forensic investigation.' I say nothing. The bastard. 'If I don't, he says he will take the story to the newspapers.'

'I see.' I pause. 'Have you forgotten, Frank? The pages on display here, at the university, are photographs of the original manuscript. Remember? I accidentally left it on a train.'

Frank looks sharply at me. 'Are you saying the manuscript was authentic? That Roberto is lying? You didn't tell him you forged it?'

'Roberto has his own reasons for telling you such a lie,' I say. 'I'm in a difficult position, Frank. The reason Professor Castelli's publishers didn't have his edition ready for the concert – well. He originally claimed that he had discovered an authentic seventeenth-century realisation by Monteverdi. He has – I know this sounds like a counter-accusation – he forged it. I saw the drafts. He changed his story when he was challenged.'

Frank doesn't ask who challenged him. 'Can you prove it?'

'No. I saw the forgery. He asked me to help him with

EPILOGUE

IT IS MIDNIGHT. I open the window. A priest hurries across the piazza far below. The door opens. Emilia comes in. She stands behind me, her arms cradling my head.

'How is he?'

'Sleeping.' She kisses my ear. 'Come to bed.'

'In a little while. I have some music to finish. I love you.'

PRIMA PARTE
FINE

❖ SECUNDA PARTE ❖

it. I refused, of course. He can't prove that I forged the James story. No-one can. There is no manuscript.'

Frank puts his cup down and sighs. 'You're not on very strong territory here,' he says. 'Emilia. Tell me the truth. Did you forge the story?'

'What do you think?' I say.

'I don't know what to think. Look. These are the options, as I see them. I can call his bluff. Tell him I already know about the story. That won't necessarily stop him from going to the newspapers. I could pretend to have a forensic check done, and pretend to have the manuscript authenticated. But then I will be colluding with the fraud, and that still doesn't necessarily stop him from going to the newspapers. None of that will do the university any good. No smoke without fire, they will all say.'

I want to kill Roberto.

'There is one further option. I remove the manuscript from the display case and ask Castelli to respect the measures we have taken. It goes without saying that his visiting Professorship will be withdrawn. That may be small consolation to you, Emilia, but it is the best I can do.'

PRIMA PARTE

❖ SECUNDA PARTE ❖

EPILOGUE

❖

I AM OFFERED EARLY retirement, with a substantial and generous pension. I am not even granted the status of Professor Emerita. I no longer play the viol. I have no further interest in early music. I do a little adult education teaching. My students like me, and I like them. Roberto published his edition of *Orfeo* in America, and it was adversely reviewed by Barton in the early music press here. Too much editorial interference, he claimed.

Some months later, I get a phone call from the East Anglian train company. They believe they have my bag. My phone number is on an old serviette in the bag. I can collect it from Liverpool Street Station.

I take a taxi. The stripey bag is a bit grubby, but I check inside, and the package, in its faded green velvet wrapper, is still there. I thank the station manager. 'I thought I had lost it forever,' I say.

'Is it something important?' he asks.

'No, no,' I say. 'It's just of sentimental value.'

'Pleased to be of service, love,' he says, beaming, and shakes my hand.

I take a taxi home and go into the kitchen. I empty the manuscript into the deep kitchen sink, and set it alight. It's a bit damp, so the flames stay low. I sit and watch it until there is no speck of white paper left.

I gather the remains and give them a decent burial in the waste bin. There is grey dust everywhere; on work

surfaces, walls, on the ceiling. There is dust on the cupboard doors, the cornices, behind door handles, and dishes on the draining board. Every speck of dust will have to be wiped away. The devil is in the detail.

SECONDA PARTE
FINE